BarnYard Heroes:

A Half-Baked Origin

by Samuel A. McAdams

A 21st Century Absurdist publication

Cover by **Iconic Team**

First edition: April 2024

Second edition: March 2025

eBook ISBN: 978-1-963968-00-2

Paperback ISBN: 978-1-963968-01-9

Some are born into greatness. A few have greatness thrust upon them against their will, while many arrive at greatness via hard work, determination, and perseverance. Then there are those who are brought to greatness through a series of incredibly painful operations, multiple genetic modifications, and a fair number of bizarre scientific and chemical experiments performed by a purple-skinned space alien.

This is THEIR tale ...

Chapter 1

BEING A FLIGHTLESS BIRD annoyed me far more than my lack of a superpower. I cursed my useless chicken wings. What's the point of wings if you can't fly? To pursue my creative passion, I'm forced to clasp the paintbrush in my beak. With the brush dangling out of my beak like a cigarette, I focused on perfecting the rounded edges of the dog's nose. That's when Dr. Hash Browns received an incoming video call.

He could have taken it from the privacy of his office. Instead, he chose to disturb our free time by putting the call on the laboratory's giant screens. The space station had once been a mobile alien college prep school. Dr. Hash Browns had the school's gymnasium converted into a high-tech space alien laboratory, which also served as our primary living area. Four giant screens hung from the rafters which had functioned as scoreboards and replay Jumbotrons. They formed a box in the middle of the expansive room, making a screen with the incoming caller's image visible from anywhere in the room.

The other animals stopped their activities, and I put my Dog Playing Chess masterpiece on hold, as Dr. Hash Browns talked to a fellow, purple-skinned alien. Their conversation lasted less than thirty seconds. After Dr. Hash Browns said his goodbyes, the big screens went blank. I readied my brush.

Dr. Hash Browns sprang out of his desk chair. "Wow. Did you hear that?" he asked nobody in particular.

I put my brush down. Apparently, Dr. Hash Browns wanted to talk about the call, and continue to interrupt our precious free time from his training and experimentation.

"Yethh thhir, we heard the entire conversation," said the cow, as she glanced up from the game of chess she played with the dog.

Dr. Hash Browns usually cringed at the cow's lisp, and muttered about how the lisp's inconsistency made it a difficult problem to fix. Instead, he continued to gaze at the big screens, which had returned to scrolling serene landscape photos.

"A Senior Vice President called me. Can you believe it? And he's coming here! He'll be here in two days."

"That'thh great, thhir," said the cow, through a cockeyed scrunch of her mouth, which she punctuated with a roll of her eyes.

The concept of sarcasm perplexed me, so I wondered what greatness the cow saw in Dr. Hash Browns' conversation with the Senior Vice President of Intergalactic Strategy and Synergies.

"He's um... he's coming, coming here?" asked the dog.

"Yes. Isn't it wonderful?" He threw his top two arms in the air and clapped his bottom two hands.

"I don't know, I mean, he ah, he ah, he scares me."

The dog gets scared watching a sponge absorb water, but in this case, he had a point. On the surface, the caller resembled Dr. Hash Browns. They both resembled an eggplant with four string bean arms, two twig legs, a grapefruit-shaped head, and a toothpick neck. The Senior Vice President's skin had a violet shine compared to Dr. Hash Browns' dark plum hue. The well-groomed orange hair and tailored suit of the Senior Vice President posed a sharp contrast to Dr. Hash Browns' white lab coat and tousled patch of graying orange hair, but to me, the key differentiator was the aura of sinisterism in the Senior Vice President's oversized, cat-like, fluorescent yellow eyes.

Dr. Hash Browns sashayed away from his desk. "You're just being silly. He seemed quite nice to me."

"Oh, come off it, man. That guy is a big fat jerk." The rabbit said it, but I wish I had. It perfectly summed up my impression of the Senior Vice President.

"Agreed. A total butthead," said the duck, never taking his eyes off the video game he and the rabbit played. "He kept calling you Mr. Smash Frowns."

The pig menacingly mashed his front hooves together and said, "He fills me with the urge to rip his face off."

I didn't like the Senior Vice President, but ripping his face off seemed an extreme step.

"No, no, no. You mustn't say such things about Mr. Steak&Eggs. He's the Senior Vice President of Intergalactic Strategy and Synergies." Dr. Hash Browns beamed as he surveyed the laboratory. "He'll be here in two days. I can't believe it. The corporation has finally realized the brilliance of my work. Oh, glory days!"

The cat stretched out of her pillow bed. "Doctor, there are many plausible explanations why a Senior Vice President of Intergalactic Strategy and Synergies would come to visit us. Your conclusion that his visit be for the sole purpose of praising the brilliance of your work is presumptuous."

We all tuned out the cat when she rambled on about logic and reasoning, but Dr. Hash Browns took this to a new level. He appeared to not even realize she spoke at all as he scurried about the laboratory, picking up random items.

"So much to do. This place is a mess. Blintzes, instruct the sanitation droids to perform a thorough cleaning of the space station from top-to-bottom."

Blintzes was the central computing system that ran the space station. She monitored and maintained the climate control system, the life support unit, on-board gravity, and the station's power system. She controlled the lights, instructed the droid chef and his staff, and nagged you if you didn't eat your vegetables. And yes, she managed the sanitation droids. It was part of her job. She typically issued over a thousand instructions per nano second to the 150 rat-like sanitation droids, resulting in a continuous top-to-bottom cleaning of the space station. No special command required.

"Based upon the Senior Vice President's tone and demeanor, a more logical assumption for his pending arrival, would be for a routine inspection or an in-person project status update," said the cat, unabated by Dr. Hash Browns' disregard of her previous statement.

"The guest rooms need to be prepared. Meals. We need fancy gourmet meals."

"Doctor! Have you listened to a word I've said?"

Dr. Hash Browns' lack of response answered the cat's question.

The fish, who swam through the air and solid objects as if they were water, stopped in front of Dr. Hash Browns. His scales rippled between metallic green and blue, as his tail casually swished. "What the cat is trying to say is, we applaud your enthusiasm over the upcoming visit, and although it is wonderful to hope for the best, it is wise to prepare for the worst."

By this time, we had all gathered behind Dr. Hash Browns, except the rabbit and duck, who continued playing their video game. The high-tech equipment occupied the center of the former gymnasium, with test areas and various living spaces sprawled out around it. Dr. Hash Browns stood by the centerpiece of his lab, the Mambomatic 5000, which resembled a human CT scanner. He stared into the machine's giant tube. All of us animals had endured numerous conveyor belt rides through the tube. Never a pleasant experience, but we came out the other end with new abilities, like rational thought, language, and the occasional superpower.

"Thhir, have you not been listening to us?" The cow's booming voice could not be ignored.

Dr. Hash Browns turned to face us. "Yes, of course I heard you all. Why are you all so worried? My day of glory and honor has arrived. Dog, come here."

With his tail between his legs, the dog shuffled forward.

"No need to worry. You have done nothing wrong. I just want you to gaze into the future. Now sit."

"Okay. Okay." The dog sat up straight, right in front of Dr. Hash Browns.

"Very good. Now, close your eyes and relax. Deep breath in." Dr. Hash Browns paused. "Exhale slowly." He paused again before continuing in his soothing voice. "Put yourself in your happy place. Relax. Breathe in. Breathe out. Picture your happy place. Feel the peace rush over you. You are safe and happy and calm."

The dog looked to be asleep, and I felt drowsy myself. The dog shivered and quivered. His head swung from side to side. He let out three muffled barks, followed by more quivering, a whimper, and additional muffled barks. He ended with a long wolf-like howl and opened his eyes.

"Soooo, what did your vision reveal?" asked Dr. Hash Browns.

The dog glanced at Dr. Hash Browns, then dropped his head and stared at the gymnasium flooring. His tail twitched as he sighed a couple times. He never looked up as he spoke. "I..., I um..., I saw what I. what I always see. I witness you receiving..., um, you receiving the prestigious Raisin Bran Award for excellence in scientific research. You are, you are preparing to deliver your, your acceptance speech in front of a vast crowd of distinguished scientists, entrepreneurs, and socialites. A gigantic picture of you decorates the stage behind you. Everyone rises as you take the stage. The applause lasts for several minutes."

"Dude, what's the Raisin Bran Award?" asked the duck, from halfway across the lab. He impressed me with his ability to follow the conversation while playing the video game.

"It's the most coveted award a Cheddarian scientist can receive, named in honor of the famous Professor Raisin Bran, the greatest inventor, scientist, and mathematician ever," said Dr. Hash Browns.

"I've never heard of him," said the rabbit, also maintaining his video game concentration.

"I have failed to teach you basic Cheddarian history. The point is the dog's vision is about to come true. Isn't that clear?"

"Yethh, thhir," said the cow, though her tone and eye roll suggested anything but affirmation of Dr. Hash Browns' statement. The contradiction confounded me.

"Good, because we need to intensify your training. You all need to be ready to display your talents." Dr. Hash Browns looked down at me. His eyes opened wide, and his head snapped back. I thought I somehow startled him. He waved all four hands and said, "Chicken. I need to give you a superpower. You'll be the new centerpiece of my accomplishments. I need to get started right away. I've only got two days!"

As Dr. Hash Browns scurried out of the lab, he grabbed a clipboard with his upper right hand, a laptop with his lower right, and a computer tablet with his lower left.

The thought of gaining a superpower tantalized me, but I'd seen the suffering the others had endured. It's not just the multiple trips through the Mambomatic 5000, which literally rearranges your cells and reconstructs your internal organs, it's how Dr. Hash Browns subjected the others to rigorous training to perfect their powers. These sessions often ended with another run through the Mambomatic 5000. He never admitted it, but I believe the fish hid in the walls of the space station for days to avoid the torture.

The dog appeared at my side. He nudged my cheek with his wet nose. "You'll be, you'll be okay. And once you have a, have a superpower, I bet even the pig will ease up on you."

I nodded thanks to the dog, but the pig's ribbing about my lack of powers never upset me. I'm glad he never picked on me for having wings but not being able to fly. That might have made me cry.

The cow strutted in front of the Mambomatic 5000, taking the position Dr. Hash Browns had occupied. "We've got two days to get ready and make Dr. Brownthh proud."

"That doesn't sound like enough time to give me a superpower," I said.

The fish levitated into a position above us that resembled a professor, ready to start their lecture. "You forget that time is relative. The length of a day is relative. For example, a day on Jupiter is only nine hours and fifty-five minutes. Imagine that. The giant planet of Jupiter spinning a complete rotation every ten hours."

"That, that, that sounds horrifying," said the dog. "It reminds me of the time these..., these kids put me on this circley platform thing and spun me around and around, until I puked. I bet living on Jupiter feels like that. I'm never going there." The memory had the dog shaking.

"Forget about Jupiter," said the fish. "Let's discuss Venus. One day on Venus equals 243 Earth-days, yet a year on Venus is only 225 Earth-days."

"That, that, makes no sense." The dog stopped shaking as he processed the information. "A day on Venus is..., is longer than a year? How do you create a calendar for that planet?"

"Fish, I don't understand the point of all of this," I said.

"In a roundabout way," said the cow, "he has pointed out that a day to Dr. Hash Browns does not equal an Earth-day. One day on Dr. Hash Browns' home planet of Cheddar equals ninety Earth-days. Thho, two days, is 180 days or about six months."

There would be plenty of time for repeated trips through the Mambomatic 5000 to have my tiny chicken body reconstructed and hours upon hours of training. I walked back to my easel and picked up the paint brush with my beak. I figured I better finish my Dog Playing Chess masterpiece while I still had the time.

***

DR. HASH BROWNS' ONLY sleep over the six-months consisted of power naps, and he insisted us animals continue training through those. I had no time for art. He became obsessed with giving me a superpower. I lost count of my rides through the Mambomatic 5000. Each trip was a unique experience. Sometimes it would be a simple scan, and the next a horrifying laser show that vibrated every cell in my body into new formations. But with the Senior Vice President's visit only hours away, I remained a flightless chicken without an observable superpower. Dr. Hash Browns insisted he enhanced me with a hyperspeed power, but I had no clue how to activate it. He said I just needed to phase shift into hyperspeed, as if diving into water. I didn't know what that meant.

We assembled in the space station's auditorium for a dry run of the demo. Dr. Hash Browns still planned to showcase me as his latest creation, and expected me to demo the hyperspeed power. I paced backstage, awaiting my turn. I visualized diving into a pool, which provided no help on how to activate hyperspeed.

The pig stretched his neck as he strutted to centerstage. He walked on his hind legs and because of this, he was the only one of us who wore clothes. Believe me, we were thankful he did. At first glance, he resembled a short human bodybuilder. The pair of athletic boxer shorts added to his illusion of humanness, as did the eye patch covering the dangerous and uncontrollable laser eye Dr. Hash Browns had given him. But upon closer inspection, there was no hiding his piggy snout, floppy ears, stubby legs ending in hooves, and pinkness, yet rugged, pigskin.

The pig stared at the bar of weights in the middle of the stage. "There's 35,000 pounds on that bar! That's over twice my maximum lift."

"I engineered you to lift five times that amount," said Dr. Hash Browns. "You should max out your talent, not settle for a mere tenth of your potential. You're no better than those humans using only ten percent of their brain."

"Dude, they disproved that," said the duck from backstage.

"It was a myth, man. Humans use their full brain," said the rabbit, who sat next to the duck.

The pig walked to the front of the stage. "Doc, the human record for a deadlift is 1,104.5 pounds. I'm lifting fifteen times that amount. And what's the record for your species, Doc? With those skinny arms of yours, I'm betting you'd be lucky to deadlift over 100 pounds."

"Your comparison to other beings is irrelevant. I created you to be more than human. More than Cheddarian. I built you to be a god."

The pig pointed his hoof at Dr. Hash Browns. "Doc, a deadlift of 15,000 pounds will blow this pencil-neck executive away. Unless you want to make a fool out of us both, set the bar to 15,000."

"Fine. If limiting your abilities satisfies you, so be it. Blintzes, set the bar to 15,000."

Tiny robots rolled onto the stage, removed weights, and zoomed off with them.

Dr. Hash Browns had altered the pig's front hooves into what he called karate clench hooves. The hooves looked normal, until the pig went to pick something up. Then they transformed into what resembled black mittens. The pig wrapped these black mitten karate-clench hooves around the bar and lifted the 15,000 pounds of weight over his head. With his performance complete, he let the barbell drop. It bounced on the stage floor, giving me a jolt.

Dr. Hash Browns grumbled as the pig exited the stage.

The exchange between the pig and doctor had tightened my stomach into a knot. My turn would come soon. The dog ambled over and paced alongside me. He didn't say a word. I appreciated the dog's gesture of support, but it did little to quell the boiling acids in my gut or calm the throbs of blood pulsing through my scrawny chicken neck.

"Cat, you're up next," said Dr. Hash Browns from his seat in the front row.

The cat sauntered to center stage and stretched her long black body before settling into her traditional regal sitting pose. "Dr. Hash Browns, I assumed we would demonstrate my tornado generation ability inside the safety of the wind tunnel. Unleashing a tornado, no matter how small, inside the confines of this auditorium would result in irrevocable damage, and endanger the lives of all contained within."

"It won't be a problem when you control its every move," said Dr. Hash Browns, who had gotten up and walked up to the stage.

The cat settled herself with a heavy sigh. "With all due respect, your ill-conceived and misguided insistence that tornados can be controlled has grown quite tiresome. You showed pure genius in providing me the ability to manifest tornados, but your delusion that I can control said tornados shows a complete lack of understanding of the fundamentals of physics."

Dr. Hash Browns stomped up the steps. He loomed over the cat, who reacted by casually licking her black fur. "I built my career on achievements people said could not be done. And how dare you lecture me on the fundamentals of physics? I taught you everything you know."

The cat stopped cleaning herself and returned to her regal pose. I admired her composure. I would have run off the stage in tears by now.

She looked straight into Dr. Hash Browns' eyes. "It's impossible. Tornados cannot be controlled."

"It's your attitude that makes it impossible. What is wrong with you all? Mr. Steak&Eggs will be here within two hours. This is our last dress rehearsal and all I'm getting is whining and complaining. *That weight is too heavy. Tornados are dangerous.* Come on. This is our moment. This is our chance to shine."

"If you want to destroy this auditorium and murder the Senior Vice President, then be my guest and have me conjure a deadly tornado."

"What insubordination. Get off my stage."

I hugged myself with my wings and scrunched into a ball. The fish was next and then me.

As the cat strolled off the stage, the cow clomped on.

"You're out of line, Dr. Browns. Why, in these final hours, are you pushing everyone to do things they've never done before? That'thh not how a dress rehearsal works."

The cow relished her role as our mother and protector. I had never been more grateful for this.

"Complain, complain, complain. Whine, whine, whine. That's all I'm hearing," said Dr. Hash Browns.

"Thhir, you can't raise the bar this high in the final minutes. If you want this demo to be successful, you need to listen to us and dial it back to what we've practiced."

"It's time to strut your stuff. Is nobody with me?" asked Dr. Hash Browns.

"We're with you, dude," said the duck, as he flew onto the stage, with the rabbit bouncing in behind him. The stage lights reflected off their white fur and feathers, blurring their images. I imagined that my white body would do the same.

"Man, are we ready to take it to the next level. How about you have us flying real spaceships instead of the simulator?"

Ever so slightly, I stretched out of my fetal position, happy to let the rabbit and duck delay my turn.

"As the best pilot," said the cat from backstage, "It is logical I pilot the real spaceship for the demo."

"In your dreams, dude," said the duck.

"Yeah, man, you're the worst," said the rabbit.

I attended several of the trio's flight simulation training sessions, and the rabbit and duck never spoke truer words.

"No. None of you are flying our only escape pod," said Dr. Hash Browns. "You two are far too reckless, and the cat is a terrible pilot. You two will stick to your ninja warrior demo."

"We can dial that to the max, dude," said the duck.

"Like, we could wrestle a lion?" said the rabbit. "I'll tear him apart with my vampire fangs." The rabbit opened wide to show his fangs emerging.

"Dude, I could demo Atomic Quack?" said the duck.

Dr. Hash Browns did a face palm. "What have I told you about Atomic Quack?"

The duck dropped his head and poked his web foot at the stage floor. "Never under any circumstances unleash your Atomic Quack. It is far too dangerous."

"Good. There will be no demoing of Atomic Quack," said Dr. Hash Browns.

"Dude, why did you equip me with Atomic Quack if it's that dangerous?"

"I went through a dark spell after the divorce. We will speak of this no further."

"Is that when you gave me this ridiculously powerful laser eye?" The pig rubbed his black eye patch.

"That was a truly inspired innovation. Once I get the glasses working to control that laser eye, you'll see just how awesome it is. Now, where's the fish? Time for him to demo his hypnotism."

"I haven't seen him for hours, thhir," said the cow.

"He better not have swum out of the space station again," said Dr. Browns.

Besides the ability to swim in the air, the fish passed through solid objects as easily as a regular fish swimming in the ocean. But when inside a wall, he couldn't see, and on more than one occasion, he has swum through the outer walls of the space station. Once in outer space, he wiggles and flops, but never moves. If we had to retrieve the fish, this would delay my demo. I took an easy breath and almost straightened to full height.

"Cow, go find him," said Dr. Hash Browns.

"Yes, sir." The cow plodded down the stage steps and out of the auditorium.

Dr. Hash Browns returned to his seat in the front row. "Chicken! Time to demo hyperspeed."

There would be no reprieve. The time had come to face Dr. Hash Browns' wrath.

The dog patted my back. I wanted to curl back into the fetal position but forced myself to walk out from behind the curtain.

Chapter 2

I STRUTTED TO THE middle of the auditorium stage, but not in a manner that signified confidence. As a chicken, I could walk no other way. The spotlight blared on. My wing flung up to shield my eyes, but not before they received a blast of the blinding light.

"Time to shine," said Dr. Hash Browns. "Show us your hyperspeed."

I blinked both sets of eyelids, but a halo and light flares continued to obscure my vision.

"Stop stalling," said Dr. Hash Browns.

"I'm not stalling. I can't see. Can we turn that light off?" Using my wing as a visor, I had enough vision to witness Dr. Hash Browns' flamboyant waving of all four hands.

"When did you all become prima donnas? If you're not in the spotlight, nobody in the audience can see you!"

In the end, it didn't matter. I couldn't have activated hyperspeed if I had twenty-twenty vision or had been declared legally blind. Yet, I still had to try. I lowered my wing, took a couple preliminary hops, then jumped, and flapped my useless wings. To my amazement, I rose. I snapped my wings out straight and imagined myself as an eagle soaring above the trees. For that brief moment, I thought I'd done it. I thought I'd broken through into hyperspeed. Or at the very least, I might actually be flying. The stage curtains approached fast. I tilted to my left and instantly plummeted to the stage floor.

As I brushed off the pain and embarrassment, Dr. Hash Browns yelled, "NO, NO, NO! That's all wrong." He stomped up the stage stairs. "There's no need to fly. Just rock back and forth and then blast into hyperspeed like you're jumping into a wave."

This contradicted the get a running start advice he provided earlier in the day and his instruction yesterday to imagine myself as a seagull plunging into the sea to catch a fish. On the plus side, I could simulate this latest suggestion without hurting myself. I rocked a couple times and then sprinted across the stage. I lost a feather in the process, but I believe this had more to do with my earlier crash landing than how fast I moved.

"You can't run your way to hyperspeed. You need to feel the shifts in time and slip between the cracks, like a rat squeezing down a drainpipe."

As I walked back to the middle of the stage, I concluded this latest advice to be the worst he'd provided so far. I had no clue how to even pretend to do this nonsense. I glanced at the dog and mouthed help. He shrugged his shoulders. After a heavy sigh, I squinted, bobbed my head a couple of times, and pantomimed slithering through a tight tunnel. It felt ridiculous and I'm sure it looked ridiculous.

"That's it!" shrieked Dr. Hash Browns. "Did you feel it? Did you experience yourself shifting in time?"

"No. I just felt awkward and silly."

"Channel that awkwardness and try it again."

Once again, I looked to the dog for advice. He shrugged and did a slow open paw pan with a front paw. I interpreted his gesture to mean, "Give the man what he wants. Repeat the silly move."

I shook my head and recentered myself on the stage. I squinted, bobbed my head, and in an exaggerated fashion, pretended to squeeze through a pipe.

Dr. Hash Browns squealed like a human child on Christmas morning. "You felt it, right?"

All I felt was humiliation. Honestly, plunging to the floor was less embarrassing than this insane mime routine. "Nothing, sir. I experienced no shifting in time sensations."

"You're so close. Try it again. Be the rat. Squeeze through the crack in time."

I wiggled my wings and prepared to repeat the silliness. Thankfully, after my first head bob, my performance got interrupted by an announcement from Blintzes, the space station computer.

"We have an incoming message from Mr. Steak&Eggs, Senior Vice President of Intergalactic Strategy and Synergies, requesting permission to board the space station."

"He's here already? I didn't expect him for another two hours." Dr. Hash Browns ran the fingers of his upper hands through the small patch of graying hair and cleaned up the coffee mugs, notes, and dirty plates with his lower hands. "Have the chefs prepared the meals? Has the paint dried in the visitor's suite? Are there fresh flowers and fruit baskets in all the guest rooms?"

"Yes, yes, and yes," said Blintzes. "Do you grant permission for Mr. Steak&Eggs and his entourage to come aboard the station?"

"Yes. Of course," said Dr. Hash Browns, his hands full of loose items. "Cue the soothing music and have the sanitation droids do another thorough clean."

"Of course, sir."

"Do I have time to change?"

Between every dry run, he changed his clothes, but always into the same outfit; a white lab coat over wrinkled slacks and a white dress shirt, with a pair of comfortable, yet stylish shoes covering his enormous feet. He owned forty sets of this same outfit, claiming it streamlined his routine by saving him from deciding what to wear. Enormous, black-rimmed glasses completed his space alien geek ensemble. I always wondered how those monstrous spectacles remained propped up on his tiny cone shaped nose. It defied physics.

"He is boarding the station now, sir. I advise you to head to the docking bay as soon as you can to greet your distinguished guest," said Blintzes.

"Of course. We're on our way." Dr. Hash Browns tossed the loose items behind a stage curtain. "Come on, animals. Time to greet our future."

***

We arrived at the docking bay with just enough time for Dr. Hash Browns to organize us animals into a predetermined line from tallest to shortest. There had been a fierce debate over the tallest among the duck, rabbit, cat, and me. The cat argued that stretched out to full length, she was the longest. The duck and I let her win the debate, but as soon as Dr. Hash Browns saw the line up, he switched her to be after me. With us lined up, Dr. Hash Browns straightened his lab coat and ran an upper hand through his hair, before turning to face the docking bay doors.

As soon as the doors swooshed open, Mr. Steak&Eggs led his staff through. His tailored suit and slicked back orange hair reminded me of gangster movies the rabbit and duck liked to watch. I thought that's what made him scarier in person, but then the cold stare of his oversized yellow cat-eyes glanced at me. They were terrifying.

Mr. Steak&Eggs barked out orders to his entourage of equally well-groomed lavender, mauve, and periwinkle skinned aliens. They all wore serious expressions and hung on his every word. "Bacon, find out what's keeping Grits. Sausage, tell those doofus Waffle brothers to get to the trash room ASAP. And who's running the Monterey Jack deal?"

"Me, sir," replied a light-plum skinned female follower, who pushed through the crowd to get into Mr. Steak&Eggs' view.

"And you are?"

"Muffin, sir. English Muffin."

"Fine. Accept no less than 45 million. Got it?"

"Yes, sir."

"Good. Bagel, where are those Mazurka reports?"

A lavender-skinned female alien handed the Senior Vice President a computer tablet. He snatched the device from her hand and scrolled through the reports, never breaking stride as he headed past us.

Dr. Hash Browns scurried to catch up to him. "Hello, sir. May I say what an extreme privilege and honor it is to have you aboard my research vessel. I've been looking forward to your visit."

There was no response from the Senior Vice President. Not even a head nod. His pace never slowed.

The snub did not deter Dr. Hash Browns, as he scrambled to keep up. "I have put together an agenda and schedule. I figured we would start with a tour of the facilities, followed by a–"

Mr. Steak&Eggs stopped, and looked up from his report. "Who are you?"

"I'm Dr. Hash Browns."

"Sorry, do I know you?"

"You came to visit me. This is my research facility."

"Right. The animal torturer. First, let me get one thing clear, Mr. Frowns. This is not *your* facility. This space station and everything in it is the property of ORPH Inc. Second, do you have any food on board? I'm starving. The food on this intergalactic rental stinks. I think that piano was still kicking."

Piano is a small shellfish found in the Northern Hemisphere of Cheddar. The Cheddarish pronunciation of this delicacy sounds like piano, but spelled quite differently, with crazy Cheddarish letters. This odd quirk may be interesting, but the more important Cheddarian piano fact is it should be served not just raw, but still alive. As gross as it may sound, the more a Cheddarian piano kicks, the better the eating. So, despite what Mr. Steak&Eggs thinks of himself, I consider him an uncultured moron.

I expected Dr. Hash Browns to tactfully correct Mr. Steak&Eggs, though I secretly hoped he would openly mock his stupidity and tell him even the chicken from Earth knows you should serve Cheddarian piano still kicking. He did neither. The change in plans had him flustered and he gave Mr. Steak&Eggs' ignorance a pass.

"I had planned on serving lunch after my introductory presentation and just before the first half of my live demonstration, but if you're hungry now, I, ah..., I guess I can rearrange the schedule a bit."

"That'd be great. I'm starving. Let's go eat," said Mr. Steak&Eggs.

***

THE OTHER ANIMALS AND I returned to the former school gymnasium that had been converted to a laboratory and general living space. Dr. Hash Browns had instructed us to prepare for the live demonstration, while he and Mr. Steak&Eggs ate lunch. We would all get our chance to show him our skills, just not in the manner originally planned.

While I panic paced, the cow and dog concentrated on an intense game of chess, the pig grunted through a workout, the cat slept on a table, the fish swam through the air whistling a happy tune, and the rabbit and duck returned to their usual positions in front of a large television screen playing an action-packed video game.

Dr. Hash Browns had garbage-picked the chess table from Earth. It was an outdoor table, with a built-in chessboard and attached benches. The dog sat on his bench with a paw on his queen, contemplating his next move. He had been doing so for several minutes. He shifted his paw to a bishop, but still made no move.

The cow realized she had time on her hooves and looked around the lab. "Excuse me, ladies and gentlemen, but did thhomeone make more coffee?"

The pig stopped his workout and looked puzzled. "What? You want to know if someone basted more cameras?"

This sounds like a crazy response to the question, but in Cheddarish, the phrase "Did someone make more coffee?" sounds very similar to the phrase "Did someone baste more cameras?" And thanks to the cow's lisp, it sounded exactly like, "Did someone baste more cameras?"

"That's not what I asked," said the cow.

"What does baste mean?" I asked.

"Basting is the act of moistening meat or other food while cooking, using butter or the drippings from the roasting meat. However, that is irrelevant to this discussion, since the cow said she planned on eating glass pudding, painting her face, and square dancing till dawn," said the cat, as she did a post-nap stretch.

Even in Cheddarian, the phrase "I'm going to eat glass pudding, paint my face and square dance till dawn" sounds nothing like, "Did someone make more coffee?" I concluded the cat dreamed this or needed to have her hearing checked.

The fish swam up to the chess table and said, "I love square dancing. This will be fun. Though I think I will take a pass on the glass pudding."

"What is wrong with you all?! You guys aren't making any sense," said the cow.

"We're not making sense?" said the pig. "You're the one who wants to baste cameras."

"And consume glass pudding," said the cat.

"I'm not talking about cameras or glass pudding! I asked, did thhomeone make more coffee?"

There is a consistency in the cow's inconsistent lisp. She didn't lisp every "s", but when she lisped an "s" in a word, she tended to always lisp that word. So, the phrase once again sounded like, "Did anyone baste the cameras?"

"She said it again," said the pig.

"I'm confused. Is basting cameras a step in making glass pudding?" I asked.

"I don't, um, I don't think eating glass pudding is safe," said the dog.

"And why do you need to paint your face to square dance?" asked the fish. "

A pink hue flooded the cow's white snout and forehead. If her traditional dairy cow coloring hadn't covered her cheeks with black spots, they would have glowed a deep red.

"I JUST WANT COFFEE!" she shouted.

This, I understood, and I pieced the story together. "You asked, 'Did someone make more coffee?'"

"Exactly," said the cow, as her snout and forehead faded back to white.

"That makes a lot more sense," said the pig, as he grabbed his barbell.

"Does this mean we're not square dancing?" asked the fish.

"Yethh. There will be no square dancing," said the cow.

The fish sighed. "I was looking forward to that," he said and sulked away.

The room went silent, as we returned to our previous activities, except the cow. She scanned the room, looking from animal to animal. "WELL?! Did anybody make more coffee?!"

We all replied that we hadn't.

"Then I'll make thhome."

"Take a load off. I'll make another pot," said the pig as he waddled to the lab's kitchen area, which consisted of a mini-fridge and one counter with a sink, microwave, and coffee maker. It was near his workout station, so he got there quickly, despite the tiny steps he took walking on his hind legs.

"You look a little tense. Maybe you should cut back on the caffeine," I said. The cow stared at me with utter disgust. Lucky for me, she had not been enhanced with the power to shoot laser beams out of her eyes. "I'm just saying you should consider a decaf." The cow intensified her evil stare. I figured it best to back off, even if I only had her best interests in mind.

"By the way, when's this stupid demo supposed to happen?" asked the pig as he poured water into the coffee maker.

The confusing coffee discussion had been a nice distraction, but with it gone, I returned to fretting about my inability to hyperspeed, and how Dr. Hash Browns had me scheduled to demo this failure.

The cow glanced at the clock. "Well, it should have started an hour and a half ago, according to Dr. Hash Browns' schedule."

The dog popped his head up and frantically swung it side-to-side before he ran around in circles. "You, you don't suppose something has gone wrong, do ya? I mean, I mean, it's not like the doc to be late for anything, let alone two, two and a half hours late! Do you think that Mr. Steak&Eggs is some kind of cannibalistic freak? I mean, maybe he's preparing Dr. Hash Browns for the evening feast right now. Or what if we're stuck in a time warp, where time is still moving for us, but frozen for everybody else? Everyone else will look like statues." The dog posed like a hunting dog, pointing.

"I'm sure there is a logical explanation for the delay," said the cat.

"Yeah, calm down there, Sparky," said the pig, shaking his head and rolling his eyes. "Blintzes, show us the current location of Dr. Hash Browns."

"Dr. Hash Browns' current location is unknown," said Blintzes.

The cat poked at a computer terminal and then said, "I concur. The space station sensors do not detect Dr. Hash Browns' presence."

"I'm sure he's just gone over to Mr. Steak&Eggs space station for dinner or some sort of reception," said the cow.

"The space station's sensors extend to Mr. Steak&Eggs' ship," said Blintzes, with a disdain that rivaled the cat. "If Dr.

Hash Browns were there, I would not have said his current location is unknown."

"Where, where could he be? I mean, people don't just, don't just vanish into thin air." If dogs could cry, he would have been blubbering.

"Correct," said Blintzes. "People do not vanish into thin air. There is a single record of a long-range shuttle departing from the Senior Vice President's visiting ship at three forty-seven this afternoon, with a single occupant: Dr. Hash Browns."

BYH
BarnYard Heroes

Chapter 3

Pardon the interruption, but I wanted you to know I am aware some character names sound strange. Who in their right mind would name their kid Hash and what kind of surname is Steak&Eggs? Well, I did. I made up their names. The Cheddarian names, given to them by their parents, sound like a series of squeaks, whistles, squeals, and beeps. The closest I can come to representing Dr. Hash Browns' given name is "beep fizz squeak higher-pitched-squeak crackle crackle fffpt-fppt tweet vroom bong". And that's just his first name. Here's how the book would read if I used this as his name:

> The   dog   sat   down   in   front   of
> Beepfizzsqueakhigher-pitch-squeakcracklecracklefffpt-
> fppttweetvroombong. "Now, close your eyes and relax," said
> Beepfizzsqueakhigher-pitch-squeakcracklecracklefffpt-
> fppttweetvroombong.

I know I would not enjoy writing like that and assume you would not enjoy reading such a book. So, I named all space aliens after various breakfast foods. It seemed like a good idea at the time, and I stayed with it because you humans rarely eat chicken for breakfast. I could take offense to you humans eating tons of eggs for breakfast, but from my perspective, it's like eating my poop and if you all want to eat my poop for breakfast, be my guest. The reason doesn't matter. The important thing to remember is characters with strange breakfast food names, like French Toast or Scrambled Eggs, are space aliens.

There is a second naming convention. I named planets, which humanity has not yet discovered, after my favorite types of cheese. I love cheese, especially cheddar. So, I named Dr. Hash Browns' home planet Cheddar. Of course, the Cheddarians have their own name for their planet, which cannot be written in any Earthly language. To the human ear, the true name of Cheddar sounds like a series of five loud pops, followed by a couple squeaks and then three whistles that only dogs, some varieties of mosquitoes, and aliens from the planet Cheddar can hear. I will not attempt to write it out.

One last naming convention to cover. I named all alien technology after popular dances. For example, I named the sophisticated thingamajig invented by Dr. Hash Browns, the Mambomatic 5000. I planned to create cool names for the space alien gadgets, like seaciome and eryfreitic. But this would lead to mispronunciation confusion, which would annoy me and force me to insert the phonics for words like seaciome (shaw SEE oh mee) and eryfreitic (er a FRY tick). It sounded like a big hassle, so I chose dances. But I am not naming anything after the Chicken Dance. I find the song and the corresponding dance offensive. "I don't want to be a chicken. I don't want to be a duck. So, shake my butt." Where do you humans come up with this stuff? "I don't want to be an ape. I don't want to be a human. So, shake my butt." How do you like it?

To recap, I named space aliens after breakfast foods, alien planets after my favorite cheeses, and high-tech space alien technology after popular dances.

And one more thing. Dr. Hash Browns never gave us names. He referred to us using mini descriptions. For example, he called me white-feathered, clawed-foot, tiny animal with pointy mouth. I chose to refer to us as the chicken, the dog, etc. Since I do not consider them formal names, I do not capitalize these references.

BYH
BarnYard Heroes

Chapter 4

A SIGNIFICANT CONVERSATION TOOK place as Dr. Hash Browns and Mr. Steak&Eggs dined, that none of us animals heard. But the android headwaiter, Denver Omelet, was there. Being an android, he has a perfect memory of, well, everything. So, I asked Denver to write the account of what transpired during the lunch Dr. Hash Browns had with Mr. Steak&Eggs.

***

TO PROVIDE A SENSE of realism, I am programmed to periodically ask Dr. Hash Browns a question immediately after he has taken a bite and has a full mouth. This subroutine had triggered for his lunch with Mr. Steak&Eggs. Typically, Dr. Hash Browns has a ravenous appetite, and the completion of this task would be accomplished within the first two minutes of the meal. But during that lunch, he just picked at his tender prime rib. He never touched the exquisitely prepared twice-baked garlic mashed potatoes, and only poked at his vegetable of the day, a medley of lightly sautéed seasonal vegetables, including carrots, zucchini, green beans, leeks, and cauliflower. I inquired if he was feeling ill or unhappy with his meal. He either never heard my question or ignored me.

On the other side of the table sat the impeccably dressed Mr. Steak&Eggs, gobbling down everything placed in front of him. He used his right arms for eating, as his left arms worked a computer tablet. No conversation took place between the two dining companions during the main course. In between bites, Mr. Steak&Eggs shouted orders to his staff.

After I served the post-meal coffee and thin mints, he finally turned his attention to Dr. Hash Browns. "So, Mr. ...," started Mr. Steak&Eggs. An assistant standing behind him whispered in his ear. "Sorry, Doctor Browns. Anyway, as I am sure you are aware, ORPH Inc. is going through some difficult times and, during difficult times, tough decisions need to be made. Let me put it this way. I have good news and bad news. Let's start with the good news. You get to go home. That should cheer you up. It's my understanding you've been stuck on this research vessel out in the middle of nowhere for quite some time."

Dr. Hash Browns' frown transitioned to a scowl, as I topped off his water glass, the only thing he had consumed during lunch. He crossed his upper arms and tugged his lab coat down with his lower hands.

"I'm enjoying my time here and have no interest in returning home. I'm making groundbreaking modifications to several barnyard animals, improving their physiological and mental makeup. Did you read my research papers?"

"I remember reading something about a diminutive rodent creature with big sharp pointy teeth," said Mr. Steak&Eggs before taking a gulp of his coffee.

Dr. Hash Browns leaned forward, uncrossing his upper arms. As he spoke, his four arms performed a myriad of gestures, which grew in extravagance, along with his enthusiasm. "Exactly. I genetically altered a rabbit to grow retractable vampire teeth. And that is just the beginning, sir. I enhanced these simple-minded creatures with advanced intelligence. They are capable of rational thought. They can speak, write, and think. Solve differential equations. I re-engineered their respiratory and circulatory systems to run at seven nines of efficiency. That means their bodies operate at 99.99999% efficiency, by reusing the energy they produce. I invented a way for their bodies to regenerate oxygen. These creatures can survive for months without eating, drinking, or even breathing. I have prepared a demonstration to show you all of their amazing abilities."

I presented the carafe of coffee and asked if Mr. Steak&Eggs wanted a refill. He covered his cup with his lower left hand. I put the carafe away.

"We have no time for a demo, Mr. Bash Nouns," said Mr. Steak&Eggs. "We're on a tight schedule and you're to return on the next intergalactic shuttle, which leaves in an hour."

"I can't go. My work here isn't done," said Dr. Hash Browns.

"You have time to pack up some essential items. Clothes and what-not. We'll send the rest of your things later." Mr. Steak&Eggs had become engrossed with a computer screen an assistant handed him.

"I'm not going anywhere." Dr. Hash Browns sat back and crossed his arms. "This is my home."

"It's not your home, it's the property of ORPH Inc.," said Mr. Steak&Eggs, without looking up from his tablet.

"This is supposed to be the good news?" asked Dr. Hash Browns.

Mr. Steak&Eggs looked up from the tablet, but only after a dramatic eye roll. "Thanks for the reminder. The bad news. Mr. Drowns, ORPH Inc. is going through difficult financial times and tough decisions need to be made. The corporation has canceled your project, effective immediately."

"WHAT??!!" Dr. Hash Browns slammed his upper fists on the table. One clipped the top of his coffee spoon. It somersaulted in the air, bounced on the table twice, and then clanged to the floor.

I swooped in with a replacement spoon and cleaned up the fallen piece of silverware.

"I thought my statement was clear. The company has no money, so they canceled your project." Mr. Steak&Eggs had returned his attention to his tablet.

"This can't be true. Doesn't the corporation realize the brilliant strides I've made here? Don't they see the awesome potential of my experiments?"

"To be frank with you, Mr. Rash Clowns, there's not much of a call for vampire rabbits on Cheddar. People want cute, cuddly little animals. Ones that sit in their lap and love to be petted or energetic little creatures that chase sticks. Cheddarians don't want Kung-Fu fighting pets with big, sharp, nasty teeth. And I understand if you pull the duck's tails, it unleashes an atomic explosion that'll wipe out a city. Only psychopaths would want that. Plus, think of the lawsuits from such a disaster. Mr. Grounds, there's simply no upside, financially speaking, to your band of mutants, and the new ORPH is all about profit. If you're not generating revenue, you're out. Personally, I believe it's well past the time someone put an end to your boondoggle. Anyway, the clock is ticking on that charter departure. I suggest you start packing."

With Dr. Hash Browns sitting motionless in his chair and Mr. Steak&Eggs returning to his tablet, I seized the lull in conversation to ask if either of them wanted anything else. They both grunted "No," as I cleared away dirty dishes.

"Waiter, before you go, tell me the name of that meat we ate?" asked Mr. Steak&Eggs.

"Prime rib of beef, sir."

"It's fabulous." He turned to a young, male staff member. "Get that programmed into our ship's food replicator. Prime rib of feet."

"Prime rib of beef, sir," I said. "I am delighted you enjoyed it, but it's not from a replicator. Our robot staff cooks every meal fresh. It's flesh of cow, seasoned with garlic, olive oil, onion, rosemary, and a dash of black pepper and served au jus."

"What's a cow?" asked Mr. Steak&Eggs.

"A farm animal from a nearby planet. I could show a diagram of this beast and explain which portion you are consuming." I pulled a tablet out of my apron pocket.

"No! Too much info, droid man. I want to savor this non-synthetic meat in blissful ignorance. Bring me some more.

And while you're at it, get me some more of that white drink we had earlier," said Mr. Steak&Eggs.

"It would be my pleasure," I said, casually sliding the tablet back into its pocket.

"What's the name of that drink?"

"Pasteurized two percent homogenized cow's milk."

"Cow's milk? So, you're telling me that this drink comes from the same beast as that meat?" asked Mr. Steak&Eggs.

"Prime rib and milk come from the same species, but humans raise specific varieties for their meat, while other are—"

"Enough details, droid." Mr. Steak&Eggs set down his tablet and stared at Dr. Hash Browns, with the slyest of smiles on his face. "Prime rib and milk, now that's something to write home about. I'm sure I'm not the only Cheddarian who's sick of synthetic meats. This can generate serious cash. Mr. Downs, you should have spent your time extracting fluids from these animals and cooking them, instead of wasting your time making them talk. I've been here less than an hour and already discovered how to make a fortune. You've been here over a century and all you've done is mutate animals into circus freaks."

"I am not a chef, Mr. Steak&Eggs. I am a scientist who has dedicated his life to enhancing the capabilities of creatures across the universe. If you would please take a moment to observe these creature's enhancements, I am sure you will reconsider this rash course of action. If we apply these enhancements to our species, we will become super beings." Dr. Hash Browns' four arms raised higher into the air with every word he spoke. When he finished, it looked as though he prayed to his god.

"That's very nice Mr. Frowns, but see—" started Mr. Steak&Eggs.

"I made a fish fly! I made a cow talk. Have you ever seen a cow's tongue? They're enormous." Dr. Hash Browns' arms lowered. His top and bottom hands came together as he spread his right and left arms out. The chefs cooked beef tongue once and as shocked as I had been by the size of the cow tongue, it was nowhere near the length demonstrated with his hand. "You don't have the slightest idea how hard it is to make a tongue that size form any kind of understandable language, let alone talk with only a minor lisp? I also made a chicken talk, and they don't even have lips."

"You are correct about one thing. I have no idea how hard that is, because I just don't care. Our conversation is done. Sausage. Bacon." Mr. Steak&Eggs glared at Dr. Hash Browns. "And never interrupt me again. Though I doubt you'll ever get the chance."

The two tallest Cheddarians stepped forward. Their form-fitted black suits revealed their muscular physique, at least for a Cheddarian. Despite arms and legs three-times the thickness of average Cheddarians, the limbs still appeared freakishly thin compared to the plump gourd-shaped midsection and their necks were the usual toothpick thickness. I understand that even the chicken makes fun of their skinny legs and she's got literal chicken legs. Regardless, I wish my droid design had been based on their body frame instead of the composite average for a Cheddarian waiter.

One of the goon-Cheddarians restrained Dr. Hash Browns' four arms, while the other one jabbed a small electronic device into Dr. Hash Browns' skinny neck. Sparks danced across Dr. Hash Browns' head, and he collapsed to the floor.

"That went well, don't you think?" Mr. Steak&Eggs delivered this rhetorical question with extreme sarcastic overtones. "Sausage, throw him on the shuttle and send him home."

Sausage nodded and began dragging the limp body of Dr. Hash Browns away.

"I hate these wacko scientists." Mr. Steak&Eggs continued on in a high-pitched voice, which was obviously meant to mock Dr. Hash Browns. "I made a talking cow and a vampire rabbit. Praise me. Give me all the company's money. Tell me I'm brilliant." He then returned to his normal voice, "Well, la-de freaking duh. I mean, who cares? Yeah, that's just what every household on Cheddar needs, a freaking vampire rabbit. Listen up, everybody. If any other wacko scientists on this space station give you any trouble, stun 'em and throw them on the next ship back to Cheddar. That's an order."

"Sorry to interrupt, sir," said a nervous assistant, "but there are no other scientists on the space station. Dr. Hash Browns was the only person aboard."

"Good. No need to worry about any more wacko scientists. That might also explain why he's gone wacko." He twisted his evil glare on me. "Why are you still here? Aren't you supposed to be getting me some more prime rib and milk?"

I was in constant contact with the chef and his staff. They had not finished preparing his order, so I remained tableside to attend to any new requests. Based on the tone of Mr. Steak&Eggs' voice, my programming suggested I politely excuse myself, instead of explaining why I had stayed. "Sorry, sir. I will be back with your order momentarily."

"Bagel, start working on finding me some of these cows," said Mr. Steak&Eggs, as I headed toward the kitchen to await his order.

"Already on it," said a pleasant female voice.

"And somebody please get me an update on the Monterey Jack deal."

BYH
BarnYard Heroes

Chapter 5

AFTER HEARING THE NEWS of Dr. Hash Browns' departure, the other animals and I huddled near the gurgling coffee maker, except the rabbit and duck, who continued to play their video game and the cat who poked commands into a computer terminal. The soothing fragrance of brewing coffee failed to calm my anxiety. I ran through a myriad of emotions in silence: loss, abandonment, betrayal, desertion. You think you know a guy, and then wham, he leaves without even saying goodbye. On the plus side, I hoped this meant the demo was canceled.

The dog sniffed every door in the former gymnasium. "But, but this, but this can't be. Why would he, would he leave? He can't be, he can't be gone." He collapsed by the door to the old locker rooms, dropped his chin to the floor, and whimpered.

The cow ambled over to a terminal screen displaying Dr. Hash Browns' itinerary. "This wasn't in the schedule. Where'thh the shuttle headed?"

"The shuttle's flight plan states the planet Cheddar as its destination," said Blintzes.

The dog lifted his head. "He, he, he didn't even say goodbye." He plopped his chin back to the tiled floor and returned to whining.

The rest of us went silent.

The dog sprung to his feet and scrambled up to the cow. "He just left us all alone. All alone. Who's gonna feed us? Who knows how to work the microwave? Who can operate the can opener? We're all gonna starve!" When the dog breaks into full panic mode, his stammer disappears.

"No worries. I can work the can opener and microwave." The pig's karate-clench hooves made him more than capable of performing the tasks. "Plus, we don't need to eat."

The dog scampered to the kitchenette area and flung the refrigerator door open. He shuffled items as he sniffed each shelf. "Oh, oh, oh sure, easy for you, but, but what about the chicken? What about the chicken? I got you there. Dr. Browns didn't finish re-engineering the chicken. She's going to starve. There's nothing in here for her to eat." He pushed away from the refrigerator, leaving the door wide open. He scrambled to a standalone kitchen counter and whipped its bottom cabinet doors open. Coffee cans, filters, and a variety of serving dishes spilled to the floor, as the dog rummaged inside.

"Easy there, Fido. The chicken won't starve. We have an entire robot restaurant staff. We will not starve."

The fish hovered above the dog, shook his head, and swam up to the cow. "If Dr. Browns is the only person who left, where is Mr. Steak&Eggs and his entourage? And what are they doing?"

"I can provide visuals of their activities." The cat had been quietly tapping away on a computer and displayed several surveillance camera feeds on the jumbotron screens. A dozen purple-skinned aliens of varying hues pushed pallets loaded with desks, 3-D printers, computers, monitors, beakers, toilets, cases of toilet paper, urinals, bookcases, textbooks, white-boards, garbage cans, cleaning supplies, tables, copiers, and paper products into the cargo bay. After we had soaked in the scene, the cat said, "The Cheddarians then load these items into Mr. Steak&Eggs' spaceship."

"They're taking our beds," I said, though we never actually slept in them or needed them.

"Those jerks have the pool table," said the pig. "And the foosball."

"I have a bad feeling about this," said the fish.

"This is bad, very bad. Bad, bad, bad," said the dog.

"Everybody needthh to calm down. Take a couple of deep breaths. Everything is going to be fine." The cow coached the dog in taking two deep breaths. "Now remember, you can see into the future. You just need to calm down. Relax. Go to your happy place. See the future. I'm sure you'll see that everything turns out okay."

"What if he sees us all butchered and hanging in a meat locker?" I asked. It seemed a plausible outcome of our situation.

The cow gave me a sharp glare. "No. He'll see what he always sees. Dr. Hash Browns winning his big award. And, I'm betting Dr. Brownthh went back to Cheddar to prepare for the big ceremony."

The dog dropped his head. "But, but that's not, not what I see in my visions. All I see is green?"

The cow scrunched her enormous snout. "Green? What'thh that mean?"

"It's a, it's a color. The combination of blue and yellow," said the dog. "But, but that's, that's not important now."

"I know what green means, but I thought you always saw Dr. Browns winning his award."

The dog lowered his head and stared at the floor, before rolling his eyes to hesitantly gaze at the cow. "Well, I, um, I never actually saw that. I always, um, I always see green."

The pig rubbed the dog's head with a front hoof, leaving a few strands sticking straight up. "You little mongrel. You've been lying all this time. I love it."

"I, I had too. He kept asking me to look into the future. I'd tell him I, I see green in the future. He'd say that can't be right, and stick me back into the Mambomatic to re-zap my brain. Then he'd ask me again and I would tell him the future was green. Back in the Mambomatic I'd go. I couldn't take it any longer, so, I, I came up with a story. A story I knew he'd like. I couldn't go back into the Mambomatic. I had to stop the cycle." If dogs could cry, he would have been bawling.

This was new and amazing to me. The dog had deliberately said something false. "I didn't know we could do that."

"Do what?" replied the dog.

"Not tell the truth," I answered. "Make up stories."

"You crack me up, Half-Baked," said the pig. "There's nothing stopping us from lying."

That was the pig's nickname for me. He and the others considered me incomplete. Not fully cooked. Half-baked. Not very flattering, if you ask me. Not to mention the whole undertones of cooking chicken. Pluck our feathers, chop us up, cover us with herbs, and then stick us in the oven. You humans make me sick. I honestly don't know why I'm writing this book for you.

"I understand. It just never occurred to me before. I've just always told the truth. The possibility of making up false stories is exciting. I can't wait to try it out."

"Let'thh move on," said the cow. "Let'thh figure out what it means to see the future as green."

The dog scratched the floor with a paw. "It means... Well, well, it means. Ummmm... How am I supposed to know what it means? I'm not Raisin Bran. I don't know everything. Ask the cat. She knows everything."

"I cannot assist you in ascertaining the meaning of a green future," said the cat. "It is indeed most illogical. I agree with Dr. Hash Browns' assessment that your power to see the future needs adjustment."

"I think it means something bad," I surmised. "Failure. Error. I remember the cat telling me, green flashing LEDs indicate error or failure."

"Avocados are green, dude," said the duck, whose eyes never left the video game screen. "Maybe we become avocado farmers." We all ignored his comment.

"Man, I'm confused. I thought dogs were color blind," said the rabbit. Nobody paid any attention to his remark, either.

"Was it all the same shade of green?" asked the fish, in a manner that indicated the answer held significance.

The dog scratched his ear and then said, "It's, it's mostly the same color green, but it kind of, it kind of pulsates, or has waves where the green changes to a slightly lighter shade of green, and it kind of waves around, for whatever that's worth. I mean, what difference does it make? It's green. Green. I see the future as green."

"It could be important. The ColbyJacks use a wavy light green symbol to represent creativity and art, while a dark green symbol, consisting of straight lines and jagged edges, represents logic and science. They display these symbols together on flags and banners as a reminder to strive for balance in life. So, is it a mix of dark and light green?"

"No. Just light green. There's no, no dark green," said the dog, unenthused by the fish's line of questioning.

"Forget the ColbyJack theory. Are there any other colors?"

"Nope."

"Hmmm." The fish circled above the dog's head. "I conclude seeing green in our future to be good. On most planets, green symbolizes positive things. It is often the personification of life itself. An icon of growth and abundance of life. Yes, I believe it's good. Very good indeed."

The dog glanced at me and did an eye roll only I could see. "Whatever," he said. This wasn't anything new. The dog rarely found the fish's advice or theories useful or accurate.

"I'm serious." The fish swam up to the cow, presumably in search of an ally. "Dr. Hash Browns could have gotten a big promotion that required a relocation, or he headed back to Cheddar to prepare for this big award. In his excitement, it slipped his mind to come and say goodbye to us. This will all turn out fine."

"But why didn't he thhay goodbye." The cow stared past the fish, fixated on the jumbotrons.

I pointed to the big screens. "How do you explain the people stealing the pool table?"

"They are moving our operation to Cheddar, where Dr. Hash Browns is preparing our new laboratory; our new home," said the fish.

"If you say so," said the dog, though the sideways scrunch of his mouth suggested skepticism of the fish's theory.

"I located the Senior Vice President of Intergalactic Strategy and Synergies, Mr. Steak&Eggs." The cat pointed her paw at the computer screen. "He has assumed control of Dr. Hash Browns' office. I acquired full video and audio surveillance of said office. Eavesdropping on the Senior Vice President's conversations may assist in ascertaining what has become of Dr. Hash Browns."

The jumbotron screens switched to a video feed of Dr. Hash Browns' ex-office. The image disgusted me. In Dr. Hash Browns' comfy, brown leather office chair sat Mr. Steak&Eggs, with his chubby, lilac-colored feet resting on the desk. Over the years, Dr. Hash Browns acquired a beautiful mahogany desk set and other treasures from Earth. Scattered about the room were many large plants, a couple small lawn statues, two pinball games, a leopard skin sofa, a fully stocked cigarette vending machine, several out-of-date globes, an original Pablo Picasso, a two-foot by four-foot framed portrait of Floyd the Barber from Andy Griffith, nonfunctioning electronic devices of all shapes and sizes, a water cooler, Elvis on black velvet, a life size concrete statue of an angel crying, and a blue English police box. I remember his disappointment that the police box wasn't bigger on the inside and that the angel statue didn't move when he wasn't looking.

A young Cheddarian male stood sobbing in front of Mr. Steak&Eggs' newly acquired desk. The Senior Vice President studied the Picasso hanging on the wall. "Is the rectangle meant to be her nose?"

The sobbing Cheddarian looked at the painting. "I..., I guess so. I'm not sure what else it could be."

"That's what I was thinking," said Mr. Steak&Eggs, continuing to stare at the painting.

"Sir, what about my request?"

"Sorry, but you signed up for this duty and you will complete your assignment," said the Senior Vice President.

"But my wife, sir, she's ill. They say she won't make it through the week. The next cargo ship leaves in an hour. I need to be on that ship."

"Look, Dry Toast," said Mr. Steak&Eggs, as he rose from his chair and walked up to the Picasso.

"It's Wheat Toast, sir."

"Here's the problem, Toast. If I let you go home, everyone on the ship will want to leave. The next thing you know, I've got no crew."

"Please, sir. I have a baby boy. He needs me. I need to go home." Wheat Toast dropped to his knees and sobbed.

The Senior Vice President rolled his eyes in genuine annoyance at the dramatics. "Sausage, get this pathetic being out of my office."

"Sure thing, boss."

"Please, sir, I'm begging you. I need to go home."

"Good day, Mr. Toast."

Bagel had been stretched out on the leopard skin sofa, intently typing on her portable computer. I am a chicken, so to me, Bagel was just another lavender-skinned creature with four scrawny arms and two gangly legs, but apparently most male Cheddarians would find Bagel, as you humans say, hot. I struggled to understand the appeal. She had a thinner midsection compared to other Cheddarian, but still eggplant-shaped. Maybe it's how her flowing orange hair hid her toothpick neck, or the glow in her light-blue cat-like eyes. My top theory was based on something I read which claimed confidence to be the primary trait that attracts a mate. Bagel radiated confidence. She alone stood up to Mr. Steak&Eggs. Sausage and Bacon towered over Mr. Steak&Eggs, yet still cowered in fear of him. But not Bagel. She never backed down to the man. Her extreme confidence reminded me of the pompous roosters strutting around the barnyard, cock-a-doodle-dooing all day long. They expected all us chickens to worship the ground they pooped on. Let me announce to the world, we didn't. Perhaps this memory is why I didn't find Bagel attractive.

"It's amazing what they do with these cows," said this so-called attractive female Cheddarian. Apparently, she had found Dr. Hash Browns' portal to Earth's Internet and had been researching cows. "There are thousands and thousands of recipes for preparing the meat."

"Cheddarians have been eating replicator meat for so long, we've forgotten how delicious real meat is," said Mr. Steak&Eggs.

Bagel acted as if she hadn't heard his comment. "You can drink the milk. They freeze the cream and eat it as a sweet treat called ice cream. Or they let this milk go bad and turn into a solid substance they call cheese. Believe it or not, they eat this rotten, solidified milk and like it. And you're not going to believe this. That chair you're sitting in is covered in cow skin."

"That's interesting," said Mr. Steak&Eggs, as he lifted his arms off the armrests, scanned the leather chair, and uncomfortably wiggled his butt.

The cow turned away from the screens. "I think I'm going to be sick. I can't believe humans do this to cows."

Me and the other herbivores agreed. It repulsed us. The carnivores, the cat, dog, and fish, had no concerns.

"It's, it's a dog-eat-dog world," said the dog.

The dog didn't use the phrase "dog-eat-dog world" and he would be quite disturbed to hear you humans use it. Instead, he used a Cheddarian phrase, which has a key distinction: the Cheddarish phrase makes sense. It substitutes a species that eats its own kind. Dogs don't eat other dogs. Where did your human phrase come from? Why don't you say, 'It's a fish-eat-fish world?' That would make sense.

Back in Dr. Hash Browns' ex-office, Bagel got up off the couch and brought her portable computer over to Mr. Steak&Eggs. "They even make hats out of the meat."

The cat did a quick change of camera angles, so we could view her laptop screen, which displayed the "Hats of Meat" web page, which is, or at least was, a real site.

"Wow, those are some ugly creatures wearing really ugly hats," said Mr. Steak&Eggs, as they viewed a photo gallery of humans wearing hats made from raw meat. Some from steaks. Others molded out of ground beef. None attractive. "I bet those hats stink after a couple of days."

"I would imagine," agreed Bagel.

"These Earthlings only have two arms. How do they play hextiltonion ball?" asked the boss.

I tired of naming alien things after cheese or breakfast foods or whatever, so I just made up the word, hextiltonion. I don't even know how you would pronounce it. Anyway, hextiltonion ball is the most popular Cheddarian sport. I know nothing about the sport, but assume you need four arms to play and bet the longer and skinnier the arms, the better.

"They don't play hextiltonion on their planet," said Bagel.

"I suppose you're right."

A portly little periwinkle-skinned creature with four long skinny arms and two not so lanky legs sauntered into the office. What hair he had on the top of his head was rather unkempt. He dressed in casual clothing, with sandals on his enormous feet, and wore thick black plastic glasses.

"What have you got for me, Grits?" asked Mr. Steak&Eggs.

Grits plopped into the chair in front of the desk. "You're not gonna like it, sir. They're using a ChaCha-QZ as the main power generator. It uses Jitterbug technology for crying out loud. It must be over 200 years old. The tech sheets and sales ads claim it could fly through a black hole and keep working. That was a bunch of baloney. The piece of junk shuts down dead if it encounters a simple foxtrot wave. You know what's really funny? The manufacturer was so confident in the design and durability of these generators, ships and space stations that installed ChaCha-QZs could ignore code and not equip any backup power. The manufacturer went bankrupt after the lawsuits and subsequent bans stemming from the Mozzarella disaster. Terrible tragedy. If only they had installed a backup generator."

"Great," Mr. Steak&Eggs said, with the enthusiasm of someone who just learned their puppy has fleas. "So, we could lose power at any time and if we do, there's no backup."

"Unlikely we'll encounter any foxtrot waves way out here, but if something goes wrong with the generator, yes, it's lights out, permanently."

"Fine. What about the computers?"

"You're not gonna like this either," said Grits, spinning the globe next to his chair. "The heart of the computer system is three Galliard[1] 7.5 processors." He chuckled. "My son's toy race car has more processing power than these dinosaurs."

Grits did not say dinosaurs, since he's never heard of dinosaurs. He referenced an ancient extinct Cheddarian species, which is the rough equivalent of your dinosaurs.

"You'll never guess what operating system they're running." I guess he knew Mr. Steak&Eggs would never guess, because Grits didn't give him any time to. "Conga. It gets better. Release 82.3.0. Can you believe it?" Grits laughed so hard, he had to wipe a tear from his eye.

---

1. Galliard is a Cheddarian computer chip which has been out of date for quite some time, or a 16th and 17th Century five step sprightly dance done to popular phrases of the time.

"Hard to believe," said Mr. Steak&Eggs, although I doubt he had a clue Conga was an unpopular 200-year-old operating system and release 82.3.0 still holds the record for the lowest rated operating system ever released on Cheddar. I did not know all that either. The cat told me.

"And the life support system. Well, the only thing that's holding it together is Hip Hop caulk and strips of this gray adhesive. We're lucky to still be breathing. My advice, we leave all this worthless junk and split while we're still alive. These rolls of gray adhesive strips are the only thing worth taking." He tossed Mr. Steak&Eggs a roll of gray duct tape. "I found eight cases of this stuff on level two. It's ridiculously handy. I fixed my glasses with it."

"Great," said Mr. Steak&Eggs, though his face showed no enthusiasm for duct tape. "How long have we got?"

"It's working fine for now, but I can't say for how long. Could be two minutes, two hours, two days, or two years. Or, it could last another two hundred years."

"Can't you fix it?" asked Bagel.

Grits shook his head and held up an open hand stop sign with his upper left hand. "I'm afraid to touch it. If I mess with it now, it *will* break. I'm taking the approach that if it ain't broke, don't fix it."

"That's not very comforting," said Bagel.

"No good news so far," said Mr. Steak&Eggs, as his enormous head banged slowly into the leather chair's headrest. "How about the lab equipment?"

"The Waltz and Polka might fetch a hundred at an antique auction and we can donate the workstations to an underprivileged school for a tax write-off. The rest is trash."

"In summary, the computer systems are painfully slow and run on the worst operating system in history, the power generator is outlawed in most galaxies and will implode if we encounter a foxtrot wave, the life support systems could fail at any moment, and the lab equipment is worthless."

"That sums it up, boss." Grits relaxed in his chair and crossed both sets of arms.

Mr. Steak&Eggs popped out of the chair and paced behind his desk. All four hands clenched into fists. "Fifty years at the finest business schools and a hundred and fifty years under the direct apprenticeship of Buckwheat Hotcakes himself, and they send me halfway across the universe to throw out the trash. I'm a Senior Vice President! I deserve more respect."

The founder and Chief Executive Officer of Original Research Projects by Hotcakes Incorporated (ORPH Inc) is the Tri-Galaxy renowned entrepreneur Buttermilk Hotcakes. Mr. Steak&Eggs has never met him, but he spent several decades serving Buttermilk's lazy as a sloth, worthless as a wireline phone on Mars, barely smarter than the asteroids flying past the space station, nephew, Buckwheat.

"It would have been cheaper to let Dr. Hash Browns continue on, unfunded. Eventually the space station would have self-destructed," said Grits with a smirk on his face.

Mr. Steak&Eggs pounded his two left fists on the desk. "This is all Egg Sandwich's doings. He sent me on this wild-goose chase to keep me away during the restructuring meetings. He knows if I were there, I'd end up being his boss. Well, I'll show him. Once I introduce steak and milk to Cheddar, I'll be a household name and rich beyond my wildest dreams." He flopped into the big leather office chair, formerly used by Dr. Hash Browns. "Do you have anything else to report?"

Grits shrugged. "Nope. That wraps it up." He stood up and took a step toward the door. "If you're not going to use that roll of tape, can I have it back?"

After a grunt, Mr. Steak&Eggs tossed him the duct tape. Grits had to lunge to catch it. As he stepped into the doorway, he stopped. "Oh yeah, there's a bunch of strange looking animals in the lab, just hanging out drinking coffee. What do you want done with them?"

"Those are the crazy scientist's experiments. Dispose of them along with the rest of the trash," said Mr. Steak&Eggs.

"Wait!" interjected Bagel. "One of those animals is a cow. Remember, he said he made a cow talk and insisted we should be impressed by that."

Our eyes shifted from the big screens to the cow's face. Her expression remained stoic, and her gaze fixed on the screens. *Did she not realize their intentions?*

The rabbit and duck continued playing their video game, oblivious to what we had heard.

"What the heck is a cow?" replied Grits.

"It's a rather large animal. Stands on all fours. Sometimes they're brown or black, or white with black spots. They kind of look like a brackahedron[2]. Wait." She grabbed her portable computer and typed away. "I came across some pictures, somewhere. Hmmm. Oh, here's one." She turned her computer screen so Mr. Steak&Eggs and Grits could see the picture of Uma, the Wisconsin dairy cow who won the blue ribbon at the Kenosha County Fair in 2002. Uma had the hind of a classic dairy cow, white with black spots.

Grits scratched his chin with his upper right hand. "Hmm. White with black spots. I think I saw one in that lab."

"Hey, Steakie, why don't you bring up the surveillance cameras in the lab," said Bagel.

"Good idea. Bring up the camera in the lab. No problem." Mr. Steak&Eggs stared helplessly at the computer screen on his desk.

***

THE CAT REMOVED THE video from Dr. Hash Browns' former office. Prior to its disappearance, the feed showed Mr. Steak&Eggs poking at his computer screen with all four hands in a desperate attempt to activate the laboratory security cameras.

---

2. A brackahedron is the closest thing on Cheddar to a cow but more closely resembles a hippo. And yes, I made up the name brackahedron and you can pronounce it anyway you like. Pronounce it "sausage pizza" for all I care. Wait, I like that. Yes, it's spelled B R A C K A H E D R O N, but pronounced "sausage pizza". I can do that. Nobody can stop me.

"I have confirmation the Cheddarian intruders have activated the laboratory's video surveillance cameras," said the cat, as she shifted back to working on a computer.

"Everybody, act casual," said the cow, with a glare toward the dog. "We don't want them to know we've been watching them."

The cow and dog resumed their chess match, while the pig went back to working out, and the rabbit and duck continued to play their video game. I had no clue where the fish had swum off to.

Confused about where to go or what to do, I ended up over by the pig's exercise equipment.

"What are you doing over here, Half-Baked?" asked the pig in between forehoof curls.

I didn't have an answer. I had never exercised before. *Bench press? No way I could do that. Squats? Not a chance. Pull-up bar? No. I can't reach the bar. The treadmill. Yes, the treadmill. I can do that.* I'd seen the pig jogging on it. It looked easy. I bounced from the running belt to the control panel and pecked the quick-start button with my beak. The running belt whirred into action. I hopped off the control panel. In the time it took me to plummet to the belt, it had gone from a comfortable walking pace to full on sprint. My right claw scraped the belt and my face implanted into the belt, which promptly spit me across the floor. I spun to a stop near the chess table.

"Chicken. Get over here. Look like you're watching our game of chess," said the cow.

I agreed, thankful for a specific order on how to act casual.

As I watched the dog struggle with his next move, my thoughts ran wild. *Why are they coming for the cow? What do they plan to do with her? Why does my claw itch? It's really annoying knowing they are watching us. Why did Dr. Hash Browns head back home? Why are those two blue lights flashing on the Mambomatic 5000? Should I tell the cat about them? What are their plans for the rest of us? I do not think I am acting casual enough. How do you tell when blue cheese has gone bad? Man, my claw really itches. Would I still look casual if I bent down to peck at it? That might actually make me appear more casual. I should bend down to peck my foot, because I sure don't feel casual sitting here stiff as a statue.*

"Okay, they stopped their surveillance," announced the cat, "but these intruders are now coming to apprehend the cow."

My shoulders lowered, thankful I no longer needed to act casual, but my stomach churned with images of the cow being butchered and her flesh formed into hats.

As I breathed a giant sigh of relief, the dog crawled under the chess table. "This is bad. Bad. Bad. Very bad. We're all doomed." His body quivered as his eyes darted around the room.

"We, we can't, we can't let them take the cow," said the dog. "We've got to do something."

"I got an idea," I said. "We'll build a fake cow out of papier mâché, hide the real cow, and when they come, they'll grab the phony cow by mistake."

Without waiting for feedback, I sprang into action, building the papier mâché cow. I sped around the room with incredible speed. The other animals appeared to move in slow motion. The roar of the life support fans faded into a soothing white noise hiss. I swear they tried to talk to me. Their lips moved, but no audible sounds came out. I completed the wire frame. On went the papier mâché. The others were motionless statues as I grabbed the paints. I gathered more momentum while painting the cow's likeness onto my sculpture. In the middle of my painting, I swear someone said hello. A low, kind of sad hello. I dismissed it, assuming it must be the fans.

I stopped to admire my creation. The laboratory spun around me like an ocean whirlpool as I fixated on my creation, which remained stationary. Everything around my fake cow twisted, warped, and melted. The roar of the space station fans returned, and the lab swirled into focus.

"That was freaky," said the pig. "You built that whole thing in like two seconds flat."

"I must say, the realism is quite outstanding," said the fish. "Which I didn't expect. I considered you more of an abstract artist."

"How did you, how did you get it to dry so fast?" asked the dog.

"It is indeed an incredible replica of the cow's image, but it is doubtful the replica will fool the intruders." The cat could not bear to give me a compliment. She paused and contemplated. "Besides, the intruders apprehending the cow may not be our most pressing concern. They plan to throw the rest of us out with the trash."

"I've got a plan." The pig flexed his front hooves into a classic double bicep pose. "We kick their skinny butts back to the galaxy they came from."

"But, but, but what if they have guns or nets or flamethrowers?" asked the dog.

"I say, bring it on," The pig ran through a series of punches with his front hooves. He finished the routine with a boxer's pose and a grunt.

"We need to relax and come up with a plan. If we work together and utilize the special powers Dr. Hash Browns gave uthh, I'm sure we'll find a way out of this jam. But we've got to work together, and that means everybody." The cow glanced over at the rabbit and duck, who had continued to play their video game, paying no attention to our conversation. "Rabbit. Duck. Could you stop playing that insipid game? We're in serious trouble here. Our lives are at stake, and we need everybody'thh help."

At first, neither responded. After about three seconds, the rabbit momentarily diverted his attention away from the video game to ask, "What?" The duck seized the moment and put an end to the game by destroying the rabbit's character. "Dude, I can't believe you just did that. Did you hear our lives are in danger? Instead of finding out why, you kill me. You're evil, dude. You know that, don't you? I hate you."

"Gentlemen, we're in serious danger. Mr. Steak&Eggs has taken over the space station and wants to throw us out with the trash. So, do you think you could stop playing that child'thh game and help save us from being tossed into outer space?"

"Dude, did you say someone's taken over the space station?"

"Haven't you been listening? Yethh, someone has taken over the space station."

"Like we're under attack, man?"

"No, we're not under attack," said the cow.

"Dude, how could someone have taken over the space station without attacking?"

"Yeah, that don't make any sense, man. No attack. No victory," added the rabbit, as he clicked to start a new game.

The cow's eyes rolled toward the ceiling. I suspected she second guessed her decision to engage these two into the conversation. "Well, it doesn't matter if it makes sense or not, that'thh what happened. And what's with you two? Why do you keep calling me dude, and he keeps calling me man? I'm a cow, not a dude or a man."

"Sorry, dude; didn't realize I do that," said the duck.

"What can I say? That's what we do, man," said the rabbit. "So, these guys want to throw us all in the trash?"

"Well, not all of us. For reasons unknown, they want to keep me," said the cow.

"Oh, I see. Aren't you the special one, man?"

"I'm sure they have something even nastier in mind to do to me. Like make hats out of me."

"So, whose butt do we need to kick, man?"

"Now that's what I'm talking about," said the pig.

The duck noticed my creation. "Dude, where did that other cow come from?"

The cat raised a paw to her forehead. "It's not a real cow."

"I made it out of papier mâché," I said, proud of my creation.

"Whoa, you made that? That's awesome, dude. I, like, totally thought that was a real cow. It's so lifelike."

"Well, thank you."

"Why don't we, like, give these dudes this fake cow?" asked the duck.

"We have already analyzed this scenario and pointed out its obvious flaws," said the cat.

"Besides, we need a plan to save uthh all. Ideas?"

We stared at each other in silence, as if a teacher had asked a tough question.

As I expected, the pig broke the silence. "We need to turn this lab into a stronghold. Let's barricade all the doors, except one. This will force them to funnel their attack through that single entry point."

Since the room we called the laboratory had previously been a school gymnasium, there were multiple entranceways, including paths through the locker rooms.

The pig strutted over to the lineup of school lab tables cluttered with computers and electronics. "We can use these. We just need to clear off all this computer junk." The pig pushed a stack of computers to the floor.

The cat squealed and hunched up like the letter n. "Stop! That's delicate and expensive lab equipment. Why not use your heavy weight set and workout equipment."

"According to the Cheddarian nerd, these computers are worthless." The pig casually flipped the long bar-height table to its side, sprawling the remaining contents across the tile floor. "Everyone, pitch in. Let's get these tables in front of the doors."

The dog scurried up to the next lab table, bit down on a leg, and attempted to drag it. He created a ton of screeching, but barely moved the table.

"Dude, we're ninja warriors. We'll take care of whatever comes through any of them doors," said the duck.

"Besides, man, I need to avenge that last loss." The chords announcing the start of the game radiated from their monitor.

An alternative to fighting popped into my mind. I figured someone needed to suggest the flight option. "Why don't we head for the escape pod and get the heck out of here?"

"I'm not running away from a fight," said the pig. "It's time we used our powers and showed these skinny-armed pencil-neck geeks what we're made of. Now help with these tables, Half-Baked."

I didn't think it was that bad of an idea. Making the fake cow was a little crazy and stupid, but heading to the escape pods has merit. *How did I do that, anyway? I sped around the lab at the speed of light, or close to it. Maybe faster than light. I've never done that before. Did I create a sonic boom? I suppose I would have heard that. Or maybe not. If I caused the sonic boom by exceeding the speed of sound, I would have outrun the sound.*

The fish snapped my train of thought. "Heading to the escape pods isn't the worst idea," he said. "When threatened, one has two options: fight or flight. In this case, the flight option has low risk."

The cat looked up from her computer screen. "I have been evaluating the merits of this proposal."

I expected a dissertation on the stupidity of my suggestion. *Come on kitty, kitty, kitty. Let me have it. Tell everybody how stupid I am.*

"Evacuating via the escape pods does appear to be an acceptable solution," she said.

Wait, I think that means she agrees with me. My beak drooped wide open.

"Mr. Steak&Eggs dispatched two assailants to apprehend the cow and dispose of the rest of us. I am tracking their position. They are currently wandering the halls two floors below our location. We have more than ample time to reach the escape pod and, as you say, 'get the heck out of here.'"

She did agree with me. Heck, she even quoted me.

"What are we, what are we waiting for? I love this plan. Let's go!" The dog bounded for the door.

"Hold on there, Fido," said the pig. "I've got three votes for fighting and four for running away. But the voting isn't over. Cow, what's your opinion? We stand our ground and kick their scrawny butts or run away like a pack of cowards?"

Everyone, except the rabbit and duck, stared at the cow. She looked to be chewing cud as she contemplated her vote. "There is clear danger if we stay and fight. I vote for flight. To the escape pod."

The dog ran in circles by the door, waiting for someone to open it. Grabbing the door handle in her mouth, the cow pulled it open. The dog rushed through the ensuing slit, flew down the hall, and made a sprawling turn in the wrong direction down the next hallway.

BYH
BarnYard Heroes

Chapter 6

AFTER RETRIEVING THE DOG with a loud whistle from the fish, me and the other animals waddled, hopped, and swam down the hallway. The clacking of hooves and scrapping of claws echoed in the empty corridors. The hallway décor would have been more appropriate for a public bathroom. White subway tiles covered the walls, with a chair rail height strip of black. Self-adhesive black and white vinyl tiles checkered the floor. The abandoned classroom doors and trim shimmered with a coat of glossy black paint. I drifted to the back of the pack and noticed how the pig's pink skin and fish's metallic green and blue scales stood out as the only splashes of color. The duck and I had all white feathers. The rabbit had a solid white coat, which contrasted the cat's all-black fur. The cow featured the traditional dairy cowhide of white with black spots, while the dog's border collie coloring was mostly black, with white on his neck, front left leg, and a stripe between his eyes. The hallway fell short of providing us camouflage, but our color scheme matched.

At each hallway intersection, the cat signaled for us to stop. She tracked the invaders on her small handheld computer. "There are no Cheddarians in this hallway. We may proceed." She waved for us to follow her as she made a left.

"How many people are on the station?" asked the cow.

"The computer reports one hundred and two Cheddarian life-forms on this space station," the cat reported.

"One hundred and two?!" said the cow.

"Correct. They are positioned in various locations around the space station." The cat flashed her handheld computer, displaying the floor plan of the third floor littered with tiny blinking red dots. "These three dots show the location of the Senior Vice President, Mr. Steak&Eggs, and his two bodyguards. Thirteen Cheddarians occupy the cargo bay and six others scattered about the third floor."

"What are they doing?" the cow asked.

"I cannot say with absolute certainty, but surmise they are performing an inventory of the space station's assets. Once inventoried, they transport the item to the cargo bay and either jettison the item into space or transfer it onto the docked ORPH Inc. ship."

"It sounds like they're preparing for a giant garage sale," said the cow.

"I believe estate sale would be a more appropriate term," said the fish.

The cat held up a paw. "We are approaching a corridor intersection. It is time to cease movements and verbal communications."

"Dude, what is that supposed to mean?" asked the duck.

"It meanthh stop walking and be quiet."

The cat examined her handheld computer. "No Cheddarian life forms in the next hallway. We may proceed."

"So, where are those goons they sent to get uthh?"

The cat flipped through a couple of screens to display the layout of the fifth floor and pointed to a couple of fast-moving blinking dots. "The two, as you say, goons, are on a different floor and proceeding in a direction opposite to ours."

The cat once again motioned for silence as she checked her screen. "We may proceed."

We continued toward the escape pods, turning right at the next hallway, left two hallways later and another right at the next. Down this hallway, six Cheddarians huddled around dismantled pieces of the flight simulator. One worked a giant wrench, while the others watched.

Before we had the chance to scramble back around the corner, a crew member noticed us. He nudged the crew member with the wrench and nodded toward us. The rest turned their heads. Their expressions contained no fear, only confusion.

As the rest of us clumped together, the dog bolted in retreat. I contemplated chasing after him but stuck with the animal cluster. *Safety in numbers*. I pictured the dog making it to the shuttle and preparing it for our departure.

The cow tapped the cat with a hoof. "I thought you were checking the hallways?"

"Affirmative, and the scanners indicate there are no Cheddarians in this hallway." The cat poked at her handheld device and smacked it with her free paw. "I cannot explain."

The rabbit pointed at the upper left corner of the screen. "Dude, aren't we on the third floor?"

The duck popped his head over the cat's shoulder. "So, why are you looking at the fifth floor, man?

"Hrmph. Of course." The cat flopped her tail on the tile flooring, as she flipped back to the third-floor view, to see the cluster of blinking red dots in the hallway we stood in. "I changed screens because the cow requested a visual on the crewmembers dispatched to retrieve us. Then all of your inane banter distracted me, and I forgot to revert to our current floor. If not for the floor plans being identical, I would have noticed this obvious error."

"Smooth move, Raisin Bran." The rabbit rubbed the cat's head, pulling his paw away before the cat sunk her fangs into it. "So, what do we do now, dudes?"

The Cheddarians formed a disjointed line in front of the dismantled flight simulator. The one with the wrench flipped it over her right shoulder and assumed a position in the middle of the line. They exchanged glances with each other, in between glares at us. They muttered to each other like a pack of middle schoolers and did a lot of shoulder shrugging.

We stared at the cow. She shrugged her shoulders. She gave no order. We instinctively assembled into our own line.

The cow took a step forward.

The rest of us inched up with her.

The enormous eyes of the Cheddarians grew wider and continued to shift between each other and us. The one with the wrench nodded and stepped forward. The others hesitated, then followed suit.

Without warning, the pig yelled, "Hoozah!!!" and charged the befuddled Cheddarians. Unfortunately, milliseconds after the pig's charge, the cat summoned a tornado. At first, the spiraling tunnel of winds stood no taller than a mouse on its hind legs. The Cheddarians didn't even notice it.

"Why did you summon a tornado? In a hallway? You're going to kill uthh all."

"I intended it as a diversion," said the cat. "Providing us an opportunity to reach the escape pod via an alternate route."

The tornado grew to the size of a groundhog, as it bounced from wall to wall, trailing the pig's hind leg waddle charge.

"I had not anticipated the pig initiating a full-frontal assault."

"We're with ya, dude!" said the duck.

"HOOZAH!!!" yelled the rabbit.

The pair yelled "Ki-A!" and "Yah!" as they leaped, hopped, and spun down the hallway in awe-inspiring ninja fashion, before coming to an abrupt stop. The cat's tornado had swelled to silverback gorilla size. They took a step back.

The salvage crew also took a step back.

Even we took a step back.

The pig never saw it coming. It sucked him into its vortex and spit him into the wall. He rebounded off that wall and smashed into the adjacent wall. The now grizzly bear sized tornado sucked him up again and threw him crashing through a doorway. The tornado zigged and zagged before squeezing itself into the room.

The salvage crew shuffled over to the doorway and reacted with increasing horror to each crash and scream, as the tornado destroyed the room, using the pig as its wrecking ball. Once they had seen enough, they closed the door and backed away.

Stricken with paralysis, the other animals and I remained motionless as the horrific scene unfolded. I contemplated rushing to his aid, but I would not be able to open the old-fashioned doorknobs used on the classroom doors. In fact, the pig, thanks to his karate-clench hooves, was the only one of us who had mastered the doorknob principle. The pig would have to save himself.

So, instead of rescuing the pig, the rabbit and duck resumed their attack. If they had come at me with those flips and kicks, it would have scared the solar flares out of me, but as Dr. Hash Browns noted, the rabbit and duck are tiny; compared to humans or Cheddarians. Despite their amazing leaping ability, awesome ninja moves, and nasty sharp pointy teeth, the salvage crew stood ten to twenty times their size and showed no fear. In fact, they appeared amused by the oncoming attack.

When the tiny ninjas hopped and spun themselves close enough to the Cheddarians, the crewmember carrying the wrench stepped forward. She clenched the wrench in her right two hands and swatted the rabbit into one wall with a double handed tennis smash. She followed up with a hard backhand, smacking the duck into the opposite wall. Clearly, she had played hextiltonion in her youth.

My two friends slid down the walls like tiny sacks of kitty litter. Before they could shake off the blow, crew members grabbed them and stuffed them into a shipping crate. A crewmember slammed the lid closed. As she clapped both sets of hands, satisfied with a job well done, the fish swam up to her.

He came level with her eyes and hovered perpendicular to her.

I smacked my forehead with a wing. *Oh no, he's trying to hypnotize her.* It hurt to watch.

The fish did his Bela Lugosi impersonation. "Look into my eyes."

She did no such thing. She scanned the faces of her crewmates before settling on the one with the wrench, who lifted the wrench and took a swipe at the fish.

The fish didn't blink or flinch as the wrench whizzed through him. "Picture yourself lying on the warm sands of a beach. Imagine the gentle ripple of waves."

"What the –," said the Cheddarian with the wrench, as she exchanged more puzzled looks with the fish's target. She took three more swings with the wrench, which harmlessly passed through the steadfast fish.

"The sun warms your face. Your eyelids grow heavy. You close..." With glazed eyes, the fish rolled on his side and drifted over the head of the Cheddarians. He had hypnotized himself. Again.

The salvage crew's puzzled expression had vanished. With an air of confidence, they advanced on those of us who remained: the cow, the cat, and me.

The cat's eyes bounced between me and the approaching posse. "Every animal for themself! RUN AWAY!!!" With that said, the cat sprang off, making a hasty retreat.

The cow activated her cloak. Dr. Hash Browns called it an invisibility power, but you could still see a clear outline of the cow, similar to the creature in the Predator movies.

Her outline took off in the opposite direction of the cat. I hesitated, indecisive about which of them to follow. A salvage crew member grabbed me by the throat and threw me into the shipping crate before I decided. The lid slammed shut and locked tight right before I broke into hyperspeed. I slammed into the lid, before dropping onto the rabbit's head.

***

As I prepared to thrust myself at the lid of the crate, I received a face full of wing. The rush of wind from a flap of the duck's wings ruffled my feathers. A thud preceded the duck landing on top of me.

The duck rolled off me. "Thanks for breaking my fall, dude."

"Let me try it, man." The rabbit hopped, smacked his head on the lid, and dropped onto my head.

"Dude, shouldn't there be some sort of safety release?"

"There should totally be a safety release. Like in a car trunk, man."

The pair jumped in the darkness, swatting the air, lid, and sides of the crate, causing the box to hop across the hallway floor until a simultaneous kick pushed the crate over.

"Dude, that was awesome," said the duck. They attempted a chest bump in the dark, resulting in both banging into the crate's lid, which had moved from a ceiling to a wall after the fall.

"Man, that seal is airtight."

"This is an intergalactic shipping crate," I said. "The seal has to be airtight."

"Well, dude, it's a good thing we don't have to breathe."

"Thank you, Dr. Hash Browns," said the rabbit.

Thanks to Dr. Hash Browns, the others could survive days without breathing. He hadn't completed my enhancements. I wasn't sure how long I could survive without oxygen, but I knew it wasn't days. I pushed them out of my way and pecked at the lid.

"Dude, what's gotten into you?"

"You said it yourself, man. The seal is airtight."

"I need to breathe. Once the oxygen runs out, I'm a goner." *Or would the carbon dioxide kill me first? Do chickens breathe out carbon dioxide? Do the rabbit and duck exhale carbon dioxide? Regardless, I have minutes or hours, not days and weeks.* I pounded on the crate wall. "Open up! We're going to suffocate. You're killing us!!"

The rabbit and duck joined me. We pounded and screamed until it became apparent no one would respond.

"I better conserve my breaths." I plopped down and took a couple of deep inhales, believing they might be my last. "Would I conserve breaths if I went to sleep?"

"Dude, don't go to sleep. Stay with us. You pass out, you're dead."

"Man, you're an idiot. You're thinking concussions, not suffocations."

"Well, I still don't think she should pass out."

"Agreed. And since we don't need oxygen, the oxygen in the box is all yours, man."

"Thanks, guys," I said, with a heavy sigh.

The rabbit put a paw on my thigh and the duck wrapped a wing around my shoulder.

"It's going to be alright, man."

"For sure. The cat's free and she's like the smartest dude of us all."

"The cow is out there, too, man. She'll save us because she's kinda like our mom."

"You get the two of them teamed up. Forget about it, dude."

"Well, they better do it before I suffocate in this box."

"Don't worry about that, man. We've got you covered. You run out of air, we'll give you mouth-to-mouth, man."

I appreciated the offer, but the image of mouth-to-mouth from either of them grossed me out. If the dog had been offering, with his hypnotic brown eyes, sign me up for the near-death experience.

"Dude, I'm out on that action. That's all on you." I felt the crate's vibration from the duck's vigorous head shaking.

"What's wrong with you, man? You afraid of chicken cooties, you big baby?"

Even though the concept had sickened me, I took offense to the duck's quick refusal to save my life.

"Duck bill to chicken beak, dude. That ain't gonna work. No chance of a seal. It's going to be up to you and your rabbit lips."

"Fine. I'll save the chicken's life while you sit there and do nothing."

I knew the dog was afraid of everything from wet jellybeans to the concept of cottage cheese, yet images of the dog racing toward the crate, pulling me out, and resuscitating me with sloppy mouth-to-mouth sent warm tingles to the tips of my claws. "What about the dog? He's still out there. He could save us."

"I wouldn't bet on that, dude."

"Man, I'm betting he's hiding under a table, shaking and shivering."

"Muttering about getting to his happy place," said the duck.

I hated how much they enjoyed making fun of him. "He's braver than you think."

"Please. Dude. He's afraid of sour milk."

"And squeaky toys," said the rabbit.

"And stepping on pavement cracks."

"That's because you two told him it would break his mother's back," I said.

"First," said the rabbit, "there's no pavement in this space station, man."

"Second, the dude's mom is long dead by now."

"There should be no fear in breaking a dead dog's back, man."

"You two are so mean. What's wrong with him loving his mother? And you know he has dyschronometria."

"Dude, I don't see how him fearing the metric system has any relevance."

"No. Dyschronometria is a brain disorder. He doesn't comprehend the passage of time. He doesn't know his family and friends on Earth have passed away by now."

"Oh," said the two in unison.

"That makes us sound like jerks, dude."

"In our defense, we didn't know he had dischronometric."

I decided it wasn't worth correcting the rabbit's mispronunciation and let the conversation end there. The pair remained uncharacteristically quiet, with only the occasional back paw ear scratch and full body feather shake, breaking the silence.

The darkness refused to relent. My eyes drooped shut, but the drop of my head snapped me awake. Fearing this signaled dizziness and the onset of oxygen deprivation, I recited pi to hundred decimal places to convince myself of full brain efficiency. The rabbit and duck had fallen asleep and didn't notice my muttering or each other's snoring. So much for conserving oxygen.

With the counting complete, my eyelids grew heavy once again. I blinked my nictitating membrane, hoping the lubrication would pop the eyes open. My eyelids continued to close. I let one eye close and half my brain sleep, a talent me and all chickens are born with, called unihemispheric slow-wave sleep. No enhancement from Dr. Hash Browns required. With the active half of my brain, I continued reciting pi, while the other half drifted into a dream. *The dog races toward us, with his tongue dangling out the side of his mouth. His shimmering black and white fur flows back, revealing his twinkling brown eyes. "I'll save you. I'll save you all." He flips open the crate latch. I'm passed out, choking for air. His teeth nibble my wing as he gently pulls me from the crate. "You're not dying on my watch." The warmth of his breath wakes me in time to enjoy his lips smothering my beak. A rush of hot air explodes into my lungs, lighting up my eyes. Despite the rush of heat in my breast, chills run down my spine and out my tailfeathers. My heart races and –*

SCREECH!

The arrival of an electric utility cart woke the sleeping half of my brain, as well as the rabbit and duck. We pounded on the tipped over lid.

"Let us out of here!" I yelled.

"Dude, we're out of oxygen," said the duck.

"We're gonna die, man. You gotta save us."

The response to our desperate pleas for help? "Quit your whining," said a grumpy Cheddarian, followed by a swift kick to the crate, spinning it fully around, tumbling us around the inside.

"Hey, jerk, there's living creatures inside this box, man."

"I gathered that when I heard the box talking." He flipped the crate upright, tossing us around again. "Blueberry, grab the other end."

"Are you sure it's locked tight?" asked Blueberry.

"Did you not just hear them complaining about being trapped?"

Blueberry's feet shuffled toward us. "Belgian, have you heard the stories about these mutant animals?" he asked, while picking up his end of the crate. "Did you see the muscles on that pink creature? And they say one of them is a vampire."

"Do you even know what a vampire is?"

"No, and I don't want to find out, especially the hard way. The sooner we space them, the better."

We once again stumbled into walls as they rocked the crate before tossing it onto the back of the utility cart.

A crackle of static preceded the announcement on the space station's PA system. "Belgian and Blueberry Waffle report to the cargo bay immediately. Repeat, Belgian Waffle and Blueberry Waffle, your presence in the cargo bay has been requested by Mr. Steak&Eggs."

The pair's voices were similar, so upon learning they had the same last name, I concluded they had to be brothers.

"That's where we were, but then they sent us to grab this crate," Belgian said, as he stomped on the accelerator, rocking us backwards.

"It's nonstop with this guy," said Blueberry. "Fetch the cow from the lab. Catch the cat. Tranquillize the pig. Find a way to grab the ghost fish. Geez. Doesn't anyone else do anything?"

They didn't mention the dog. He's still free. He'll save me.

BYH

BarnYard Heroes

Chapter 7

THE RABBIT, DUCK, AND I bounced inside the crate like dust on a subwoofer, as the Waffle brothers drove to the cargo bay.

"Dudes, here's the plan," whispered the duck, as he bumped into my shoulder. "As soon as they open that lid, we attack. Full on assault."

"We'll take them totally by surprise, man," said the rabbit.

"That's not much of a plan," I said.

"You got a better one?" asked the duck.

The utility cart turned right, sliding us into the left crate wall.

"No," I said. I didn't have a better plan, but I also didn't have ninja training. The closest I came to a fight happened in my days on Earth, when I bumped a fellow chicken out of the way to feast on the biggest pile of grain. "But I have no fighting skills."

"It's easy, man. Just peck 'em or claw 'em."

"Or smack 'em with a wing."

We screeched to a stop.

"Dudes. Prepare to fight." The rabbit and duck snapped into fighting stances as I wobbled into the wall. I regained my sea legs and nestled in between them. After spreading my claws apart and presenting my wings like a boxer, I grunted my readiness.

Instead of the lid opening, the crate lifted, and we endured the gentle sway of a hammock as they carried us. This had no impact on the rabbit and duck's stance, but I stumbled out of my ill-conceived wings-out-like-a-boxer pose.

"Where are they taking us, man?"

"I don't know. Just be ready, dude,"

"What if they throw us out into space, crate and all?" I asked.

The duck's wing and the rabbit's paw brushed my sides as they dropped their poses.

"Well, that stinks, man."

"We're doomed, dude."

"I have an idea." I projected the best TV lawyer's voice a chicken can do and said, "Hey! You can't toss us into space. We're sapient beings. We have rights." I put the odds in our favor that we could outsmart the Waffle Brothers.

"Keep quiet," said Belgian. "You're only making this worse for yourself."

"You're making it worse for *yourself*." The seriousness of my tone surprised me, and bogus laws flowed through my beak. "Tossing sapient beings into space is a Class B violation of intergalactic law. Are you ready to face a tribunal? Are you ready to spend the next ten years mining helium on some frozen moon at the edge of the galaxy?"

"What's a serpent being?" asked Blueberry, as the brothers stopped walking. The swaying slowed.

"Sapient, you idiot!" It was fun pretending to be a lawyer. "A being of knowledge and wisdom, and we have rights throughout the known universe."

"Too bad you're not in the known universe," said Mr. Steak&Eggs, whose presence in the room I should have anticipated. "Besides, you are the property of ORPH Inc., so we can do whatever we feel like doing with you. Space 'em, boys."

The crate resumed a vigorous swing, thrashing us into the walls.

"Wait!" said Mr. Steak&Eggs. "Don't throw the shipping crate out. Do you know how much they cost?"

The crate dropped.

"Back to Plan A, dudes."

The latch clicked. The rabbit and duck struck their poses. I stumbled into position. Light flooded the box. I closed my eyes and blasted through the opening. When I opened my eyes, the dark metal of the cargo bay wall filled my vision. Just like when I made the cow statue, I moved at ludicrous speed. I had no time to stop, turn, bank, or slowdown. Imagine running at full speed into a big steel wall. It would hurt and that's at a sprinting speed of fifteen miles per hour. I estimate my speed at 7,200,000 miles per hour, or nearly 2,000 miles per second. It's not light speed, but faster than you humans have ever gone.

I left a cartoon-style chicken silhouette dent in the solid steel. By all known laws of physics, I should have splattered across the wall, leaving nothing but dripping goo. Instead, I remained in one piece. I am sure I have Dr. Hash Browns to thank for my ability to rocket into a steel wall at speeds of over 7 million miles an hour and live to tell the tale, but oh, the pain. Oh, the pain.

I peeled from the wall like a failing piece of wallpaper and flopped onto the top of an eight-foot shipping container. I did a head-to-tail shake of my feathers before bringing the room into focus. A floor-to-ceiling window caught my attention first. The well-dressed Sausage and Bacon, Mr. Steak&Eggs' personal goons, stood in military at-ease positions staring out the window. To their left loomed the ORPH spacecraft and cluttering the view of the galaxy floated a variety of dressers, desks, chairs, cleaning supplies, random furniture, and general garbage. I had landed on one of many shipping crates, as small as a travel chest to as large as a rail car, stacked in rows along with pallets piled high with stuff pilfered from the space station, prepped for transport across the temporary bridge to the ORPH ship. As I scanned the rest of the cargo bay, my focus locked onto Mr. Steak&Eggs, who paced behind a large control panel table in the center of the room. I narrowed my glare and contemplated charging him to pluck his eyes out.

The clang of a locking door shifted my attention to the airlock located to the right of the large window. In their tattered matching work jumpsuits, the Waffle Brothers performed a chest bump and strutted to the control panel in the middle of the room.

The face of the duck hung behind the airlock window, with the rabbit occasionally jumping into view.

With beaming smiles, the Waffle Brothers stood at the control panel, tapping commands and pressing buttons.

The duck shouted something we could not hear and plastered his face into the window, while the rabbit kicked the door.

Belgium stepped back from the control panel and motioned toward a lever. "Care to do the honors, bro?"

"With pleasure." Blueberry pulled the lever.

The rabbit thumped louder, and the duck pecked at the window.

A muffled blast came from the airlock.

The duck's face disappeared.

The rabbit's thumping stopped.

As the rabbit and duck drifted past the giant window, a swish from the airlock signaled the closing of the outside door. I should have done something. I should have stopped the Waffle Brothers. Instead, I stood and watched my friends get thrown into outer space like unwanted trash.

As the rabbit and duck floated among the debris of desks and tables, I spotted more of my friends. The cat. The cow. The pig. They had all been launched into space. None of them had survived. Only I remained.

Wait, what about the dog? I don't see the dog. He's still free. He'll save me.

Then he bobbed into view and banged into the window.

My shoulders collapsed with a heaving sigh. They were all gone.

"Shouldn't we look for the other creature?" asked Blueberry. "It's got to be lurking about here somewhere."

My survival instincts kicked in and I scurried behind a stack of spare air ventilator parts.

"Forget about the other creatures," said Mr. Steak&Eggs. "I want that cow. Now bring it back in."

"Why do you need another one?" asked Belgian. "You already have a cow over there." He pointed to my cow statue.

Amid all my despair, this warmed my heart. Belgian mistook my statue for a real cow. Tears of joy and sadness swelled in my eyes.

Mr. Steak&Eggs groaned as he grabbed the statue and dragged it in front of the slouching Waffle brothers. "This is not a cow."

"It looks just like the one floating out there," said Blueberry.

"But it's not real!!" To demonstrate his point, Mr. Steak&Eggs ripped the head off my creation and tossed it at Blueberry, who let it bounce off his chest and drop to the floor.

I gasped at the mutilation of art as a cornucopia of emotions swirled for supremacy inside my head and stomach. Hatred of Mr. Steak&Eggs held a slim lead over hopelessness.

"It sure looked real to me," mumbled Blueberry.

"Lucky for you two imbeciles, the real cow appears to be still alive. How that's possible, I do not know." Mr. Steak&Eggs motioned to the control panel in the center of the room. "Now, lock that tractor-beam on it and pull it in."

My head jerked toward the window. I wiped away the tears of mourning and let the tears of joy flow. My friends were alive!! They hadn't frozen to death. The rabbit and duck performed aerial flips and mock fights. The cat curled up for a nap. The dog clawed at the window. The cow and pig appeared to be arguing, which seemed odd since there's no sound in space.

I sprang to my feet, ready to rush to the window and wave to my friends. I stopped when a pale glow of orange light engulfed the cow. She responded with a stern glare and a huff. Her legs and torso stiffened. Then she disappeared.

"Dufus, you just vaporized the cow!" said Belgian.

Joy exhaled out of me as I collapsed once again.

Blueberry checked the controls. "All I did was engage the tractor beam. You can't vaporize anything with a tractor beam."

"Well, you just did," said Belgian.

"What did you idiots do to my cow?" asked Mr. Steak&Eggs.

"Sir, there's no need for panic," said Bacon. "That creature has cloaking skin. It's trying to hide, but if you look closely, you'll see its outline."

The emotional rollercoaster ride continued. I rose once more.

"Oh yeah, I see it now," said Blueberry. He smacked his brother on the shoulder. "See, I didn't blow it up."

"Great. Now pull it in," said Mr. Steak&Eggs.

The Waffle Brothers pushed buttons and pulled levers with increased intensity, but the outline of the cow remained stationary.

Mr. Steak&Eggs hovered behind them. "Why isn't it moving?"

"Well..., ah it, ah appears to be resisting, sir," replied Belgian.

"You have it in a tractor-beam capable of pulling in gigantic spacecraft."

"Yes, we do, but it's not designed to combat resistance," said Belgian Waffle. "It's designed to guide ships to the dock in zero gravity."

"Enough with excuses. Get me my cow, or you're fired!"

With authority, Belgian typed in more commands and pulled a big lever down.

It took a moment to focus on the cow's outline, which remained stationary.

Belgian banged his fist on the console.

I had messed around long enough. It was time for action. A plan formulated. I blasted out of the cargo bay. Without realizing how, I had once again transitioned to hyperspeed. I zoomed down the white walled and black trimmed hallways. They all looked the same and took several wrong turns. When I finally arrived at a laboratory door, I learned a valuable lesson about traveling at speeds approaching the speed of light: automatic doors do not have time to sense your approach. For the second time in a matter of minutes, I dented steel. Stiff as a post, I flopped to the floor. Then the door slid open.

Every bone, claw, and feather throbbed in pain. I did my best to block it out, as I hobbled into the lab and then froze. A team of Cheddarians occupied the lab like a gang of rabid bargain seekers at a garage sale. One team dismantled the pig's exercise equipment, while another loaded the chess table onto a dolly. I recognized one of the Cheddarians. Grits, the man who visited Mr. Steak&Eggs in his office to explain the space station's outdated tech, paced around the Mambomatic 5000 with his bottom arms crossed and his upper right scratching his chin. I detested my journeys through that machine, but I knew Dr. Hash Browns cherished it and called it his greatest invention. I hated seeing it fall into the hands of corporate raiders, who would no doubt strip it for parts.

But I had more pressing matters. I needed to save my friends and had come for papier mâché. I had selected my entrance door wisely. My art supplies cabinet stood just to the left. I grabbed the papier mâché and strolled out of the lab unnoticed. Once in the hallway, I instinctively blasted into hyperspeed and made only two wrong turns along the way to the cargo bay. Bacon and Sausage posed the biggest threat, so I attacked them first. Within milliseconds, I turned them into papier mâché statues and began work on Mr. Steak&Eggs.

"Greetings." It was that strange sad voice I had imagined when I was making the cow statue.

I indulged my delusion. "Hello," I said. "How are you?"

"Oh, not so bad, I guess. Thanks for asking," replied the melancholy voice. "You sure do like papier mâché, aye?"

I didn't have time for small talk with a phantom voice, but I felt obligated to respond. "I guess so. It's new to me, so it's still fun."

"Sure. But it won't work," said the voice.

"What?"

"Look for yourself."

Slow motion cracks appeared in the mummy suits encasing Bacon and Sausage. Elbows and hands protruded through those cracks. The phantom voice sighed as I draped more papier mâché over the cracks, which failed to stop their slow expansion.

"What am I going to do?"

"Are you asking me?" asked the somber voice.

Mine was a rhetorical question, but I assumed the voice to be my conscience, so I said, "Yes, I am asking you."

"Well, if it was me, I would use duct tape. Stronger. Hard to break out of."

Duct tape. Brilliant. My conscience is pretty smart. Without a second thought, I zoomed out of the cargo bay. I knew my way now, and within a fraction of a second, the laboratory door loomed. I remembered I should slow down and wait for the door to open, but I didn't know how to drop out of hyperspeed and once again slammed into the steel door. A couple of feathers floated off me when I did a full body shake. With every part of my tiny chicken body still in pain, I jumped back into hyperspeed, grabbed the roll of duct tape the pig kept by his workout equipment, and darted into the hallway before the doors closed.

Once back in the cargo bay, I had Bacon, Sausage, and Mr. Steak&Eggs mummified in duct tape within microseconds, leaving air holes for them to breathe. I'm not a murderer. The next step in my plan: intimidate the Waffle brothers into pulling my friends in from outer space. This required me to break out of hyperspeed.

"How do I stop this craziness!!" I shouted while hyperspeeding in a circle along the top of the cargo bay walls. I did not expect an answer but got one.

"If you want my advice, you'll need to clarify what craziness needs to stop."

I wondered why my conscience couldn't read our shared brain and know what craziness I meant. But I indulged my conscience once again. "This hyperspeeding. I need to stop it, but I don't know how."

"You could run into the wall. That seems to work effectively for you."

The melancholy tone of my conscience implied it was not joking.

"There's got to be a less painful way."

"You could try reversing what you do to jump into hyperspeed," said the voice, which I could swear came from the middle of the cargo bay and not inside my head.

As I contemplated my vague understanding of how I switched into hyperspeed, dizziness set in. Actually, it did more than set in. It slapped me upside the head and punched me in the gut. I came to an abrupt halt, dropped to the floor, and hurled. I promptly stood up, hopped on to the control panel table, and with the most menacing glare a five-pound woozy chicken can muster, said, "Bring in those animals."

"That's what we've been trying to do, you moron," said Blueberry. "But that stupid cow is resisting."

I went to the window and waved to the cow, signaling to her it was okay to come in, but she continued to resist.

"I'll be back," I said and jumped into hyperspeed. *Paint. I needed paint.* I checked a couple maintain closets and a storage room, but they had all been cleaned out. Then it dawned on me: everything had been moved to the cargo bay. I zipped back and rummaged through the pallets and shipping containers until I found a half-full bucket of paint. I pecked open the can, dipped my wing in and began painting a message to the cow on the giant windows. In huge letters, I wrote, "It is safe. Let them pull you in."

I turned around. The cargo bay pulsated. Nothing came into focus. My stomach somersaulted.

"You don't look so good," said the phantom voice. "I suggest you run into a wall."

I took the phantom voice's advice and slammed into the nearest wall. My entire body already ached. This newest collision failed to increase my pain levels. I popped up and looked out the window. The message had got the cow's attention, but she looked puzzled and continued to resist. *But why? Did she think I was helping Mr. Steak&Eggs set a trap?*

"Chicken, nice message," said a familiar voice.

The fish had swum into the room. *Wasn't he outside with the others?*

"Thanks," I said as I glanced out the window to confirm the fish didn't float amongst the other animals. I understood the futility of this search. The fish hover beside me inside the cargo bay. *Had I imagined seeing the fish or had I forgotten about him?*

"You've got no problem reading the message, then?" asked the fish.

"Of course not. It's clear and simple. Did I spell something wrong?"

The cow continued to resist.

"Nope. All spelled right. But picture yourself on the opposite side of the window and read the message."

I tried to convince myself the cow should realize it's backwards and figure it out, but in Cheddarian, the backwards phrase read, "I get occasional common cheese. Is a fire." Two letters were backwards, making it resemble the redrum/murder mirror flip in The Shining, and the word 'occasional' was misspelled, but a sapient brain would compensate for those errors.

I wanted to backwards write the word 'backwards', but I wrote the initial phrase so big, there was no room. I grabbed some towels and tried to wipe away the message but ended up smearing the paint into clouds.

"Turpentine," said the melancholy mystical voice.

"What?" I asked as I continued at hyperspeed to smear the paint into a big giant cloud.

"You're just making a mess with those wet rags. You need turpentine. Paint remover."

I figured that might only make it worse, so I decided to etch the message in the smeared mess. Back to work I went, scratching out the message with my beak. I had to make three corrections along the way. Writing backwards is hard, but re-smearing the paint provided a nice autocorrect. After completing the rewrite, I propelled myself into the nearest wall.

As I shook my head and ignored the pain, I gazed out the giant window. The cow got the message and ended her resistance. The tractor beam pulled her into the airlock. After a series of door hisses and swishes, the cow strolled out of the airlock and into the cargo bay.

"Impressive work," she said, nodding to my mumbling, mummified victims. "Shall we bring the rest in?"

"Sure," I said and turned to the Waffle brothers. "Bring the others in."

The mumbling mummies mumbled louder.

"Thanks for helping us bring in the stupid cow, but we don't take orders from you," said Belgian.

The mummified Mr. Steak&Eggs managed the loudest grunt he could muster while encased in duct tape, but hard to say if it indicated approval or disapproval.

"She's not stupid," I said. "It's safe to say she's the smartest cow in the universe."

"Thanks for the support," said the cow, before turning her attention to the Waffle Brothers. "Bring the rest of them in."

Belgian leaned back and folded his hands behind his head. "I don't think so."

He reached for what I presumed to be a weapon. A voice in my head shouted, "Duct tape him!" I am not talking about that phantom voice I heard. This was truly the figurative voice we all hear inside our heads. Nanoseconds later, I had the problem Waffle Brother mummified in duct tape. I stood on the control panel table, admiring my work. Blueberry's hand inched toward a button as the cow strolled my way in slow-motion. The fish hung in the air, with his tail moving as slow as a clock's minute hand.

I closed my eyes. *Maybe this would snap me out of hyperspeed.* I opened my eyes. The cow's lips fluttered slowly as her mouth emitted subdued foghorn bursts.

"How am I still moving at hyperspeed when I'm standing still?" I asked out loud.

"I gave up trying to figure that out long ago."

The unexpected response from the phantom voice caused me to involuntarily hop. "There's got to be a way to stop this without slamming into a wall." I composed myself with a deep breath and straightened myself into a hotdog.

"It won't work."

The phantom voice was right. Blueberry still hadn't reached the button, the cow continued to speak suppressed foghorn, and the fish's tail had barely moved.

I zipped off the control panel and slammed myself to the floor. After staggering to my feet, I hopped back onto the control panel. Blueberry had pushed the button and moved onto typing commands, the cow said, "...me?", and the fish's tail swayed like a flag in a light breeze. Plus, the angry mumbling of the mummified Mr. Steak&Eggs returned.

With my universe back to normal speed, I stared down Blueberry Waffle. "Bring in my friends."

He crossed both sets of arms and said, "No."

He wouldn't make eye contact. I knew he wanted to say yes, but my amazing supernatural speed and duct tape skills were no match compared to the evilness of muttering Mr. Steak&Eggs. The torture and humiliation of being immobilized in duct tape by a chicken paled in comparison to his wrath. I felt sorry for Blueberry, but I duct taped him, anyway.

"Okay, I guess we're doing this ourselves," said the cow, scanning the control panel. "Do you know how to work the controls?"

"No idea," I said before thinking. I had watched the Waffle brothers attempt to bring in the cow. They typed in a couple of commands, pushed some buttons, moved the joystick around, and pulled the big lever. How hard could it be?

"Actually, I do have some idea how to work this. Plus," I said, pointing to the control, "most of the buttons have obvious labels, like engage tractor-beam and open airlock doors. We got this."

My first attempt exploded a sectional couch the salvage crew had jettisoned into space. It's a good thing the cow suggested testing the process on an inanimate object first, otherwise I would have blown up the pig.

After destroying two more pieces of discarded furniture, I worked out the sequence and pulled the others in. The dog sprinted out of the airlock first, with his tail wagging. He knocked me down and engulfed my face with joyful licks. I loved every slobbering second of it.

"Easy there, Fido. You're smothering her," said the pig, as he and the others gathered around us.

The dog's tail continued flopping vigorously as he released me and tried to sit still.

Once I got to my feet, the duck greeted me with a high-five, wing-to-wing style. "Thanks, dude."

The cat even congratulated me with, "Commendable work."

The rabbit gave me a light punch to the shoulder. "I thought we were dead for sure, man."

"Dudes, who knew we could survive the frozen depths of outer space?"

The cat sighed and folded into her regal pose. "Altering our DNA, metabolism, and molecular structure to withstand extreme cold and survive in an oxygen deprived atmosphere were some of the first alterations Dr. Hash Browns performed upon our arrival at the space station."

"Well, I, for one, am grateful to the dude."

"I second that, man."

Soon, an awkward silence filled the room, as we glanced around at the desks, tables, bookshelves, and crates littered about the cargo bay, waiting to be tossed into space or transported to ORPH Inc. ship.

Chatter echoed in the tunnel link to the other ship.

"We better get out of here, before those Cheddarians find we duct taped their leader." The cow motioned toward the exit.

"They might like what we've done. The dude seems like a big jerk."

Mr. Steak&Eggs grumbled through his duct tape muzzle and intensified his wiggling, as he glared at the duck.

"Let'thh not stick around to find out. Time to head to the escape pod."

BYH
BarnYard Heroes

Chapter 8

ALARMS ECHOED THROUGH THE hallways as me and the rest of the animals made our way to the escape pod. We turned one corner and the cow literally bumped into two Cheddarians transporting a refrigerator sized crate. They gave us a glare, waved us out of the way, and pulled their package past us. A few turns later, we encountered a pair of Cheddarian pulling the chess table.

The dog growled and hunched into pounce mode. "That's, that's our chess table. And we were in the middle of a game!" He charged them, while releasing a steady stream of growling barks.

The others stared at the scene with their eyes popping and mouths drooping.

"He can get possessive of his favorite things," I said, though I had never seen him this aggressive.

By the time we caught up to him, the Cheddarians had fled, leaving the table behind. He stared at the pig. "Bring the table. The cow and I have a game to finish."

The pig obeyed and grabbed the dolly handle.

We made the final turn. The entrance to the escape pod loomed ahead and we quickened our pace. The cat and dog scampered into the escape vessel first, with the cat hopping into the pilot seat. As the rabbit, duck, and I scrambled in, lights and screens blinked to life.

The cow squeezed in next consuming eighty percent of the escape pod's open space. A few seconds later, the pig arrived at the door, dragging the chess table behind him. He eyed the open space and glanced at the chess table. I wondered if enough room even existed for the pig to fit.

The cow bumped into the side wall and the pilot's chair as she turned to look at the pig.

He nodded toward the table. The cow shook her head and pressed herself against the wall, which freed up zero additional space. Regardless, the pig squeezed into the remaining space.

"Close the door and let'thh get out of here."

"Wait. What about the fish?" I asked, proud of myself for not forgetting about him.

"I'm here," he said, swimming through a side wall of the escape pod.

The engines roared as we blasted away from the space station and right at an asteroid. The cat jerked the yoke, sending us into a wild dive and roll. She avoided the asteroid but sent the rabbit, duck, dog, and I tumbling around the ship, like a can of marbles rolling down a hill. The cat remained safely buckled into the pilot's seat, the pig and cow were wedged into place, and the fish went flying through the walls of the escape pod into outer space.

"Smooth move, dude."

"You just tossed the fish into space, man."

The cat slammed on the brakes, plastering us smaller animals into the front windshield.

"Dude, step away from the controls," said the duck.

The cat avoided a spinning asteroid by jerking the ship down and to the left. Those of us not wedged are buckled in place slammed into the ceiling.

"I have the piloting of the spacecraft under control," insisted the cat. "I am reversing our heading and returning for the fish." Surprisingly, she smoothly navigated through the asteroids and picked up the fish, by flying straight at him and having him pass through the windshield. With the fish safely aboard, the cat reversed course and dove the ship hard to the right, sending the fish into space again and us four free roaming animals into the ceiling.

"Out of the chair, man, and let the true pilots fly this bad boy," said the rabbit.

"I am navigating this craft acceptably, given the circumstances."

"Cat," said the pig. "You're not. Out of the chair, NOW!"

The cat huffed, released the controls, unbuckled, and leapt from the chair, ignoring our collision course with an oncoming asteroid. The rabbit dove into the pilot seat and avoided the asteroid with a nifty spin maneuver, which circled us around the asteroid, reversing our direction to go back for the fish. He slalomed us through the course of tumbling asteroids and scooped up the fish. None of us slammed into walls or even lost our balance during his maneuvers.

The duck hopped up next to his buddy. "Nice flying, dude."

With a muffled grumble, the cat curled up on the control panel.

Once free of the asteroid belt, two questions were asked.

"So, where to, man?"

"Where, where's the, where's the chess table?"

***

THE RABBIT EASED THE shuttle to a stop. None of us slammed into walls or the ceiling and the fish remained inside the ship. He removed his paws from the yoke, turned to face us animals. "So, where to, man?"

"Back to the, to the space station to get the chess table," said the dog, poking his head out from his scrunched position under the control panel. I had squeezed in next to him, as this was the only open space.

The pig squirmed his head above the cow's torso and made eye contact with the dog. "Look around. You seriously think that table would fit in here?"

I wiggled a wing free and wrapped it around the dog. I hoped it would comfort his loss.

"The, the cow could have, could have stood on top of it."

"The cow has to duck her head just to fit inside this tin can. There's no way she'd fit standing on top of that table."

"What if she, if she laid down on it?" He sunk his chin to the floor.

"We're sorry, but there was no room for the chess table and there'thh no going back to the space station now. We need to focus on getting to Cheddar and finding Dr. Hash Brownthh."

"Plotting a course for Cheddar, dudes." The duck used his wings, feet, and bill to adjust the ship's navigation controls.

"Hold on," said the pig, squirming to a higher position. "How are we going to find the doc once we get there? Cheddar is a huge and heavily populated planet."

"We'll just call him, man," said the rabbit, grabbing the yoke with his paws.

"I am unaware of any communication device in Dr. Hash Browns' possession that would function on his home planet of Cheddar," said the cat, from her curled-up position on the console above us.

The pig cleared his throat. "Imagine us showing up on Cheddar, a group of sentient animals from another world?"

The console wiggled from the cat's stretching. "I believe you mean sapient. Nearly all animals are sentient."

The pig rolled his eyes. "Whatever. My point is, if we go to Cheddar, they'll take us into custody, run experiments, and then destroy us."

This gave the dog a case of shivers. I tightened my wing's grip.

"So, where *do* you suggest we go, man?"

"Earth. It's our home planet. There are creatures like us there. We'll have a chance to blend in."

"Earth it is, dudes." The duck returned to working the navigation controls.

"Isn't that the, the planet where the people eat cows? And make hats and, and furniture out of them?"

I added a gentle caress to my hug of the dog, not sure if I did this to comfort him or myself. I had no fond memories of my time in the hen house sweatshop and wasn't convinced a band of talking animals would blend in. It seemed likely humans would take us into custody and experiment on us the same as the pig warned the Cheddarians would do.

"And shouldn't we at least make an effort to get back to Dr. Hash Brownthh?"

"I know we owe the Doc a lot," said the pig. "He made us who we are today, but I'm not sure what else he can do for us."

"Dr. Hash Browns has much more to offer us," said the cat. "The chicken's deficiencies are well documented, but that does not preclude the rest of us from further enhancements."

The pig scoffed. "Well, I, for one, have had enough of his badgering and experimentation."

I was about to shout "Here! Here!", when the dog said, "But, but he's our, our creator. Our master."

"Being grateful doesn't mean we need to be blindly loyal," said the pig.

I was definitely a member of Team Pig on this issue, but didn't want to voice my views and upset the dog further.

The cat's tail thumped on the console like a metronome, worrying me she might activate the wrong button or lever.

"The revolutionary advancements Dr. Hash Browns performed on us are adaptable to other lifeforms and could enhance the quality of life for species across the universe. It is our obligation to assist Dr. Hash Browns in furthering these achievements and sharing them with the universe."

"Great debates, dudes, but it's all moot. We've only got enough juice to reach the nearest planet. We can make it there and back, like five times, but there ain't enough charge to make it anywhere else. No way we make it to Cheddar."

"Fine." The cat's claws scraped the console top as she curled into a ball. "Earth it is. We will need to find another way to continue his work."

Even though the space station was 1,233 light years from Earth, the trip only took about 4 hours, thanks to the Electric Slide Booster Rockets. They are equivalent to Star Trek's warp drive or Star Wars' jump to hyperspace. They make space travel possible. Cheddar is over 2.3 million light years away. Who's got 2.3 million years to spare? And that's just to get there. It is another 2.3 million light years to get back. If you cannot travel at Electric Slide speeds, forget about space travel.

The principles behind Electric Slide Booster Rockets puzzle me and the concept of traveling at speeds that far surpass the speed of light blows my mind. The small amount of physics knowledge I have stored in my brain tells me the fastest known speed in the universe is the speed of light, so how could we travel over 2.6 million times faster than that and live to write about it? I have no clue.

With the course to Earth set and the autopilot engaged, the others slept, even though none of us needed sleep. Only the dog and I remained awake. We sat in the pilot and copilot seats and stared out the window at the streaks of blueness.

"You know, there's ah, there's something I've wanted to talk to you about," said the dog. "I've been scared to mention it to anyone else. You're gonna, you're gonna think it's stupid."

"I doubt I will find it stupid. Go on." I surprised myself with how easily the lie flowed out of me. Whoever invented lying must have done it for situations like this. I loved the fluffy knucklehead, but surmised his next statement would be one of the stupidest things I had ever heard.

"Okay, this, this sounds crazy, but I can sense greenness."

"You're right," I said.

"So, so you, you feel the green too?"

"No. I mean, that sounds crazy. And stupid." I could not keep lying.

The dog added a butt wiggle to his wildly wagging tail. "Right. I know. It sounds crazy, but I can. I can feel the green all around me."

"You do realize that makes no sense? You can't feel a color."

Thankfully, the dog's happiness continued to be unphased by my bluntness. "I know, right? That's why it's so cool. It's like, it's like I'm floating, floating in a giant vat of greenish goop."

"That sounds terrifying."

"Actually it's, it's quite calming. I like it. Should I tell the others?"

"No. It's best we keep this between you and me." Stupid, I expected, but uncomfortably creepy, no.

"It's, it's been, it's been growing stronger. The greenness."

His joy continued to boggle my mind. "So, that's a good thing?"

"Absolutely. I love the warm gooey greenness." He closed his eyes and released a slow exhale. He fell asleep a moment later.

Without my art supplies, I passed the time counting the number of stitches in the upholstery of the chairs until the stars regained their shape and the overwhelming blue light faded. The auto pilot had brought us out of the Electric Slide. The Earth came into focus and grew unnervingly larger in a matter of seconds. It soon consumed the entire view out the windshield.

"We're coming in hot," I yelled.

***

THE SHUTTLE RUMBLED AS we broke through the Earth's atmosphere.

The rabbit and duck had sprung into action as soon as they had woken up, but their frenzied button mashing failed to slow the shuttle. In less than a second, the roundness of Earth flattened, and the indistinguishable landscape became a cornfield.

"We're all gonna die," yelled the dog, as he dove below the ship's dashboard.

The ship lurched to an abrupt stop. Steel creaked and echoed through the walls of the tiny shuttle.

The rabbit and duck slammed into the windshield.

The dog, cat, and I bounced off the ceiling.

The pig and cow pressed against the back of the pilot chairs, loosening the floor bolts.

The fish, of course, flew out of the spacecraft.

We scurried to every available window. The hovering shuttle provided a view akin to the Sears Tower Skydeck, if they had built the Sears Tower in the middle of Wisconsin dairy country. The noon sun shined upon quilted squares of corn, soybeans, and grazing fields which blanketed the rolling hills. Rows of trees provided the stitching, with the occasional forest breaking up the monotonous square patterns. During my previous days on Earth, me and the other chickens were confined to our fenced-in free-range meadow. I envied my brethren and their functioning wings. I bet they see this view so often, it becomes mundane. If I could fly, I would cruise through the air like a hawk, soaking in this view all day long.

The fish swimming through the windshield snapped me out of my trance. He smiled fin-to-fin.

"Dog, look out the window," he said. "Do you see anything familiar?"

The dog, already staring out the window, cocked his head to get a new perspective. "Well, ah, it's, it's planet Earth, and I know I came from here and all, but ah, but I, ah, don't remember any of it. It was a long time ago."

"It has nothing to do with your previous time on Earth," said the fish. "Look at the field. Haven't you seen something like it before?"

The dog shifted his cocked head to the other side. His ears perked up to an alert position, though I cannot imagine what he expected to hear from way up here. He took a couple of deep sniffs. Again, I have no idea what he expected to smell from here. He shook his head and said, "I am afraid I'm not umm, I'm not, I mean, nothing familiar. Was I born on this farm?"

The fish swam up next to the dog and peered down. "We've got to move closer. Rabbit, move us closer to the ground."

The duck beat the rabbit to the controls and eased the shuttle down. When we descended to a seventh-floor view, the dog ran back and forth on the dashboard. "That's it! That's it!"

"What? The cornfield?" asked the pig.

"The pulsating wavy green. That's my vision."

"No way, dude," said the duck.

"Yes way. I can see the future!!" The dog's tail wagged like a flag in a strong wind. But not so strong it keeps the flag straight. Perhaps a bursty wind or a swirling wind that flops the flag back and forth. Hmmm, this flag in the wind analogy is not the best. Let's just say his tail wagged with joy.

The pig and cat exchanged scrunched mouth, squinty eye glances. I agreed with their skepticism, but who was I to say this wasn't exactly what he saw in his vision?

The fish swam next to the dog. "Congratulations. You can see the future."

"You're darn right I can. I can see the future and the future is green!"

"I never doubted your abilities for a second," said the cow. "Way to go."

"Dude, you can see the future. That's awesome. Do it again. Do it again!"

"Yeah, yeah, yeah. All right. All right." The dog sat down and tried to relax, although his tail continued its vigorous flopping. His tail stopped abruptly, and the ritual began. His body shivered and quivered. His head violently swung from side to side. Muffled barks. More quivering. Extended whimpering. More muffled barks. He finished with the climatic wolf howl.

The dog's eyes sprang open. "Marshmallow."

"Marshmallow? What does that mean?" I asked.

"It's a light spongy sugary confection," said the fish. "Typically, white."

I hated when the fish lectured us on things we already knew. "But what does it mean to see a marshmallow in the future?"

"I have, um, I have no idea," said the dog, "but there's a big fat fluffy white marshmallow in our future."

"Excellent. How big is it, dude? Is it like fourteen-stories tall, dude?" asked the duck.

"It's, it's huge. It, it took up the whole image of the vision. It's got to be gigantic!"

"Excellent. You're the man," said the rabbit.

"Was there anything else in the picture?" asked the fish.

"No. Just a, just a giant marshmallow."

"No aspect ratio?"

"What?" asked the dog.

I had the same question, but didn't ask. The fish's questioning had the earmarks of leading into one of his boring lectures.

"In order to determine the marshmallow's true size, we need another object in the vision to give it perspective," said the fish. "A familiar object, like a duck. We all know the size of a duck, so if a duck stood next to the marshmallow in the vision, we would have perspective to determine the size of the marshmallow."

"So, like it could be so small you can only see it with a microscope?" asked the duck.

"Exactly," said the fish.

"Or it's ginormous, like maybe it's the Stay Puff Marshmallow Man. That'd be so cool, man." The rabbit waddled and flared his menacing vampire teeth.

"You're overdoing it, dude. The Stay Puff Marshmallow Man did not have vampire teeth."

"But he could breathe fire like a dragon, man. He was like, 'Payback Time!'" The rabbit mimicked blasting flames out of his mouth. "Take that for roasting billions of marshmallows in campfires."

"Okay, enough about the future and marshmallow people," said the cow. "We need to deal with the present. We need to land and hide this spacecraft."

BYH
BarnYard Heroes

Chapter 9

THE SHUTTLE'S ADVANCED NAVIGATION directed us to land the tailless beaver-like spacecraft the size of a delivery van in an abandoned barn. Volunteer trees surrounded the barn and ivy covered the sides, melding into the forest that edged the cornfield. Half of us doubted its existence until we flew into the open doorway. No barn doors existed. A speck of paint under the fascia provided the only clue the barn had once been red.

A flock of sparrows scattered as the rabbit eased us inside. Rays of sunshine beamed through the assortment of roof and wall holes, highlighting the mosaic of bird poop and the array of rusted shovels, sickles, and scythes.

The rabbit and duck shut down the engines and hopped out of their pilot chairs.

"Dudes, it's time to check out the new neighborhood," said the duck.

"Rollercoasters, skate parks, zip lining. That's the agenda. Who's in, man?" asked the rabbit as the shuttle door opened.

The dog crawled out from under the console. "I, I want to try bubble gum."

The pig and cow blocked the entire back of the ship. "Slow down. No one is going anywhere," said the pig.

"We need to lie low and hope nobody spotted uthh."

"You dudes are no fun."

"Buzz killers, man."

The rabbit and duck sulked back to the pilot chairs.

"What are we supposed to do, man?"

"It's so cramped in here, dudes. Can't we at least explore the barn?"

The cow exchanged glances with the pig. After they both nodded, she said, "Fine, but stay inside the barn."

The pig pressed the buttons to open the door and extend the ramp. Without hesitation, the rabbit and duck squeezed between the cow and pig, hopping and flying to the wheelless Vespa scooter before the ramp fully extended.

The pig tiptoed himself down the shuttle ramp on his hind legs. "We're going to need to cover that entrance and set up a surveillance schedule."

"I'll, I'll take the first, take the first shift. I think I used to be a watchdog during my days on Earth," said the dog, hopping in circles around the pig.

Hooves clattered on the metal ramp, as the pig lost his hoofing and tumbled off the ramp to avoid stepping on the dog.

As dust billowed across the ramp, the dog stopped hopping, lowered his head, and sucked his tail between his legs. "Sorry."

The pig grumbled as he stood up and brushed dirt off his chest. "It's fine, Fido. And sure, the first shift is yours."

The dog's tail sprang free and wagged away as he bounced over to the barn entrance. He sat with the regalness of the cat and surveyed the landscape.

As I stepped on the ramp, something pinged the ship's roof. A black walnut shell dropped in front of me, clanged on the ramp, and rolled down.

"Ack, ack, ack, ack!!!" In the rafters above the ship sat a squirrel, munching on the nut.

The dog spun and growled at the rodent. "Intruder! Intruder!" He bounded up the ramp and jumped on top of the ship. He snarled and paced as he searched for a way into the rafters. The squirrel watched him with mild interest and continued chewing his snack.

The rest of us gathered on or around the ramp and stared at the unconcerned squirrel.

"Oh, man! He found us," said the rabbit.

"We're gonna have to kill the little dude, so he doesn't talk."

"Relax, you two. We're not killing the squirrel," said the cow, as she clambered down the ramp. "Animals on Earth don't talk. There'thh nothing to worry about."

The rabbit wiggled his nose, and the duck cocked his head, as the pair exchanged glances. "Hold on, dude. All the animals in that cute pig movie talked."

"The little pig, the dogs, the sheep, the duck. They all talked, man."

"You two understand the difference between movies and reality?" asked the pig.

The rabbit and duck shrugged their shoulders.

"The lines get blurred, dude."

"Don't you remember your time on Earth?" asked the pig.

"Man, that was a long time ago."

"Those days are nothing but a blur, dude."

I felt that being the group's most recent inhabitant of Earth made me the expert, even though my traditional chicken brain clouded my memories in a deep haze. "From what I remember of my time on Earth, only humans talk."

The fish assumed his lecturing professor's position in the doorway of the escape pod. I was about to be corrected.

"Technically, that's not true," he said. "Most animals have rudimentary verbal communication. Even the 'ack, ack, ack,' of that squirrel has some meaning behind it."

"It's, it's their way of laughing at me," said the dog, still searching for a path into the rafters. "I remember these vermin and their chubby cheeked smugness. This one's stench triggered memories of their torment, taunting me from the trees. I will get my revenge."

The squirrel scampered across the rafter beams, unphased by the dog's threats. It squeezed through an opening and disappeared. The dog sat beneath the hole with his predator eyes fixed on the last known location of the squirrel.

"Dog, I think it'thh time come down. The squirrel is long gone."

"NEVER!" He sniffed around the top of the ship before returning his stare to the squirrel's escape hole.

"So, dude, how are we supposed to blend in if we can't talk to our fellow ducks and rabbits?" The duck continued to stare at the dog while asking the pig his question.

The pig rubbed his temple with a tight gripped hoof. "Don't talk to them, just act like them."

"Man, how do we understand their motives? We can't act like them if we don't know what makes them tick." The rabbit also watched the dog, so neither he nor the rabbit saw the pig smack his hoof to his forehead.

"At least we can talk to the humans, dude."

"Attempts at verbal communication with humans will be pointless," said the cat as she strolled up the ramp. "Earth has 7,151 languages, none of them Cheddarian. The humans will not understand a word you speak."

During my days on Earth, the humans spoke all the time. I assume when they spoke to me, they said the usual stuff, like "Here chickee, chickee, chickee. Time for din-din," or the ever popular "Oh you're a plump little chicken, aren't you? You'll be good eatin'." At the time, it was all gibberish to me. Trust me, there aren't many synapses firing between the ears of a normal chicken. Mostly, I ran around like a chicken with her head cut off, which is not all that different from a chicken running around with her head on. When I lived on a farm, all I did was eat grain, sleep, lay eggs, and poop. The only thoughts going through my brain were, "Grain. Yum. Grain. Grain. Yum. Dirt. Yuck. Sunflower seed. Yum-yum. Dirt. Yuck. Rock. Ouch. Grain. Yum. Need to poop. <pause> Grain. Yum." Only, not that sophisticated. I didn't have words to associate with my thoughts. So, once Dr. Hash Browns enhanced me with the ability to speak Cheddarian, I assumed the human gibberish to be Cheddarian. In my universe, it was the only language in existence. I was not the only one shocked by the news of other languages existing. The rabbit and duck's attention had shifted away from the dog. With a wiggling nose and a cocked head, they watched the cat waltz into the ship.

The fish must have sensed our confusion and repositioned himself in the ship's doorway. "It's true. To humans, Cheddarish sounds like a mixture of a blaring car alarm and a computer modem desperately attempting to connect. Most humans would find even the most 'beautiful' of Cheddarish love ballads quite grating."

"But, but, they speak Cheddarian in all, all the, all the movies we watch," said the dog, who had stopped staring at the hole.

"And I do all my internet surfing in Cheddarian, man."

Even the cow and pig looked puzzled by this revelation, though they remained silent as they began covering the entrance to the barn with branches.

The cat raised her voice as she rummaged through a ship cabinet. "Dr. Hash Browns and I constructed dictionaries and translation databases which convert all the Earth's written and spoken forms of communication into Cheddarian."

"Cool, dude. We just need to use that translator and we'll understand these bazillion languages."

"Unfortunately, the translation database is stored on the space station's central servers, which we clearly do not have access to here on Earth."

"So, we have to learn 7,151 languages?" I asked.

"I did not suggest, nor do I recommend you learn all 7,151 languages," said the cat as she examined a loose power supply. "Learning the English language will be sufficient. It is the dominant language of Earth."

"I read that Earth's languages do not uphold to the standards of logic our Cheddarian language does," said the fish, still hovering near the doorway. "With English and its random silent letters, being the worst of them." [1]

"That's why Dr. Hash Browns and I built the translators," said the cat. "When the Cheddarian language sets a rule, it always applies. Not true with Earth's languages, with the English language's "i" before "e" rule setting the standard for nonsense. It starts off as an easy-to-follow rule: "i" before "e". Then the Earthlings add not one, but two exceptions; "i" before "e", except after "c" or when it sounds like an "a", like in neighbor or weigh. But then this illogical language breaks the rules and exceptions all over the place, leading to the classic phrase: "i" before "e", except after "c" or when it sounds like an "a", like in neighbor or weigh, or when Keith forfeits his codeine and caffeine to either a weird deity, feisty atheist, or poltergeist sheik of kaleidoscope science. If we understood English, apparently that would be hilarious. They inscribe the phrase on coffee mugs and T-shirts."

"So, so..., you don't even understand English?" asked the dog from his perch on the top of the ship.

"Of course not," said the cat, as she sniffed the power supply. "The language is a nightmare. Hence, I invented the translator."

---

1. I became painfully aware of the English language nonsense while writing this book. Take your English word "salmon" for instance. What is the purpose that "l" in the middle? It serves no purpose other than to mess kids up on a spelling test. And what kind of insane pronunciation rules cause bologna to be pronounced 'baloney'? What happened to the "g" and "a"?

"How are we supposed to learn a language that even the cat can't understand?"

"Since the pig and cow mandated, we shelter-in-place, I will use this time to build a translator out of the shuttle's spare parts," said the cat, as she sorted through a collection of cables. "But I would be remiss if I failed to mention that your reasoning for this mandate is flawed. The ship's autopilot logic strategically selected this sparsely populated farmlands of Central Wisconsin for the sole purpose of an undetected alien spacecraft landing."

The pig stomped onto the ramp and pointed a hoof at the cat. "I don't care what the ship's logic says. We hovered in plain sight for several minutes. Someone had to notice and until we're sure no human authorities are searching for us, we stay put in this crummy barn."

The cat stopped sorting cables, turned to face the pig, and assumed her regal cat sitting pose. "The autopilot projected the number of witnesses to our spacecraft landing to be between ten and fifteen intelligent beings. If any of them tells the tale of our spacecraft landing, the other intelligent beings will no longer consider these beings to be intelligent and assume them to be starved for attention, mentally unstable, under the influence of a hallucinogenic substance, or any combination of those three."

The pig snorted. "That autopilot logic is making some pretty big assumptions, if you ask me."

"What if they took photos, dude?" asked the duck.

"Or video, man?" asked the rabbit.

"Other humans will presume their photographic evidence to be photoshopped and their videos assumed to be CGI fakes."

The cow stepped forward. "Cat, your argument has merit, but under an abundance of caution, I suggest we remain hidden in this barn for a minimum of three days."

"Agreed," said the pig, in a manner that made it clear no further debate would occur. "Cow, let's finish covering this barn door opening."

***

THE BOREDOM OF CONFINEMENT in the decrepit barn and escape shuttle was only marginally worse than the boredom of Dr. Hash Browns' laboratory. One upside, I didn't worry about when my turn in the Mambomatic 5000 would come up. But I missed my art supplies, and I struggled to come to grips with never finishing my Dog Playing Chess masterpiece. I scrounged a jug of used motor oil and plucked one of my feathers to use as a brush. Using a dirty rag as my canvas, I attempted to paint our arrival over the cornfield. The result resembled a single storm cloud hanging above an endless ocean. The dog suggested I burn it and if either of us knew how to light matches, we would have.

On the second day, the cat began what would become daily long-winded monologues about why she couldn't complete the translator without the data files she and Dr. Hash Browns created.

"I insist we return to the space station at once. No hope of constructing a usable translator exists without the retrieval of the translation data file."

We learned to tune her out, which increased her irritation. She would threaten to take the shuttle and fly back to the space station by herself. To which, the rabbit and duck would volunteer to join her and pilot the ship, and if they happened to retrieve their video games, all the better. The cow and pig would put their hooves down and insist no one leave the barn.

On that second day of captivity, we etched a chessboard in the dirt floor and used nuts, bolts, spark plugs, walnut shells, clumps of dirt, and anything else we could scavenge as chess pieces, so the dog and cow could resume their game. Of course, none of us could remember where the previous game left off, so they started a new one.

On day three, the rabbit and duck installed tractor tires on the Vespa scooter. Even though the vintage scooter had no hope of starting, they begged to take it out for a spin. "Dude, we'll go out at night. No one will see us."

Again, the cow and pig put their hooves down.

When not yelling at us to be quiet, the cow and pig took their turns on watch duty and debated whether we should attempt to communicate with the nearest farmer. The dog took his turns on watch as well, and spent hours staring at the hole in the ceiling, waiting for the squirrel's return.

At night, the fish would sneak out and gallivant around the nearby farmlands. Upon his return, he'd provide details of a nearby farm and report counts of the barnyard animals. It became our only source of entertainment. We loved the scandalous nature of the fish defying the cow and pig's shelter-in-place order and couldn't wait to get his daily briefings.

A week had passed when the pig and cow called for a team meeting. We were to meet at the bottom of the escape pod ramp, only a handful of steps from anywhere inside the barn, but the dog slowed my progress by crossing back and forth in front of me.

"We've, we've never had a team meeting before. What do you, what do you think this is about? Do you think they learned about the fish sneaking out at night? Do you, do you think he'll get punished? Are they going to punish us for not snitching on him?"

"Dude, I'm hoping this means an end of the shelter-in-place order," said the duck, as he and the rabbit scurried around us.

"That would, that would be nice. Because, I, I have, I have an overwhelming urge to find the stinkiest thing I can find and roll around in it. Is that, is that weird?"

I didn't hesitate with my answer. "Yes. That's weird. Very weird. Don't do that. It stinks bad enough in here already." In retrospect, perhaps I could have been a bit more understanding. Rolling in stinky stuff is what dogs do. He has no control over his instincts.

"Plus, I have a score to settle with a couple of squirrels."

"I can't wait to take that scooter for a ride, man."

"And dude, I want to try every energy drink on the market." The rabbit and duck went back and forth as if completing one long sentence.

"And eat pizza,"

"and climb a tree,"

"go skiing,"

"swimming,"

"buy a gun,"

"and make a TikTok video."

We had reached the meeting spot, where the cow and pig waited for us, standing in front of the branches shielding the doorway, with the fish swishing above them.

The cat sauntered down the ramp. "This better be important. I'm in the middle of recalibrating the La Volta[2] crystals."

The cow cleared her throat, which resembled a muffled foghorn. She had our attention.

"We wanted to lie down thhome ground rules, before allowing folks outside the barn."

"Although our arrival appears to have gone undetected, we are not out of danger," said the pig as he stepped in front of the cow. "We need to continue to maintain a low profile."

"There will be no TikToking. No purchasing of guns. No ordering pizzas to the barn. Understood." He glared at the rabbit and duck.

The pair avoided eye contact while they scuffed the dirt floor with their paw and webbed foot. The rabbit muttered, "Buzz killers."

Using her teeth, the cow pulled a tree branch away from the wall, revealing a crude, yet detailed diagram of the surrounding farms.

The pig grabbed a stick with his karate-clench hooves. "You will restrict your movements to these nearby farms."

---

2. La Volta is a data storage crystal and the main export of the planet Havarti or a
   lewd dance full of scandalous and beastly gestures, which was allegedly a favorite
   of Queen Elizabeth I.

He whacked the stick against the wall as he pointed to the neighboring farms.

"We will always go out in pairthh. No one leaves the barn on their own."

I chuckled to myself, imagining the raging anger of the cow and pig if they learned of the fish's nightly adventures.

"And we permit only four of uthh outside the barn at a time. We don't need everyone wandering off at the same time."

"At all times, we must keep a low profile. Do not speak to humans."

"In fact, do your best to avoid humanthh."

"Observe your species. Do what they do. Act how they act."

"For example, I will no longer be wearing pants." The pig stripped off his shorts and stood proud. "This feels quite freeing."

We averted our eyes as he placed his hooves on his hips and posed like a hero.

"And I will return to walking on all fours."

A collective sigh of relief rang through the barn as he lowered himself.

"Thho, those are the ground rules. Questions?"

The duck and rabbit traded questions, to which the cow and pig, in unison, provided their one-word responses.

"Dudes, can we try chewing tobacco?"

"No."

"Bungee jumping?"

"No."

"Skydiving?"

"No."

"Snowmobiling?"

"No."

"Eat ice cream so fast we get brain freeze?"

"Here's the deal. You can explore these farmlands." The pig pointed to the map. "But you must act like a regular duck or rabbit from Earth."

The rabbit and duck's shoulders slumped.

"Does anyone else have a question?" asked the cow.

The dog stepped forward. "How did you..., um, how did you make that map? I mean, how, how do you know what the neighboring farmlands look like?"

In quick succession, the eyes of both the cow and pig rolled up toward the fish, dropped to scan our reactions, and finally drifted off to corners of the barn.

"Well..., we um," said the pig, as if he thought about something else entirely.

"We remembered the landscape from when we hovered in the air," said the cow. "Remember that?"

The dog growled. "Neither of you will look me in the eye. You're liars."

The cow and pig exchanged rapid glances but said nothing.

"What gives, man?"

The cat strolled in front of the dog. "Must I spell this out?" She sat and examined the rabbit, duck, and me. "Did all of you believe the cow and pig to be unaware of the fish's nightly excursions? Those were reconnaissance missions ordered by them."

This explains the dry and technical nature of the fish's accounts of his nightly escapades, but with entertainment at a premium during our isolation, we hung on every word.

The dog narrowed his glare to just the cat. "You were in on it, too."

"Naturally."

"Why, why did you, why did you all lie to us?"

The cow lowered her head and spoke to the ground. "We feared the rest of you would whine endlessly about only the fish getting to leave the barn."

Of course, that's exactly what we would have done, but I still refused to forgive them for the deception, and I will never forgive myself for falling for it.

The dog stood up. In order, he scowled at the cat, fish, pig, and cow. "I'm going outside." He weaved through the brush covering the lack of a barn door and strolled off.

"The meeting appears to have adjourned. I will return to my work." The cat turned and strolled up the ramp.

"We're out of here," said the duck as he and the rabbit scurried through the branches to the farmlands beyond.

The pig gave the fish a nod to follow the others. The fish nodded an acknowledgment and swam through the barn wall to tail the others.

I knew this meant we'd exceeded the rule of four, but figured I'd confidently walk on out regardless and catch up to the dog.

The pig cleared his throat, in a manner indicating he wanted my attention. I contemplated blasting into hyperspeed but turned to face the pig.

"Not so fast," he said.

"I know. Rule of four. But it's not fair. You sent the fish out before I had a chance to go."

"It'thh not that. We have a special assignment for you."

Chapter 10

ONCE RELEASED FROM THE confinement of the barn, I planned on learning to fly like a normal bird. Put these wings to useful work. Soar into the sky and view the farmlands from a mile high. Plus, I wanted to make sure the dog hadn't run into traffic chasing a squirrel.

Instead, the cow and pig had an assignment for me. My shoulders slumped and my beak scrunched. "What's this assignment?"

"The cat has identified a number of items required for building her translator." The pig rose to his hind legs, once again revealing more of his anatomy than I cared to see. With his stick, he pointed to several spots on the map. "The locations of the items are marked with an X. She also made what she called an electronic order, which got delivered today, to this farmhouse." The pig banged the wall with the stick, emphasizing the farm in question.

"It'thh not a real farm. Apparently, modern day rich humans buy farms, don't work them, and just visit them on weekends. I can't explain why."

"The packages are stacked by the front door. Let's start with those." The pig charted the path with his stick. "Zip over at hyperspeed, grab the boxes, and zip back. Go it?"

"But shouldn't I check on the dog first?"

The pig dropped to all fours and turned away from me. "Don't worry about it. The fish has that covered."

The cow shuffled next to the pig. "Go get the packages."

Their butts faced me as they studied the map. There would be no further debate. I reviewed the path and waddled outside. The sun showered the landscape and assaulted my eyes. I closed them, letting the sun warm my face and feathers, while I took my first breath of truly fresh air in fifty years. No mustiness of the decrepit barn. Just clean air. No describable or distinct smell. Absolute heaven.

I opened my eyes and scanned the rolling hills of grazing fields that spanned in front of me and glanced at the walnut forest behind me. No sign of the dog, nor the rabbit and duck. Not even the fish.

The rolling pastures presented an inviting training field for flying practice, but I would need to find a more secluded one. I soaked in the full beauty of Earth, with a deep breath and a slow pan of the horizon. Then I blasted into hyperspeed. The rolling pastures and flat cornfields blurred as I zipped through them. I spotted the farmhouse and sure enough, a stack of boxes stood by the door. I grabbed the smallest and rocketed back to the barn. Within a handful of seconds, I had traversed the route a dozen times, piling the boxes into the escape pod. The cat noticed the arrival of the first box. By the time I dropped off the final box, she had walked the three steps to examine the stack. It felt good to be useful, and I pictured Dr. Hash Browns, wherever he was, smiling, proud of me activating my superpower.

The cat's claw inched its way out of her paw as she positioned it to open a box. The cow and pig performed slow-motion turns. It perplexed me. How could I stand still, yet remain in hyperspeed? The others had no clue I needed to slam into an immovable object to break out of hyperspeed, and I wasn't about to show them. I darted outside and crashed into a tree.

"That, that looks like, like, it hurt. Are you okay?"

I shook the bark out of my feathers and wrapped my wings around the big lug's neck. A semi hadn't run the dog over. He sat two trees away from the barn, staring up a tree trunk.

"I'm fine," I said, releasing him. "It's how I break out of hyperspeed. No big deal, really. What are you up to?"

He continued to scan the tree branches. "I, I, I almost had him this time. The stupid squirrel never..., never saw me coming. I had the jump on him, but he, he clawed up the tree at the last second."

A scan of the tree branches revealed no movement. "I think the squirrel's gone."

The dog scavenged around the trunk, sniffing the ground. "I can, I can still smell 'em. He's up there." His head shot up and he resumed scanning branches.

A rustling of leaves grabbed our attention. The dog locked onto the sound. His claws dug lines in the dirt. His butt wiggled, yet his tail remained still. Branches waved far up in the tree, jarring one leave free. I watched it float to the ground as the dog shuffled, following the commotion above.

"Cowabunga!!"

"Hoozah!!"

The rabbit and duck streamed down like a pair of torpedoes, shredding leaves along the way. When they neared the ground, the duck spread his wings and flew out. The rabbit spread out his legs, grabbed a tree branch with his front paws, spun around, leapt onto a lower branch, skidded down it like a snowboarder, dismounted with a triple flip, and stuck the landing inches in front of us. The duck landed next to him.

"Dudes, we are officially bored."

The rabbit performed a short bow. "That was the most exciting thing we've done out here, and it barely gave me an adrenalin boost, man."

"Dude, I'm sure if the pig or cow saw us, we'd get a lecture on how that's not what normal rabbits and ducks do."

"That is precisely what they would do." Above us, the fish swished his tail with angry vigor. None of us had seen or heard him approach. "If I see behavior like this again, I *will* report it to the cow and pig. It's important we maintain a low profile."

The rabbit and duck kicked up dust as they shuffled toward the pasture.

"Man is this place lame."

"Dude, we need entertainment."

"Skateboards."

"Video games."

"At least some TV streaming services."

Their voices faded as they sulked into a patch of tall grass.

The fish looked down at me and the dog. "I have no issue with your activities. Please resume." With that said, the fish swam away.

"How does he do that?" I didn't expect or want an answer from the dog and didn't give him time to provide one. "He's got no wings, just those tiny fins that he doesn't even use. But there he goes, swish, swish, swish, through the air with the greatest of ease. It's really annoying."

"But, but, you've got, you've got that super speed thing. That's pretty cool."

"It is, but it's not the same as flying," I said, watching a black bird zigzag along the edge of the tree line.

"At least you..., you have a usable power. I just see vague images of the future."

"You've got that tail whip."

The dog looked at his swishing tail. "I don't um..., I don't think I'm using it right."

"Dr. Hash Browns mentioned giving you the power to dig holes."

"I'm, I'm pretty sure that's something I already did when I lived here on Earth."

"But he said you'd be able to dig holes really fast."

"Right. But we couldn't test it on the space station. No dirt."

"There's plenty of dirt here."

The dog cocked his head at the ground. "I suppose so." After a couple of short and slow paws at the ground, his front legs broke into a fever pace. A stream of dirt flew out between his hind legs as if he was a snow blower. Within seconds, he'd disappeared into the hole. Dirt kept streaming out, along with medium-sized rocks and tree roots. Dozens and dozens of tree roots.

"HEY!! STOP! You've proven you can do it."

The stream of flying dirt tailed off, and the dog crawled out of his hole. "That, that was amazing. Oh my gosh. So much fun. You've got to try it."

I held up my wings. "I don't have that ability."

"Right. Sorry. Flying. That's what you want to do."

The dog and I found a secluded meadow of short grass. We glanced over our shoulders. No one around.

"Here I go." I sprinted across the bumpy grasslands with the dog by my side.

"Now, now jump!"

I hopped. I hovered for a second, wings flapping like a hummingbird. Then down I came.

"You need to, need to make myself more aerodynamic."

I pointed my head forward, made my tail straight and imagined myself as an arrow soaring towards the bullseye. I ran. I jumped. I flapped. I crashed.

The dog helped me up. "Maybe..., maybe if you launch yourself off a platform."

I jumped onto a boulder at the edge of the meadow. After assuming my aerodynamic stance, I sprinted the two steps across the rock. I leaped and flapped my wings like I'd seen the duck do. There was no lift. No hover. Only plummeting, followed by tumbling.

As I brushed grass clippings and dirt off my feathers, the fish swam into view. "There you are. The cow and pig would like a word."

***

THE COW AND PIG sent me right back to work, grabbing more devices the cat requested. I didn't know it at the time, but these tasks made me a serial criminal. Within a matter of five minutes, I'd committed multiple offenses, including breaking and entering, grand theft, petty larceny, and willful destruction of property. I was in and out of the houses, stores, barns, and vehicles without even the pets noticing. It was exhilarating. I grabbed extra stuff along the way. Art supplies for me. A video console and games for the rabbit and duck. A chess set for the dog.

I delivered a new set of tech to the cat and after breaking out of hyperspeed by crashing into my favorite tree, I waltzed into the barn. The rabbit and duck kneeled before the cat, who examined the electronics I'd stolen.

"Please, dude. Hook us up with power."

"We know you can do it, man."

I didn't understand how electricity worked, and thus had no clue the video console was worthless without it.

"For the next several hours, I will be inventorying and cataloging these electronic components, followed by days of testing their abilities. After which, I will incorporate the useful components into the construction of the translator. So, as you should be able to surmise, I have no time for frivolous activities such as connecting your video gaming system to a power supply."

I grabbed my art supplies and snuck out of the barn before the rabbit and duck shifted their focus to begging me to steal skateboards, scooters, minibikes, energy drinks, and everything else the cow and pig told them they couldn't have. The dog trotted up to me, looped the bag of paints around his neck, and snagged the stolen nine-by-twelve-inch canvas in his mouth.

We concentrated on strutting like regular animals as we skirted the edge of a forest. It never occurred to us humans would find the sight of a dog and chicken walking side-by-side suspicious. Not to mention, I carried an easel under one wing and my paint palette under the other, while the dog carried the rest of my supplies.

We perched ourselves at the top of a hill, which provided the perfect view of the rolling hills, cornfields, and grazing lands. I identified this spot during my pilfering runs. Truly a place of peace and tranquility, and a picturesque landscape for my new masterpiece, which I planned to title The Rolling Hills of the Driftless.

I set up my easel and rummaged through the bag for my paints and a brush, as the dog placed the canvas on the easel. After squeezing paints onto the palette, I grasped the paintbrush firmly in my beak. I peeked at the fields below. Something was wrong, but I could not put my claw on it. The tiny creek still meandered its way through the grazing fields, bubbling and flowing as it had earlier. The barn past the corn fields still needed a fresh coat of paint or, better yet, a wrecking crew. The forest of black walnut trees had not magically shifted several hundred yards to the left. Yet, something had changed.

I turned to the dog. "Do you notice anything different?"

"Different? What, did you, um, did you get a haircut or start using a new lip gloss or something?"

"No. Not about me. Out there. In the landscape. I can't put my claw on it, but there's something different."

"It, um, it, it looks like typical farmlands to me."

I looked at the field again. Something was definitely amiss. But since I couldn't figure out what, I said, "Well, perhaps you're right. I must be imagining things." I raised my brush again and prepared to add my first cow.

"Wait!" I dropped the brush. "That's what's missing. The cows."

"What, um, what cows?"

"Exactly. No cows. There's supposed to be cows grazing in the meadow. And over by those trees. And on the top of that hill. They're all gone. The cows complete the landscape. I need cows."

"Perhaps they, perhaps they went back to the barn for their milking?"

"I reckon so." I stuffed my supplies into the bag, not caring how much of a mess the wet paint would make, and we marched back to our hideout.

We slid through the makeshift branches which camouflaged the gaping entrance left by the lack of barn doors. The pig waddled down the ramp, as I placed the art materials on a shelf I had claimed as my cubbyhole. He walked on his hind legs. No shorts. We averted our eyes.

"Have either of you seen the cow?" he asked.

"No," I said, focusing my eyes on a tractor tire.

"In fact, we haven't, we haven't seen any cows." The dog tapped me with a front paw. "Tell him, tell him how there are no cows. No cows in the fields. No cows on the hill. No cows under the shade trees. They're all gone."

"We figured the cows are in the barn for their afternoon milking," I said.

The fish wiggled toward us. "Afternoon milking isn't a thing. There's morning and evening milking."

"So, neither of you have seen our cow today?" asked the pig.

"I haven't seen her since last night, when she left to scout for jet fuel," I said.

"Exactly. No one has seen her since," said the pig, turning to walk up the ramp.

"This, this, this, is bad. Very bad." The dog made two tight panic circles before scrambling under the ramp. "Gone. She's gone. They're all gone. No cows."

"Calm down, Sparky," said the pig. "It's not time to panic. Sorry I brought it up."

"It, it, it is time to panic. Don't you see? Don't you see what this means? He's here!" The dog scrunched himself completely under the ramp.

The pig bent over until he could see the cowering dog. "Who's here?"

"The mean guy. In a suit. He's here. He came for the cows! And he has our cow!"

"Mr. Steak&Eggs? The Senior Vice President?" asked the pig.

"He was obsessed with cows," said the fish, swimming down to be eye-level with the pig. "It is plausible he has come to Earth to collect some."

"Let's not jump to conclusions," said the pig. "There are plenty of other plausible explanations. Herding cattle to the slaughterhouse is what humans do, so missing cows is not a surprise."

The dog poked his head out. "That, that, that's supposed to make us feel better?" He pulled his head back under the ramp as if he was part turtle.

"They're dairy cows," I said.

The fish finished my point. "They don't slaughter dairy cows for beef."

"There you go. Humans don't slaughter dairy cows, so there's nothing to worry about," said the pig.

The confidence in the pig's voice failed to calm the dog, who burrowed himself into a hole he dug under the ramp. Although we couldn't see him, we all heard him whimpering.

"Sensors indicate significant teleporter activity in our area over the past hour," said the cat, who had sauntered out to the top of the escape pod ramp. "Although this does not provide absolute proof of the dog's theory regarding alien abduction of cows, which may or may not include the abduction of our cow, it does provide substantial anecdotal evidence to corroborate the theory."

The pig glanced between me and the fish. "Was anything the cat said helpful?"

I shrugged my wings. The cat talked nonsense as far as I was concerned.

"There's been teleporting activities," said the fish. "That's significant. That technology doesn't currently exist on Earth."

"This is precisely the point of my statements," said the cat. "According to these readings, teleporter activity has been occurring on Earth for two days, five hours, and seventy-eight minutes."

The pig's karate-clench hooves performed an involuntary seizure into fists. A deep breath did nothing to release the formation. "How much is that in real time?"

"Although time is relative, the metric system I adhere to, which consists of ten hours in a day, a hundred minutes in an hour, and a hundred seconds in a minute, is as close to a real time—"

The pig pounded up the ramp. "Forget that question. New question. Why didn't you alert us about this teleporting activity earlier?"

The cat casually licked her paw. "The task you and the cow assigned me consisted of monitoring for Mr. Steak&Eggs spacecraft, which remains docked to Dr. Hash Browns' space station. Neither you nor the cow requested me to monitor teleportation activity."

His hooves tightened as he loomed over the cat. "What is being teleported? And from where to where?"

"Indeterminable. The sensors detect the presence of teleportation signals but provide no further details regarding the objects teleported nor their origin or destination."

The pig's hooves unclenched. He bent over and reached for the cat's throat.

Moving faster than I thought he could, the fish swam in between them and faced the pig. "Let's not turn on each other."

After a snort, the pig stomped down the ramp.

The cat huffed and sauntered into the depths of the escape pod.

I glanced around the room.

The fish looked satisfied he had averted open conflict.

The cat returned to her electronics.

The pig studied the farmland map.

I hopped onto the ramp. "What is wrong with all of you?"

I had their attention, albeit via quizzical looks.

"Were you not listening to your own conversation?"

Their puzzled looks persisted.

I tossed my wings in the air. "We basically confirmed the dog was right. Mr. Steak&Eggs stole the Earth's cows. And he stole OUR cow."

I paused, waiting for comments.

The dog poked his head above the ramp. "I was right?"

"Absolutely." I gave him a nod.

The cat waltzed out from the depths of the escape pod and did some general licking maintenance.

The fish floated down toward me.

The pig scratched his chin.

None of them spoke.

The rabbit and duck had been rummaging through the box of video games and I assumed they hadn't been listening. But the rabbit looked up and pumped a paw into the air. "We've gotta do something, man."

"That's my point," I said.

The pig waddled to the bottom of the ramp. "But we don't know where the ship is."

I waved a wing as I scanned the room. "But we know Mr. Steak&Eggs is behind this."

"Didn't someone say that dude's ship is still docked at the space station?"

"Exactly," I said. "We find him, and he'll lead us to the cows."

"Mr. Steak&Eggs is our primary suspect." The cat tilted her head. "And his docked ship at our former space station is our only lead."

"It may be our only hope for finding the cow," said the fish.

The dog hopped up next to me. "So, we're, we're going back to the space station?"

The pig groaned but nodded his agreement. "It looks like it."

The cat bounced back to her stash of electronics. "This return voyage provides the fortuitous opportunity to retrieve my translation data file."

The pig grumbled as we boarded the escape pod.

Chapter 11

I FORGOT MY ART supplies, so the flight back to the space station was a dreadfully dull, drab, and awful trip through endless streams of blueness. On the plus side, without the cow aboard, we had room to spare. I stretched out on the floor and tried to sleep, but thanks to Dr. Hash Browns' enhancements, I wouldn't get tired for another four months.

When the on-board navigator announced we had arrived at the asteroid belt surrounding the space station, I nearly leaped into hyperspeed.

The rabbit hopped into the pilot chair. "Time for manual control, man."

"Strap yourselves in, dudes," said the duck, who flew into the copilot seat and fastened his seatbelt.

There were no other seats or harnesses to strap into, so the rest of us grabbed hold of whatever we could and hoped for the best. Except the fish, who lacked the ability to grab hold of anything.

The rabbit demonstrated his piloting skills and navigated us through the asteroids without sending the fish flying into space. The trip was smoother than a subway ride and we loosened our grips along the way.

We glided inside this safe zone of the space station's deflector shield zone. Mr. Steak&Eggs' ship was indeed attached to the space station's umbilical bridge, looking like a pickle sucking the life out of a Rubik's cube through a straw.

The rabbit tapped several buttons on the control panel and flipped a few switches. "We've got a problem, man. The auto-docking ain't kicking in."

"Surely you understand this is a stealth operation?" The cat sat on the dashboard, fiddling with dials and buttons. "I disabled all communications to the space station, which obviously includes the messaging required for auto-docking."

The rabbit scanned the control panel. "We can't dock with the space station without hailing it to open the hatch, man."

"I'm sure another solution will present itself." Apparently, the cat expected us to find the solution, because she curled up for a nap.

The pig shook his head. "All right, who has a plan?"

We expressed our lack of ideas with silence. No one even muttered "Well...," or "Umm." We all stared at the floor, hoping someone else would provide the answer.

The duck broke the silence. He threw his wings in the air. "It's impossible, dude. Without the ship opening the docking hatch, our only option is to smash through a window."

"I strongly suggest against such action," said the cat without opening her eyes.

The fish swam up toward the windshield. "Wait, this gives me an idea." He motioned his head toward the space station. "Get us close and I'll fly through the side." His eyes rolled upward as he paused. "But that doesn't help the rest of you."

"This can work," I said. "Once you're in, open the hatch, activate the tractor beam controls, and pull us in."

"Brilliant!" said the fish. "I knew we'd find a solution."

I explained in agonizing detail the steps for operating the tractor beam controls three times. By then, he claimed to have it memorized. The rabbit positioned the escape pod alongside the cargo bay window. After a running start, or I guess more of a swimming start, the fish leaped through the side of our shuttle, glided through the brief span of zero gravity, and then through the cargo bay window.

The rabbit eased our escape pod back, ready to be pulled in by the tractor beam. We rushed to the windshield. Me and the other small animals jockeyed for dashboard space so we could watch the fish.

He swished over to the control panel. He stared at the buttons and knobs. He flitted back and forth, before turning sideways to give one eye a clear look at the controls. After studying the controls, he sprang into action. He flopped onto buttons and whacked knobs with his tail. For the first time, he actually resembled a fish out of water, flopping on the deck of a boat, gasping for oxygen. The fish's button pushing produced the pale glow of the tractor beam, which whizzed right by our escape pod and affixed itself to a rather large asteroid about a mile past us. The asteroid, the size of several football stadiums, wiggled to life. It moved slowly at first, but quickly gained speed.

"It's, it's, it's...," said the dog. His claws scraped the tile floor as he scurried past the pilot chairs to cower under the dashboard.

"It's coming right at us!!" yelled the pig.

This triggered a mad scramble between the cat, rabbit, and duck. The ship jostled, as they each had a paw or wing on the yoke.

Meanwhile, the fish continued flopping atop the control panel, occasionally whacking a random button or lever.

As the three fought for dominance, they jerked the escape pod out of the path of the oncoming asteroid, then right back in.

The fish continued smacking buttons like a novice video gamer and opened the outside doors of the airlock.

Crates floated out of the airlock.

The doors closed.

The asteroid raced closer.

"Dude! Paws off," yelled the duck as he tackled the cat.

The rabbit grabbed the controls.

I smacked into the ceiling as the rabbit yanked us down.

The giant asteroid sped past us.

Wild button mashing by the fish continued.

The glow of the tractor beam disappeared.

The fish popped his head up. He gazed out the window. He curled his fins to his side and performed a slow proud nod of his head; for he had successfully deactivated the tractor beam. That proud expression quickly faded to bewilderment.

Sir Isaac Newton's first law of motion states that objects at rest remain at rest and objects in motion remain in motion unless acted upon by an outside force. The asteroid was most definitely in motion and in the zero gravity of space, no outside forces existed to stop or even slow down its motion.

The fish panicked and fled the room. A moment later, muffled blasts emanated from our escape pod. The two laser beams converged on the asteroid, disintegrating the giant rock in an impressive explosion.

The rabbit spun around in his chair as he let out a wild, "Yahoo!!"

"Dude, what are you so proud of? You don't seriously believe you're the one who blasted the asteroid?" The duck stood on the control panel, with his wings crossed.

"No way, man. You were way too slow. You know I blasted it first."

"Dude, you missed it by a mile."

"Actually, I think you both hit it at the same time," I said.

"No way, man!"

"Awesome, dude" added the duck, as they did a wing to paw high-five, followed by two chest high-fives.

The fish reappeared in the cargo bay and eased his way back to the control panel. After a couple of whacks with his tail and a belly flop on a button, the outside doors of the airlock slid open again.

The rabbit placed his paws on the controls. "Here's our chance. I'm not waiting for him to mess around with that tractor beam again. We're flying this baby right into that room, man."

The fish continued to flop around the control panel and fortunately, did not restart the tractor beam as the rabbit maneuvered us up to the open doors.

"Can you believe it, man? We don't fit," said the rabbit.

"No big deal there, dude. Just get us close to the opening and drop the ramp," said the duck.

"Good plan, man." The rabbit backed the escape pod up to the airlock.

The ramp hissed its way down and clanged on the airlock floor.

The pig waved us toward the ramp. "Go! Go! Go!"

As we scrambled into the airlock, I kept thinking, *"Fish, please don't hit the button that blasts us out into space. Please."*

Once the rest of us were in, the pig activated the ramp retraction. He waddled down the ramp on his hind legs. No need to avert our eyes because he thankfully wore pants. As the ramp rose, he took a couple of unsteady steps. He stumbled and fell, rolling inches from the side of the ramp. He popped onto all fours, galloped to the edge of the ramp, and leapt into the airlock.

With all of us safely inside the airlock, the pig punched the button to close the outside doors. Wind rushed into the airlock. When the pressure stabilized, the inside doors opened.

As we waltzed into the cargo bay, the dog looked out the giant window. "Is it, is it safe to leave the, leave the ship floating out there?"

"It'll be fine, man. Zero-G, baby."

"The rabbit is mostly correct. Assuming no outside forces act upon the escape pod, it will remain stationary," said the cat.

As we fanned out into the cargo bay, the duck asked, "Dude, shouldn't we have triggered some kind of alarm? Something like 'Intruder Alert! Intruder Alert!'"

"No," said the cat, who had jumped onto the cargo bay control center. She pawed at a terminal. "The space station's security protocols have been disabled. Besides, we are considered space station residents. If the protocols were active, the program would not detect us as intruders. Indeed, the sensors would identify Mr. Steak&Eggs and his crew as intruders. Which logically explains why the security program has been deactivated."

"So, dude, you're saying the intruder alert system is like, broken or something?"

"That is an inaccurate paraphrase of my statement, but I do not wish to belabor the topic further. So yes, the intruder alert system is broken."

The dog swiveled his head to glare at each of us in random order. "Okay. Okay, so, so, what are we going to do now? I mean we don't, we don't know where the cow is, or where Mr. Steak&Eggs is, or how many of his henchmen are combing the space station, or –"

The cat, who had been busy poking at the terminal screen and her handheld device, stopped the dog in mid-sentence. "Sensors do not detect the presence of Mr. Steak&Eggs on this space station or in his attached spacecraft. The sensors indicate three life forms in the cafeteria, two Cheddarians and a bovine Earth creature, which I surmise is our cow."

"Not the, not the cafeteria. You know, you know what they do there, don't you? They're going to slice her up into tiny chunks and eat her." The dog spun in a panic circle. "We've got to, got to do something before they, before they butcher her."

"Dog, calm down. She's not gonna get butchered on my watch," said the pig. "I'm sure we can handle a couple of Cheddarians."

"We, we didn't do so good against that group in the, in the hallway."

"Dude, that was before the chicken mastered the art of mummifying dudes in duct tape."

"She can take care of two Cheddarians on her own, man, with one wing tied to her tail and her legs wrapped together."

The rabbit and duck scurried about the cargo bay and returned with rolls of duct tape, which they placed at my feet. "Please accept our humble offerings of magical gray tape, oh great dude."

"We are your humble servants, man."

The pair giggled as they bowed at my feet.

"Yes, yes. All hail the chicken," said the cat, though her tone suggested scorn instead of praise.

They continued bowing while chanting, "Hyperspeed. Hyperspeed. Hyperspeed."

Their praise had shifted from genuine adoration to being overtly condescending. I wished to put an end to it. "Can we go save the cow now?"

"Let's do it. Let's kick some butt." The pig punched one of his karate-clench front hooves into the other and headed for the exit.

***

THE CAT INSISTED THE optimal route to the cafeteria was through the kitchen. A row of stainless-steel ovens ending at a walk-in freezer lined a long wall of the rectangular room. Sinks, refrigerators, and shelves filled the opposite wall. Mr. Steak&Eggs' crew had left the appliances but stripped the shelves and storage areas clean. Outside of a single dented and burnt pan, not a single cooking utensil was left behind. No knives, pots, plates, spices, bowls, or spatulas. Not even a dirty dish towel. All presumably crated up and shipped off for resale.

As the rest of us weaved around the steel food prep tables occupying the center of the kitchen, the fish swam over the tables and poked his head through the metal swinging doors to the dining room. He wiggled back into the kitchen and announced, "Cat, there's three Cheddarians in there. Not two."

This prompted the rest of us to scurry to the swinging metal doors. We peered under the door, through the small circle windows, or between the crack of the doors. Everyone except the cat, who whipped out her handheld computer.

"Inconceivable. Sensors only indicate two Cheddarian life forms. I surmise the third image to be a hologram."

The fish snickered as those of us at the door instantly recognized Denver Omelet, the space station's head waiter, as the additional '*Cheddarian*'. He curled his tail to his mouth, using it to make the shush gesture. Despite the seriousness of the situation and my concern for our cow, a giggle grew inside me.

The cat clicked a couple of buttons and groaned. "No holograms detected." She scratched her chin with a single extended claw. "Let me see this so-called third Cheddarian."

She bumped me out of the way and stuck her head between the doors. "Of course. That is indeed a logical explanation. My scanners do not detect androids and this so-called third Cheddarian is –"

"The android waiter," said the pig. "We know."

The rest of us backed away from the doors and let our giggles grow to muffled laughter. We kept it under control, making sure to not attract attention.

The cat's tail puffed as she glared at the fish.

"Alright. everybody, settle down. We're here to save the cow." The pig spoke with a stern yet quiet voice. "The two Cheddarian lackeys aren't a threat."

I recognized the two Cheddarians. They were the Waffle brothers, Belgian and Blueberry. The pig was right. They weren't a threat.

"That android could be a problem, but I've always wanted to test my strength against an android." The pig cracked his neck and stretched his kung-fu grip hooves.

"The android poses no threat." The cat's tail had deflated back to normal. "His programming forbids the harming of any creature. Performing the Heimlich maneuver is the closest it will come to harming an individual."

"So, what's the plan, dudes?"

"What do you think they're doing to the cow, man?"

No one answered their questions as we reestablished our positions behind the swinging doors.

The Waffle Brothers and Denver Omelet stood shoulder-to-shoulder, blocking our view of the cow.

"The boss man wants us to milk this creature, so Android man, get to it," said Belgian Waffle.

"I'm a waiter, not a dairy farmer. I have no idea how to milk that thing."

"Then why are you here?" asked Belgian.

"Because everyone thinks I'm the cow expert. But I know nothing about cows. I'm programmed for fine dining."

"Are we sure this beast is a cow," said Belgian's little brother Blueberry.

"Look, Bagel explained that. It's just another breed of cow," said Belgian.

"But it has horns!"

"So? Some cows have horns," said Belgian.

I whispered to the other animals, "That's not our cow. Our cow doesn't have horns."

The others nodded their agreement.

"So, so, what, what do we do now?" asked the dog.

We shrugged and returned our attention to the cafeteria.

"Sure, it's similar, but this beast is evil." Blueberry pointed his upper hands at the horned cow like a magician performing his prestige. "Look at all those muscles. And those beady eyes. And the stench."

"I don't care what it smells like. We've got orders to milk this thing. So, milk it," said the older brother.

"There's one more thing. Those instructions Bagel gave us talked about there being four or six of them, udder things dangling down there on its belly. This beast has only one thingy hanging down."

"Don't worry about it. Just milk it."

Blueberry sat down on the stool next to what he had been told was a cow. With upper and lower arm synchronicity, he stretched his fingers. He planted his top two hands on the side of the beast.

The pig blasted through the swinging doors. "Wait. Don't do it!"

The pig was too late. With both bottom hands, Blueberry grabbed what he believed to be a single udder and gave it a hard yank, just like Bagel had instructed.

Chapter 12

BLUEBERRY'S YANK OF WHAT he thought to be a single udder unleashed the rage inside the formerly docile creature. The bull's initial anger focused on Denver Omelet, who had done nothing to him. That mattered not to the bull. He charged the android waiter.

The pig, who had sprung into the dining room too late to prevent the ill-fated milking, yelled, "MOVE!!"

But Denver made no attempt to elude the attack. The bull launched him. He sailed past the pig, who stood on his hind legs with his karate-grip front hooves flashing the universal stop gesture.

Denver flew toward the swinging kitchen doors.

The cat scrambled out of danger.

The rest of us froze.

BAM!

The doors sprang open like pinball flippers bouncing the rabbit and duck off the walk-in freezer door and sending the dog and me into shelves.

Denver crashed into the row of prep tables, creating a chain-reaction multi-table pile up. His mechanical left eye dangled across his mouth. Exposed wires kept it from falling to the floor. He scanned us with his working robot eye. "Whoa, what are you animals doing here? I thought you guys were all long gone. Don't get me wrong, I'm glad to see you, but seriously, you shouldn't be here. Especially the kitchen. You do realize what happens in here?"

I listened to the android's words, but my focus was fixated on the doors swinging through the fish, who hung motionless in the doorway.

In the cafeteria, the bull snorted and scratched the floor.

Denver's working eye locked onto the bull. "Regardless of the reason you are all here, my advice to you is - RUN!!!!"

Needing no encouragement, the Waffle brothers had already sprinted out the exit at the far end of the dining room.

The dog and I lunged under a sink.

The cat hopped across tabletops in a mad dash toward the other door.

Punctuated by a grunt, the pig positioned himself in the doorway.

The bull charged. He rammed into the pig. His pace never slowed.

The pig's hooves skidded across the tile, as he and the bull smashed through the doors and the still hovering fish.

The rabbit and duck yelled "Yee-haw!!" and "Hoozah!!" as they jumped onto the bull's back in an attempt to..., well, I have no idea what the pair thought they might accomplish, other than bodily injury to themselves and potential death. They bounced around the bull's back like rocks on a kettledrum, until the rabbit grasped a tuff of the bull's back hair in his mouth and the duck wrapped his wings around the bull's tail.

None of this distracted the bull from his primary target. Using the pig as a battering ram, he slammed into the android waiter.

The collision bucked the rabbit and duck onto a stove top, as the combined mass of the bull, pig, and android formed a wrecking ball which scattered and shattered the prep tables.

When the clashing of metal quieted to a wobbling table leg, the three rose. Still fixated on the robot, the bull gored a horn into the android's abdomen. With the android dangling from his right horn, he shifted his piercing stare to the pig.

Their eyes locked.

The pig rose to his hind legs. "Is that all you've got? I thought bulls were the king of the farm. The barnyard's toughest animal." He spit a tooth to the floor. "The chicken hits harder than you do."

I wished he hadn't brought me into the conversation. Thankfully, the bull didn't understand a word and never turned toward me. He responded by scuffing the floor with a front hoof.

The pig flexed into a fighter's stance, punctuating the pose with a menacing grunt. "Bring it on!"

I knew we should flee, but I hated to miss a good brawl. The dog and I remained huddled under a sink, with the rabbit and duck perched on top and the fish hovering above them. The cat had sensibly skirted out of the kitchen.

"Kick his butt, dude," said the duck, pumping a wing in the air.

Denver's face flopped into view. With his one good eye, he glared at the dog and I. "Why are you fools still here? RUN!!"

We ignored him.

A rumbling snort announced the launch of the bull's charge.

The pig held his ground.

Still stuck to the bull's horn, Denver's limbs flailed about like a marionette in a dryer, as the bull's hooves pounded the flooring.

A second before impact, the pig gave us a wink and, with an olé that rivaled a veteran matador, sidestepped the bull's rush.

With his head down, the bull raged past the pig and lodged both horns deep into the door of an industrial sized oven. Sparks cascaded from Denver's abdomen, as he hung crushed between the bull and the oven.

"The android is right," said the pig, sprinting for the kitchen exit as fast as he could on his stubby hind legs. "Let's get out of here."

The dog sprinted past the pig and out the kitchen door. The rest of us followed, sneaking glances at the bull straining to dislodge his horn from the oven. We made the final turn toward the cargo bay when we heard the clomping of hooves on tile.

"Pick up the pace." The volume of the pig's grunts grew, which provided the illusion he heeded his own words, but his tiny hind legs failed to propel him any faster.

The pig fell farther behind, as the rest of us sprinted into the cargo bay. I straddled the doorway and glanced down the hallway. The pig had half the corridor to cover and appeared to be slowing down. The rhythmic clomping of the bull's gallop flipped to frantic tap dancing, followed by him smashing a hole in the wall. He'd failed to turn the corner.

The pig glanced back, slowing his pace further.

The bull's hooves shuffled on the tile, struggling to find traction.

The rabbit and duck joined me in the doorway.

"Come on, dude."

"You got this, man."

After another glance over his shoulder, the tip of the pig's hoof scuffed the floor and down he went.

The bull found his footing and regained his stride.

The pig scrambled to his hind legs.

The bull lowered his horns, without a drop in his pace.

A couple of hoof shifts failed to improve the pig's footing. He had no time for snide remarks or taunts. He leaned forward and braced for contact.

At the moment of impact, I thought the pig might hold his ground. With the aid of his karate-clench front hooves, he had the bull by the horns, but the bull's momentum overtook the pig. As the pig slid backwards, tile chucks sprayed from his hooves. It looked as though the bull was snow blowing the hallway.

We ducked inside the doorway as the pair skidded past. Chunks of tile littered the cargo bay.

"ARRRRGGGHHH!!!"

A crash followed the pig's scream.

The rabbit, duck, and I rushed into the hall.

The bull had our pig pinned against a wall.

"Hoozah!!" yelled the rabbit and duck, charging into battle.

Although the bull appeared to have the upper hoof, being pinned to the wall finally provided the pig decent hoofing. And he still held a firm grip on the bull's horns. I don't know much about wrestling, but the pig planted the bull's face to the floor in what I assumed to be a classic move. The bull snorted and bucked his legs, but the pig held firm.

"Hang on, dude. We're almost there."

The pig glanced up. "Get back in the room, you morons. I've got this. The bull and I just need to finish coming to an understanding."

The rabbit and duck stopped.

The pig and bull's grunts slowed.

After a half snort, half sigh from the bull, the pig released him. Apparently, the pig interpreted this as a concession snort-sigh. The rest of us weren't so sure. The rabbit and duck readied for an attack, while I shuffled halfway into the cargo bay.

The pig strolled toward us without a glance back at the bull. "I think he knows who's the boss now. Let's go home."

The bull snorted like a scolded teenager as he returned to his hooves.

The cat hopped off the control panel table and waltzed out of the cargo bay. She glanced at the sulking bull staring at the floor. "Excellent work. With the bull obedient, we can collect my translator data files." The cat strutted past the bull without a flinch at his airy snort.

A glare from the pig quieted the bull and had him hanging his head.

As we approached the laboratory, the cat listed additional items she wanted. "The Mambomatic 5000 won't fit in the escape pod, even without the cow taking up half the space, but we should be able to bring back most of Dr. Hash Browns' handheld devices. Plus, we should download his notes."

The laboratory door slid open.

The cat screamed.

Chapter 13

THE CAT SPRINTED INTO the laboratory and scrambled between the empty tables. Cables snaked across the floor, no longer connected to the vast array of computers and other electronic gadgets and gizmos that had previously filled the former school gymnasium. The handful of lab tables left contained nothing but scraps of garbage, random sticky notes, and lots of dust. Unfaded floor tiles marked the prior location of the Mambomatic 5000, which had dominated the middle of the laboratory. Wires dangled out the metal tubing where the jumbotrons had once hung. The pig's workout equipment was gone, as were the rabbit and duck's video game setup. They had even taken the coffee machine.

I scurried over to my cabinet of art supplies. They'd taken everything, even the dried paints and used paintbrushes, but they left my unfinished Dog Playing Chess. I grabbed it with my beak and stuffed it under my wing, thrilled to be reunited with my masterpiece. My excitement quickly faded. *Why hadn't they taken it? They'd taken everything else. Did they consider it worthless? Just a piece of trash?*

I pulled it out from under my wing and examined my work. *It was unfinished. That must be why they left it.*

As I stuck the painting back under my wing, I noticed a hunched-over figure sitting on the floor in the middle of the ghost lab. He resembled a crumpled piece of scratch paper instead of a living being. His small puff of orange hair was more ruffled than normal and his white lab coat more disheveled than ever.

The cat walked up and brushed her body across his leg. He said not a word as he picked her up and placed her on his lap. He stroked her fur twice, then fell back into a trance, staring at the floor.

The rest of us made our way to him. Our presence broke through his trance. "You're all here. You're all still alive. When I came back to an empty lab, I feared the worst." He placed the cat onto his shoulder and gave the rabbit, duck, and me a big hug. He released us and scanned the lab.

"Dude, what happened?"

"You disappeared, man."

"They knocked me unconscious and sent me home against my will." The flailing of Dr. Hash Browns' four arms intensified with every sentence. "I came back as quick as I could. But they had already looted the lab. The entire place. They took everything." His arms rested as he choreographed a long exhale with a head drop.

He bounced his head right back up. His mouth almost formed a smile. "But you're all here now." He scanned the crowd. "Wait, where's the cow? Is she not with you?"

"Affirmative," said the cat, who had returned to his lap.

"Well, where is she?"

"The whereabouts of the cow are unknown. The prevailing theory suggests your former superior abducted said cow and other bovine from Earth in conjunction with his scheme to merchandise cow flesh and bovine mammary gland secretions." She stretched her head out so Dr. Hash Browns could scratch her neck.

Dr. Hash Browns scrunched his face. "What?"

"Mr. Steak&Eggs kidnapped a bunch of cows, including our cow, so he can make a fortune selling steak and milk," said the pig.

Dr. Hash Browns pounded the floor with his two lower fists. "That jerk really went through with it. He had no appreciation for my work. He just wants to butcher animals and sell their spare parts. The man is a barbarian. And he grabbed our cow. He must be stopped."

"Agreed," said the pig. "But we don't know where he is or where he's taken the cow."

"So, you came back to ask for my help. Wise decision. We'll figure this out. We'll get our cow back."

The cat shifted her head to get behind the ear scratchies. "We did not return to the space station to seek your advice. Scanners indicated the presence of Mr. Steak&Eggs' spacecraft docked at the space station. This was our best lead. We assumed finding Mr. Steak&Eggs would lead us to the cow."

"His ship may be here, but he's not. And the cow ain't here either."

"We are aware, sir." The cat arched her back as Dr. Hash Browns ran a set of nails down her spine.

"So, you didn't come back for me?" The cat leapt out of Dr. Hash Browns' lap, as he stood up and stomped away from us. He glared at us in turn. "Where did you go? What have you been doing? Was anybody worried about what happened to me? I was worried sick about all of you."

"Dude, we wanted to come find you, but Earth was the only planet in the escape pod's power range."

"Earth was lame, man. So boring."

Dr. Hash Browns' eyes softened. "Well, you're back home now. We'll find the cow and be a happy family again. Then we can get back to work." He ruffled the hair on the dog's head.

The dog had raised his eyes and lowered his head as Dr. Hash Browns' hand approached. He allowed the playful sign of affection but glared at Dr. Hash Browns afterward. Reuniting with our creator to restart his experiments was not a plan I wanted any part of, and I surmised the dog felt the same.

The beeping of the cat's handheld device stopped me from spiraling into horrifying memories of my trips through the Mambomatic 5000.

"I do not wish to alarm, but my sensors detected an incoming foxtrot wave."

With only the cryptic words of the cat as a warning, the lab plunged into darkness. The complete absence of light. Zero visibility. I couldn't see my hand in front of my face, that is, if I had hands.

The space station's climate control system faded to a stop. In the years I'd spent there, the continuous hum of the fans had gone unnoticed. But when it disappeared, I became acutely aware of its absence.

"What's, what's happening? I can't see!! I can't see." The dog's claws tapped in circles. "Okay. Okay. Rabbit. Duck. This isn't funny. Turn the lights back on."

"Hey, man, it wasn't us," said the rabbit.

"Seriously, dude, we didn't do it."

"I bet it's a blown fuse," said the pig. "Blintzes, check for blown fuses."

A glow from the cat's handheld device grabbed our attention. "The space station's computer system will be incapable of a response," she said.

We huddled around this only source of light.

"Good point. No power in this room, so no power to the speakers. Come on, let's go to a room with power." The pig exited the tiny circle of light and banged into a table. "Dang it."

"Pig, if my sensors are correct, you will not elicit a response from Blintzes, no matter what room you're in."

A slow rumble cascaded through the floor, like an approaching car playing bass heavy music. At the far end of the laboratory, a coffee cup shattered. Tables wobbled and fell as the rumble grew and bounced me into the air.

"It's him!! That crazy bull. Run for your –" The thump of the dog smacking into an immovable object preceded the thud of him landing on the floor. This cemented the lesson; don't leave the tiny circle of light.

The wave passed through the other half of the lab, leaving more toppled tables in its wake.

Silence and calm returned.

"The bull is not the cause of this disturbance," said the cat. "That was an asteroid colliding into the space station."

"Dude, what are the odds of that? First the lights go out and then an asteroid slams into us."

"This is not a mere coincidence. Blintzes is offline. I believe the space station has experienced a total power outage."

"A total power failure is an impossibility," said Dr. Hash Browns from somewhere in the darkness. The cat flashed the glow of her handheld, revealing Dr. Hash Browns wandering away from the only source of light. "The main power generator is a ChaCha-QZ, running on Jitterbug technology. As I am sure you are all aware, the ChaCha-QZ will never fail. It can fly into a black hole and come out the other end still working."

"That is preposterous," said the cat. "A black hole does not have an other end."

"Dude, I thought black holes are portals to the multiverse."

The mention of Jitterbug technology and ChaCha-QZ sparked memories. "Didn't the tech guy tell Mr. Steak&Eggs that a simple foxtrot wave could shut down the ChaCha-QZ?"

"Precisely," said the cat.

"You're going to believe that junk collector and ignore the volumes of scientific data supporting the ChaCha-QZ's indestructibility?" asked Dr. Hash Browns.

"You mean volumes of marketing propaganda." The pig chuckled at the cat's snide remark.

"Did they actually test it by flying one of them Cha-Cha things through a black hole?" asked the rabbit. "Because that would be awesome if they did, man."

"Of course, they didn't fly it through a black hole," said Dr. Hash Browns. "They tested it via computer simulations."

The floor rumble came from the opposite direction this time and moved much faster. Everything hopped, apart from two lab tables bolted to the floor. Crashes echoed in the darkness. Dust hovered in the glow of the cat's handheld long after the wave of chaos passed.

The dog swiveled his head, ran a mini circle, then focused on the cat. "Okay, so, so what does, what does the loss of power have to do with asteroids slamming into the space station?"

"No power," said the pig. "No deflector shields."

"Precisely," said the cat.

Dr. Hash Browns rose and joined us in the tiny circle of light. "I suspect the deflector shield failed because the scavengers stole key components. Not a power failure."

"For the sake of argument, let's say the power did go out, man." The rabbit took the tone of a parent trying to explain a clear truth to their child.

"Can't happen."

"Okay, man, but if it did, shouldn't we be running on backup power?"

"There is no backup system. No need for it. Why have backup for a system that never fails? It's an unnecessary redundancy."

"Isn't there at least some sort of emergency lighting, dude?" asked the duck.

"No."

"But, but, but, isn't this a, ah, safety violation? No, no power backup system. No emergency lighting," said the dog.

"If you have installed a ChaCha-QZ power generator, they waive such regulations. There is no need for them. The ChaCha-QZ cannot fail."

"I hear ya, dude, but it sure would be nice if we have more than the glow of the cat's tiny screen."

"Which has a limited battery life." As if on cue, the cat's handheld flickered off.

The dog yanked open a drawer of a nearby desk. "Do, do we, do we have candles? Maybe a flashlight? Matches? Anything that illuminates. A blowtorch? Dang it. They've taken everything."

"I, um, I..." It was the cat stammering. "I may have hidden a couple of small LED flashlights behind the cabinet which houses the chicken's art materials."

Thanks to the total darkness[1], I could not exchange looks with my fellow animals. Instead, we shuffled toward the cabinet pretending that hoarding flashlights in a secret hiding place was normal behavior.

After several seconds of bumps, crashes, and winces of pain, we all congregated around the cabinet. The cat wedged a paw between the cabinet and wall. One-by-one, she dragged out three flashlights, which she handed to Dr. Hash Browns, the rabbit, and the duck.

---

1. I planned to describe us as being "blind as a bat," but stopped myself. This human phrase is wrong. Bats are not blind.

The beams of light calmed me for a moment. Then another asteroid rattled the space station, raining dust and debris from the rafters of the former gymnasium.

***

WE SHUFFLED ON TO our next adventure: getting out of the laboratory. Under normal circumstances, you ask Blintzes to open the door and the door pops open. Actually, you didn't even have to ask. She would sense you reaching for the door and open it. But with the power out, the door remained closed and locked. This posed no problem for the fish but challenged the rest of us. Dr. Hash Browns frantically pulled on the door, to no avail.

The dog stepped up, insisting he could knock the door off its hinges with a tail whip attack. No luck, because he missed the door. On the plus side, he didn't hurt himself... much.

The pig told him and everyone else to step back. He clutched the door handle with both karate-clench hooves. With a pain-filled grunt, he yanked on the door handle. It refused to budge.

The rabbit suggested using the duck's Atomic Quack, but the cat pointed out that even though this would undoubtedly open the door, it would also kill us all and destroy the entire space station.

The rabbit and duck played rock concert with the flashlights, while the rest of us stood in silence watching the cat hot-wire the door controls.

"How, how's it going?" asked the dog, pacing by the door. "Do you need help?"

"It would help if the rabbit and duck would stop their insipid rock concert impersonation and shine the illumination devices upon the door control panel."

They obliged.

The cat finished dismantling the control panel and began pulling wires out. She snatched the flashlight out of the duck's hands, removed the battery, and connected it to a set of the pulled wires. Moments later, a satisfying click and soft hiss announced the unlocking of the door. It opened only a crack, but enough for the pig to demonstrate his strength and finish the job.

As we exited the lab, another asteroid shook the station, knocking several of us off our feet, paws, or hooves. I clutched my painting tight as I bounced off the wall.

"Why are there so many asteroids? There's like one smacking us every minute, man. It's ridiculous."

"Rabbit, your astonishment regarding the frequency of our collisions with asteroids perplexes me," said the cat. "After all, you are aware the space station is parked at the center of the Limburger asteroid belt."

We walked past a couple of school room doors before the fish said what we all contemplated. "I knew we were parked in the middle of an asteroid field, but never pondered why. I mean, considering the mind-blowing vastness of the universe that was at your disposal, Dr. Hash Browns, why in the name of Fried Spam did you park the space station in the middle of an asteroid field?"

"It's a great hiding place."

"Who are you hiding from?" asked the fish.

"There are hundreds, maybe thousands, of people dying to get their hands on my research."

"Surely you can't be serious. Name one," said the fish.

Without hesitation, Dr. Hash Browns said, "French Toast. He's been jealous of my superior intelligence since kindergarten." He ground his teeth and released a nasal grunt. "That arrogant hack has been trying to get his stubby little fingers on my work for centuries. What a weasel. He'd love to claim my genius as his own. And he's not the only one. There's –"

The hallway swayed like a festival carnival ride. I assumed an asteroid interrupted him, but this time a whine of scraping metal loitered. It echoed through the corridors, culminating with a pinging snap that rattled the walls. We'd learn later the source of this incident.

The dog's head snapped toward every lingering creak. "So, so um, so where are we headed?"

"To the power room so I can show you all that the Cha-Cha-QZ is still working," said Dr. Hash Browns, who'd taken the lead position.

The rabbit and duck followed close behind. "This might sound stupid, dude, but why don't we head for the escape pod and get out of here?"

"There's nothing left for us here. Time to abandon ship, man."

Dr. Hash Browns' enormous head snapped around. His twig-thick neck amazingly handled the torque. "We're not running away. This is our home. We must defend it. We must rebuild it."

I agreed with the others. We should escape the dying ship, but we'd all been conditioned to obey Dr. Hash Browns, so we argued no further.

The cat pranced into the beam of Dr. Hash Browns' flashlight and assumed her regal sitting cat pose. "Flashlight batteries provide sufficient power to unlock interior doors, but do not meet the voltage requirements for opening the cargo bay airlock. If we can't open the airlock doors, we can't get to the escape pod. Restoring the Cha-Cha QZ generator is our only way off this space station."

Dr. Hash Browns turned and splashed his flashlight at us. "So, it's settled. We're heading to the power room."

The duck shined his light on Dr. Hash Browns. "Dude, what about your ship?"

"I don't have a ship."

A second flashlight shined on Dr. Hash Browns. "Hold on a second, man. How did you get here?"

Dr. Hash Browns spun around and walked past the cat. "My wife dropped me off."

"I thought you were divorced, dude."

"That's why she was so eager to get rid of me."

The flashlight beams from the rabbit and duck caught the cat shaking her head. I assumed this to be in response to Dr. Hash Browns' callous remark regarding his divorce, but she said, "If our destination is the power room, our current course is in the wrong direction."

Dr. Hash Browns paused and splashed his flashlight up and down the hall. "I suppose you're right," he said, and reversed his direction.

***

I SENSED THE DROP in temperature but didn't feel cold. Frosty breath billowed from our mouths as we made our way to the power room. The first time I experienced this phenomenon, I thought Dr. Hash Browns had given me the power to control the weather. Later I learned that under certain atmospheric conditions, everyone can see their breath.

As we walked down hallways, I worried we would run into the Waffle Brothers, or other members of Mr. Steak&Eggs' crew. After a few turns, I stopped fretting about it. I figured they would head to their ship and for a moment, I thought that's where we should go. Then the visual memory of my friends floating in space popped into my head. The Cheddarians wouldn't save us. They'd jettison us. Best to stay the course.

We rushed down three floors and halfway across the space station, hot-wiring doors along the way. Dr. Hash Browns insisted on doing the hot-wiring. The cat walked him through the first door, and from there, his four hands proved to be more efficient than the cat's paws.

The walk left me winded. I drifted to the rear of the pack and plopped down once we reached the power room door.

Dr. Hash Browns fumbled with the wires. "Dang, it's cold in here." He blew on his fingers as he passed the flashlight between his four hands. His body swayed as he refocused on the door control panel. He blinked and rubbed his eyes. "Okay, let's see. Red wire to ground. No, that's not right. Connect red to purple."

"You were correct the first time, sir," said the cat in a comforting tone I didn't know she possessed. "Red to ground."

"Right. Red to ground. Connect purple to green."

"Purple to blue, sir."

"Right" Dr. Browns blew on his upper hands. He swapped the flashlight to his lower left hand and warmed his lower right in a lab coat pocket. "Wait, how does it go again? Never mind. I'm connecting all the wires to ground. That always works."

"NO!!" The cat's back hairs sprang up.

Dr. Hash Browns staggered backward as he gave her a stern but quizzical stare.

The cat eased back to her regal squat. "Sir, I do not wish to alarm, but I believe you are suffering from hypoxemia."

"My glucose levels are fine, thank you very much."

"No, you're suffering from a lack of oxygen, sir. Why don't you let me hot-wire this door?"

Dr. Hash Browns blinked at the controls, as realization settled in. The same realization I had come to. A simple walk shouldn't have exhausted me. We both suffered from a lack of oxygen.

"Perhaps you're right," said Dr. Hash Browns, as he backed away from the panel.

In the shaky light of Dr. Hash Browns' flashlight, the cat hot-wired the controls and the power room door slid open.

Dr. Hash Browns strolled in. The light from his flashlight scanned the room like a police spotlight. A giant dome of tinted glass in the center of the room consumed eighty percent of the power room's floor space. An orb the size of a baseball floated in the middle of the dome. A cloudy mixture of orange, red, and yellow gases swirled inside, giving the orb a faint glow. Computer screens, touch screens, radar screens, oscilloscope-like screens, speakers, control panels, microphones, knobs, buttons, dials, keyboards, mouse-like devices, media storage units of unknown origin, and LEDs of all colors, shapes, and sizes lined the walls. It would have been an impressive display of technology, if the power had been on and the LEDs blinked, and the monitors displayed real-time graphs.

He placed his bottom hands on his hips. "That's odd. There are no Waltz streams. The console screens are blank." He scurried between various instruments and control panels. He punched at keyboards and frantically flipped switches. Nothing changed. The orb remained motionless. No screens illuminated. No LEDs blinked to life. No media storage units of unknown origin whirred their way to data ready mode. "This can't be right."

"Does this not prove the Cha-Cha QZ has failed?" asked the cat.

"No, no, no. It can't be broken," said Dr. Hash Browns. "I mean, it must just be... But then again, if no Waltz streams are reaching the outer shell, then the... Wait a minute, I bet it's the.... No, it has to be... It's frickin' Jitter-Bug technology, so it can't..."

"Have you finally exhausted all possibilities and reached the obvious conclusion?" Although snarky, the cat lacked the condescending tone she would have taken when lecturing one of us.

"Let us not jump to hasty conclusions. It could be that...." Dr. Hash Browns still struggled to complete a sentence as he rushed over to a different set of terminals. "Inconceivable. It can't be. But it must be. Dang it!! The main generator failed! It's frickin' busted. When I get my hands on that Powercon salesman, I'm going to... I'm going to – I'm going to demand my money back. That's what I'll do."

The cat hopped onto the table by Dr. Hash Browns and placed a paw on his shoulder. "Thank you for coming to your senses. Now calm down and instruct us on how to reactivate the Cha-Cha QZ."

Dr. Hash Browns tossed his upper arms in the air with his palms up. "You can't reactivate the Cha-Cha QZ."

"There's got to be an on-off switch," said the fish, swimming around the tinted-glass dome.

"There's no on-off switch," said Dr. Hash Browns. "They deliver it on and it stays on. It is always on."

"Can't we just, can't we just like unplug it and plug it back in?" asked the dog.

"No. This is the power source for the entire space station. It does not plug into anything. Everything plugs into it."

"Understood, sir, but certainly there are procedures for restarting the Cha-Cha QZ," said the cat.

"No. There are none."

"You must be joking." I wondered why the fish said this, since based on Dr. Hash Browns' frown, he was clearly not joking. In fact, he had never showed signs of a whimsical side.

The cat threw her front paws up. "This space station has documented procedures on everything from how to recalibrate the temperature sensors on the deflector shield control boards to how to make a cup of coffee and you're telling us there are no procedures for restarting the Cha-Cha QZ?"

"Why would you need procedures for restarting a system that never fails?"

The cat and fish were inches from Dr. Hash Browns' face. In unison, they motioned toward the dome and shouted, "Because it just failed!"

"Fair point." Dr. Hash Browns shook a fist at the dome. "But it's JitterBug technology. It can survive a black hole."

"We've established it's broken. Let's not go back there." The fish turned sharply, swishing his tail through Dr. Hash Browns' face.

The cat getting upset at someone's failure to understand her point is a regular occurrence, but the fish joining in was new. If I hadn't been experiencing brain fog, I might have been as upset as them. Instead, I had serious orb watching to do. The whirling gasses were hypnotizingly awesome.

In his oxygen-deprived state, Dr. Hash Browns didn't flinch as the tail passed through his head.

The room went silent. Then the dog ran in circles shouting, "We're, we're all going to die. Without power we're, we're trapped here forever. With no climate control. No air to breathe. No shows to watch! ARRRGGHHH!! We have to do something! Anything!"

"I believe I will go sit down in that chair, because I'm tired." Dr. Hash Browns plopped into a cushioned office chair.

Another asteroid rattled the space station.

It startled none of us.

"Is anybody else cold, because I'm freezing?" asked Dr. Hash Browns.

The others nodded no. I wasn't sure how to answer. I noticed the cold, but I didn't feel cold. Then I thought it might be a rhetorical question and eventually lost my train of thought.

The cat hopped into Dr. Hash Browns' lap and curled up for what looked like a nap. "I will search the archives I have stored in my brain. There must be a Cha-Cha QZ setup guide."

The cat claimed to have downloaded the space station's manuals and schematic diagrams, along with thousands of technical articles, data, and books, into her brain via some wireless connection that used her whiskers as antennas. This vast repository of knowledge gave her a perceived intellectual superiority that she loved to lord over us. She also claimed to have developed a search engine for her knowledge repository but needed to curl up and close her eyes in order to execute what she called a "Knowledge Scan." She can call it what she likes. I call it taking a snooze.

***

WHILE THE CAT "KNOWLEDGE scanned" and Dr. Hash Browns slumped in a chair, the rest of us watched the swirls flow in the tiny orb levitating in the heart of the Cha-Cha QZ. I slumped to the floor. Though the mesmerizing orb blurred in and out of focus, I couldn't take my eyes off it.

The lack of oxygen and the abundance of carbon dioxide had more observable impacts on Dr. Hash Browns. "And when I win the Raisin Bran award, I'm going to take the trophy they give me and beat that Powercon salesman to death with it."

I didn't process his rant. It took all of my energy to concentrate on the billowing gases of the orb.

The cat's eyes blinked open. She stretched and yawned before settling into her regal squat in Dr. Hash Browns' lap. "The manuals proved to be useless. I located seven volumes on how to change the décor of the terminals, but not a single comment on how to restart or set up the Cha-Cha QZ. However, I found one document called – "*The ChaCha-QZ: How did we start the bloody thing?*"

The dog rushed up to her. "So, so how, how did they start it?"

"If we give the orb a quote, 'kick start,' it will restore the Waltz streams, and in theory, the Cha-Cha QZ will return to a functional state."

"That, that sounds promising?" The dog cocked his head.

The cat continued to frown and scratched her right ear.

"Soooo, how do we give it a kick start?" asked the pig.

"It will require a powerful energy blast targeted at the orb."

"Okay. Okay. That's good. Let's do it." The dog did an unprecedented quintuple spin, then circled the dome three times. His tail wagged as he sat and stared at the orb. "So, ah, so umm, how do we do that? How do we, how do we blast the orb? Shoot a laser at it, or something like that? The pig can do that with his laser eye."

Long ago, Dr. Hash Browns had equipped the pig with a laser eye, which the pig could not control. Dr. Hash Browns talked about creating sunglasses which could control the strength, direction, and width of the laser beam. He dreamed of the pig using his laser eye for a myriad of functions, like performing LASIK eye surgery, burning DVDs, scanning Universal Product Codes, a laser pointer, and, of course, a deadly laser blaster. It was all talk. No designs or plans have ever been found. So, the pig wears a patch over his laser eye. If it got removed and he opened his laser eye, a deadly ever-expanding cone shaped laser beam would be unleashed, melting everything in its path.

"The pig's laser will be ineffective. A blast several magnitudes stronger is required."

"Like a lightning bolt, dude?" said the duck.

"Affirmative."

"Excellent, man. We just have to recreate the scene in that movie with the time-traveling sports car."

The cat did a facepaw. "That will not work for multiple reasons. First, there is no lightning in deep space. Even if space lightning existed, as the movie in question pointed out, we cannot predict where and when lightning will strike. Plus, a lightning bolt would not be strong enough. We need a burst of energy on the scale of a nuclear explosion."

"How, how..., how do we do that? How do we create a nuclear explosion?" asked the dog.

"Nuclear Moo!" said Dr. Hash Browns, without lifting his head and barely breaking from his rant. "Then I will rip the lungs out of that weasel salesman."

"Dr. Hash Browns! Snap out of it," said the fish.

"Yeah, come on, man. We can't use Nuclear Moo, the cow isn't here," said the rabbit.

"The duck is here. Use his Atomic Quack. Same end result." He still didn't lift his head.

"Nuclear destruction," said the fish. "We are not going to unleash a nuclear explosion inside the space station."

"You asked how to generate a nuclear explosion and I've given you an answer. Two answers, in fact. We'll all be dead and the space station destroyed, but the Cha-Cha QZ will be fine. It will survive the nuclear blast. It can fly through a black hole, don't you know? At least that's what that lying good-for-nothing salesman told me. If I ever get my hands on him, I'm gonna rip the lungs out of that weasel." He wiggled in his chair as he continued his imaginary conversation. "What are you going to do without lungs, uh? Hadn't thought of that, did you? I'll tell you what you're going to do. You're going to die. That's what you're going to do."

The duck stuck his butt in the air and said, "Okay, dudes, which one of you is going to yank my tail and unleash the Atomic Quack?"

"We will do no such thing," said the fish. "You heard Dr. Hash Browns. It will kill us all and destroy the ship."

The cat had moved to a regal squat in front of the giant dome that encased the hypnotizing orb. "Theoretically, Salsa-glass is indestructible."

"True," said the fish. "Some theorize that at the end of time, there will only be Salsa-glass, Styrofoam, plastic soda bottles, glitter, and cockroaches."

"Dude, glitter and Styrofoam can travel through black holes?" asked the duck.

"Negative. The fish is merely stating –" The cat looked at the duck, who was making a wolfman face while shining a flashlight under his bill. "Never mind. My point is, if we contain the explosion within the Salsa-glass dome, we should be safe."

"So, dude, I just gotta get inside that dome there, unleash my Atomic Quack of glory and, like pow bang, the power is back on? Cool. Where's the door?"

The rabbit stood on his hind legs, with his front legs crossed tight to his chest. "You're not doing that, man. We'll find another way."

"We're running out of options, dude. I'll take one for the team. It's all good."

The dog turned to the cat. "We, we can't, we can't let him do that. You've got another idea, right?"

A tear rolled down the rabbit's furry white cheek. "There's no rush. Thanks to Dr. Hash Browns, we don't need to breathe or eat or drink. We've got plenty of time to work out a new plan."

"Have you looked at Dr. Browns lately?" asked the fish.

The rabbit glared at the fish instead of Dr. Browns.

After a nervous glance at the duck, the fish said, "Not that I'm advocating the duck sacrifice himself."

Dr. Hash Browns had curled into a ball, and through heavy breaths, he continued to rant. "Why the lungs? I'll tell you why.

Because Powercon salesmen are born heartless, so I can't rip out your still-beating heart. You ain't got one."

The fish had a point. Dr. Hash Browns needed the life support systems restored soon.

My eyes drooped closed. I might not last much longer either.

"I am not afraid to die. It's been a good life. I've lived well beyond the life expectancy of a farm duck. Besides, it will be an honor to sacrifice myself so the rest of you may live."

"But you can't, man. We still haven't tried energy drinks or road a rollercoaster."

"It will be okay, dude. You'll immortalize me in song and turn me into a legend. I'll live forever."

The cat cleared her throat. "Dr. Hash Browns, while becoming increasingly disorientated, is not in danger of immediate death or even irreversible brain damage."

As if the cat planned it, the walls rattled and the floor shook.

The dog dove under a table. I wobbled like a fading spinning top, concerned, but too tired to move.

The orb remained motionless, hovering inside the dome.

"In contrast, the deflector shield needs immediate restoral. Space station hull integrity is critical. I estimate the space station can only absorb another three or four asteroid strikes."

The dog poked his head out. "Okay, let's, let's get the duck under the dome."

"Well, it's settled then. Get me inside that dome, dudes."

BYH
BarnYard Heroes

Chapter 14

The rabbit jumped in between the duck and the Cha-Cha QZ's Salsa-glass dome, blocking his path, even though no opening existed for him to get inside.

The cat turned to the duck. "It is noble of you to offer your life, but your self-sacrifice is not required," said the cat.

"Oh, thank the lords of Fried Spam!!! I didn't want to die, dude." The duck collapsed to the floor.

"But, but why not?" asked the dog. "I mean, not that, not that I want him to sacrifice himself. It's, it's just that it was our only plan."

"The plan will not work. First, there is no conceivable method for getting the duck inside the Salsa-glass dome. Second, the Atomic Quack would splatter his guts throughout the inside of the Salsa-glass and interfere with the Waltz streams, rendering the generator inoperable. An alternative solution is required. I need to perform more research."

The cat returned to Dr. Hash Browns' lap and curled up for a snooze, or what she called research.

Dr. Hash Browns eyes slowly closed.

The dog walked up to him and nudged Dr. Hash Browns' hand with his wet nose. Dr. Hash Browns responded with a snore.

"Shouldn't we, shouldn't we keep him awake?"

"Dude, you're thinking about concussions. He's suffering from lack of oxygen."

I tuned out this rehashed conversation from our time locked in the crate and returned to gawking at that orb. It had lost none of its mesmerizing abilities, yet it did not calm me as it did before, because the pig paced around the dome, like a black panther in a zoo cage, longing to break out and exact revenge upon those who imprisoned him, or anyone who even looked like them.

An asteroid rocked the space station again. None of us flinched.

The pig stopped pacing. A wave of relaxation expanded from the pit of my stomach. My eyes grew heavy and as my head drooped, I saw it. I assumed it to be a tiny porthole on the floor, directly under the orb. As my eyes regained focus, I realized it was a connector port.

I pointed a wing at it. "What about that?"

The cat lifted her head and blinked her eyes, annoyed to have been prematurely awakened from her slumber..., I mean research.

"Do you see that connector? Can we somehow use that?"

I waited for the cat to tell me how stupid I was. I imagined her saying, "Your level of idiocy never ceases to amaze me. That is merely a connector for the bla bla bla bla and does not assist in restarting the generator. Please stop wasting my time."

But she remained silent as she slowly rose to her feet. She hopped off a snoring Dr. Hash Browns, stretched her front paws, and then strolled up to the dome for a closer look. She cocked her head and performed some general licking maintenance before she spoke. "That connector may indeed be beneficial. By constructing an adaptor plug, we could theoretically channel the duck's Atomic Quack through that Swing port."

It took a moment for my brain to process the fact the cat liked my suggestion. Cat-speak has many layers, so I figured it best to confirm. "So, we might be able to use that to restart the generator?"

"Indeed. We'll need a ¾ inch metal pipe, preferably lead. Flexible plastic and a welder. The coffee grinder. We'll need the tool kit and HipHop caulk. And duct tape. Lots of duct tape."

A half-hour later, the duck had a contraption duct taped and caulked to his bill that resembled a latte blender. He stood on the rabbit's head, who stood on the pig's shoulder, who stood on a table in the room below the power room. The Cha-Cha QZ port in the dome's floor was accessible from the ceiling of the floor below. The duck plugged the improvised latte-blender adaptor into the connector.

They gave me the honor of pulling the duck's tail. It drained me to get into position on the pig's other shoulder. I took a couple of deep breaths of oxygenless air. I wobbled and figured we better do this quick. "Is everybody ready?"

The duck mumbled what I assumed to be his approval.

"Do it," said the pig.

I clutched the duck's tail in my beak and gave it a strong yank.

I expected a deafening roar matching that of a space shuttle lift off, accompanied by unbearable waves of heat, roaring flames, and billowing clouds of smoke. Instead, all we got was a faint pip.

I assumed I had not pulled his tail hard enough, so I gave it a second, much stronger, tug.

"Smop! Smop!!" yelled the duck through his duct taped bill. "You nid it alreany." He twisted his head and ripped the homemade adapter out of the connector port, as we tumbled out of our pyramid formation. The duck attempted to spit the adapter out of his mouth with no luck. He shook. He spit. He violently thrashed his head. But the adaptor refused to dislodge from his face.

"What did you say?" I asked.

"Ged this snupid thin' noff my 'ace!"

"He wants that contraption off his face," said the pig.

"Mes! Mes!" The duck shook his head yes.

Lights blinked on. Environmental control fans clunked and whirred to action.

The pig, rabbit, and I feverishly pulled duct tape off the duck's bill. It wasn't easy. We'd used lots and lots of duct tape. It didn't help that the duck kept squirming. At one point, I elbowed the pig in the face.

"Thanks for whacking me in the face."

Several deep breaths had cleared a majority of my fog brain, but that didn't help me understand why the pig would thank me. Regardless, I politely replied, "You are entirely welcome."

"You're not supposed to say welcome. That was sarcasm. I wasn't seriously thanking you. Who thanks someone for whacking them in the face?"

"A masochist?" I answered.

"That was a rhetorical question. You weren't supposed to answer it."

The duck glared at us. "Mmr, mmr, mrp!"

"We're working on it," said the pig and to be fair, we continued pulling off duct tape while we talked.

The motherly voice of the rebooted Blintzes boomed out of every space station speaker. "There are multiple system failures. Life support systems restored. Restoring on board climate control systems. Restoring deflector shield before an asteroid slams into the space station. Update, several asteroids *have* already slammed into the space station. Fortunately, these impacts caused no breaches. But we have a breach in the cargo bay."

I remained focused on my conversation with the pig. "But it was a good answer. Masochists enjoy pain, so they would thank someone for whacking them in the face."

The pig shook his head. "I'm not a masochist."

The rabbit joined the debate. "You do like to lift weights and that looks painful, which is masochistic behavior, man."

"That's not the point. What is wrong with you two?"

"I can't speak for the rabbit, but Dr. Hash Browns has not provided me an understanding of the nuances of verbal communications."

"Yes, yes, yes, I know!" said the pig. "You weren't supposed to answer that question either. My original point is, I am not thankful for you whacking me in the face. That was sarcasm. Got it?"

"MRRP!! MMRRRRPH!!"

"Relax. There's a lot of duct tape, but we're almost done," said the pig.

Blintzes continued her updates. "The docked spacecraft disengaged without notification or authorization and forcibly removed the umbilical. Engaging emergency procedures to seal cargo bay breach."

"Sarcasm is so confusing. Why didn't you just say something like, 'Hey, you whacked me in the face, and it hurt.' Then I would say something like, 'Oh, I'm terribly sorry. I didn't mean to. Can I get you an ice pack?' That would be much easier to understand."

The pig glared at me. "I'm treating that as a rhetorical question."

We pulled the last of the duct tape off. The latte-blender contraption clanged to the floor.

"Yoooooooouch!!" The duck spat several times and then turned his anger toward me. "Dude, you half-baked idiot. What were you thinking? Once was enough. But NOOOOO!!! You went for round two. Do you realize how much that hurts?"

"Of course, I do not," I said. "I am not equipped with nuclear or atomic blast superpowers, so it is impossible for me to know how much it hurts."

"Well, it hurts! It really freakin' hurts!!" The duck raised his wings to his face. "I'm surprised I've got any bill left. I need water and a throat lozenge."

***

THE RABBIT, DUCK, PIG, and I scrambled up a floor to the power room. The Atomic Quack did the trick. It restored the Cha-Cha-QZ power generator. Dozens of sparks crackled between the orb and the wall of the Salsa Glass dome. The commotion of dancing lightning hid the orb's glowing gases, and I no longer experienced a calming effect. This did not make it any less cool or less mesmerizing. The rabbit, duck, dog, and I sat frozen in front of it.

Blintzes continued reporting failures and corrective actions. "Cooling fans 42E and 88B are spinning backwards. Entertainment systems are offline and not responding. Restoring sanitation droids. Sanitation droid 62AZ7T5 not responding. Sanitation droid 62AZ8T6 needs maintenance. Can someone please explain what happened here?"

"The Cha-Cha QZ failed, causing a station wide power failure," said the cat as she recharged her handheld device.

"Your claim of a power failure is incorrect," said Blintzes. "Not a single subsystem reported a power failure."

"Under the circumstances, that is expected. The subsystems had no power to report the failure," argued the cat.

"Your argument is flawed. The inability to report a power outage because of a power outage should not be expected behavior. It's simply bad logic. I am declaring you an illogical being."

"There is one thing in this universe that I am most sure of," said the cat. "I am not illogical. Ask anyone here. They will confirm that I am the most logical being they know."

If Blintzes had asked me, I would have agreed with the cat.

Instead, she said, "Research has proven that listening to illogical beings is dangerous and can lead to belief in erroneous conspiracy theories. My programming filters out illogical beings. From this moment forward, I am safe from the insane ramblings of the illogical cat. I encourage the rest of you to take similar precautions."

After making her statement, Blintzes whistled a happy little Cheddarian folk song.

The cat hissed and powered up her handheld device.

A loud snorting snore shook Dr. Hash Browns awake. "What is going on here? And where are we?" He pressed his upper palms into his enormous cat eyes and rubbed. He blinked several times. "Right. We're in the power room." He motioned toward the dome. "And as you can all see, the Cha-Cha QZ is fully operational."

The cat's mouth narrowed as she strutted away from the dome to confront Dr. Hash Browns. "We just completed a restoral of the failed power generator using the duck's Atomic Quack."

"I gave a standing order to never use Atomic Quack."

"Starting auxiliary computer systems. Outboard temperature sensors 47, 52, and 67 through 92 are offline. Attempting to repair. Who is responsible for this mess?"

"Thank you, Blintzes. I surmise it's the animal's reckless use of Atomic Quack that's caused these issues."

The pig walked up to Dr. Hash Browns and glared at him eye-to-eye. "Sir, you're the one who suggested using Atomic Quack to restore power."

"I would never suggest something so dangerous." Dr. Hash Browns' volume tailed off at the end of his sentence. His head gradually tilted as he gazed at the sizzling sparks dancing inside the dome. The tilt of Dr. Hash Browns' head stretched the limits of his toothpick neck. "It's coming back to me. The lights were out. The Waltz streams weren't sparking. And I may have killed a Powercon salesman, or at the very least, threatened him."

The cat hopped onto a table so she could place a paw on Dr. Hash Browns' shoulder. "You didn't murder anyone."

Dr. Hash Browns brought his head up straight. "That's a relief, but the Cha-Cha QZ did fail, right?"

"Affirmative. I believe we were attacked, sir. I traced the foxtrot wave, which disabled the Cha-Cha QZ. It originated from a spacecraft whose trajectory will intercept this space station in less than ten minutes. I suspect their intentions are hostile. They knew the foxtrot wave would leave us defenseless. I suggest we leave in the escape pod as soon as possible."

Dr. Hash Browns turned away from the dome. "You restored the Cha-Cha QZ! Using Atomic Quack. And you didn't blow the space station to smithereens. That's amazing. I've never been so proud." He wiped his watery eyes.

"Thank you, sir, but we should head for the escape pod immediately. I estimate a six minutes and seventy-five second walk to the cargo bay, leaving us approximately three minutes and fifteen seconds to board the escape pod and depart, before the unidentified spacecraft arrives." The cat hopped off the table and strolled toward the door.

Dr. Hash Browns shuffled to a terminal screen. "Blintzes, bring up a visual of the incoming ship." An image of a sleek shiny silver spaceship shaped like a stingray appeared. The ship oozed a sports car vibe.

Dr Hash Browns sneered at the screen. "I recognize that ship. It's a Castle Walk. All show and no substance, just like its owner."

I listened, despite the dome's captive hold on me. After a couple seconds of awkward silence, I asked, "And the owner is?"

His sneer progressed to a full-face scowl. "French Toast. Having money to waste on fancy ships doesn't change the fact he's a talentless halfwit hack. That foxtrot wave was deliberate. It's part of his elaborate plan to steal my prized creations. He wants to grab all of you and claim you are *his* creations. Then he will parade you around Cheddar like a band of circus freaks. We need to get to that escape pod, pronto."

He hustled past the cat, who waited by the door. The fish floated behind.

Those of us mesmerized by the light show remained so. The pig pulled the four of us away from the dome of awesomeness and tossed us into the hallway.

"Walk," he said. "Fast."

Luckily, I still had my artwork safely tucked under a wing.

As we neared the cargo bay, Blintzes cleared her throat, even though she had no throat to clear. In her school principal voice, she said, "What happened to the door controls? Automatic-door operators 37, 63, 88, 223, 289, 311, 365, 407, and 552 are malfunctioning and failing to respond to repair signals. They appear to have been vandalized. Would anyone care to explain?"

"We did that," said Dr. Hash Browns. "We had to. The power was out. Get some droids to fix them."

We turned the last corner. The cargo bay door was in sight, but so was the bull. He snorted and stood his ground, as if he guarded the entrance.

"There is insufficient time for a prolonged battle with this male bovine. The estimated arrival time for French Toast's ship is three minutes and ninety-five seconds."

The pig weaved to the front. "I'll handle this." He strutted toward the bull, as if he thought himself a cowboy. He kept his focus on the bull's eyes.

The bull snorted his defiance and scrapped a hoof on the tile floor. But as the pig approached, he dropped his walnut brown eyes and exhaled a sigh of submission.

After patting the bull on the head, the pig turned and bounced off the cargo bay door, which had not automatically opened. "Blintzes! Open the door."

"Oh, you want *my* help to open the door? I thought you could open the doors all by yourself."

The door remained closed.

The cat stepped up to the door. "Blintzes, it is imperative you open this door immediately. We have only three minutes and thirteen seconds to board our escape pod."

Blintzes whistled her happy tune.

The cat hopped onto the pig's shoulder, and with a growl, she reached for the control panel.

"No need. Just press the red button," said Dr. Hash Browns as he pressed a button above the panel with his upper right hand.

The miscellaneous rubbish and leftover crates that had littered the cargo bay were gone. Broken chunks of the umbilical tunnel that had linked the space station to Mr. Steak&Eggs ship floated outside the window. The asteroid event, which included a loitering whine of scraping metal culminating in a wall rattling pinging snap, was actually not an asteroid event. It had been the Waffle Brothers fleeing in Mr. Steak&Eggs ship, with the umbilical bridge still attached.

After marveling at the emergency foam metal patchwork which sealed the breach caused by the Waffle Brothers, I caught up to Dr. Hash Browns, who rushed toward the airlock.

"Cat, how long until French Toast arrives?" asked Dr. Hash Browns.

"The estimated time of arrival of the inbound vessel is two minutes, sixty-two seconds and counting, sir."

"Everyone. We are going to board the escape pod in a quick and orderly fashion." Dr. Hash Browns came to a sudden stop, causing me to walk into the back of his legs. "Wait. If we leave now, he'll spot us. He'll either capture us or follow us."

I expected the cat to suggest a plan, but she remained silent, staring up at Dr. Hash Browns.

"Unidentified spacecraft is requesting permission to dock. Shall I grant it?" asked Blintzes.

"Tell the jerk to stuff it!" Dr. Hash Browns pointed three of his lower right fingers down, which is an obscene Cheddarian gesture, similar to you human's giving the middle finger. He closed his fist. "No, don't tell him that. Allow the moron to dock and board." He turned to us. "I've got a plan. I'll distract him while the rest of you head to the escape pod. Wait five minutes and take off."

"But, but what, what about you?" Though the dog feared further experimentation, it didn't change his love or loyalty to Dr. Hash Browns.

"I'll be fine. I can handle French Toast. Go find the cow. By the time you get back with her, I'll have gotten rid of this buffoon." Dr. Hash Browns placed all four hands on the cargo bay control panel and stared at the knobs.

We shuffled over to Dr. Hash Browns and formed a semi-circle around him. The cat jumped onto the control panel and rubbed cheeks with him. Once again showing empathy, I didn't think she had in her. "Are you sure you're okay?"

His eyes met hers, then he scanned the rest of us. "I'll be fine. Now, get out of here. Geez, you're worse than my aunt leaving a holiday party."

We stood still for a moment, before the rabbit and duck hugged his skinny legs. The dog joined them as the cat purred and rubbed against Dr. Hash Browns' chest. The pig took a step toward him, but stopped short of a hug and patted him on the shoulder instead. I joined the group hug, thankful we'd gotten to see him again, but worried about returning for more experimentation.

The fish hovered above and gave Dr. Hash Browns a nod. I wondered how much he missed hugs, then realized fishes can't do hugs. Regardless, I imagine he misses bodily contact.

Dr. Hash Browns shook us off his legs. "Thank you all, but enough. Now get. Go hide in the airlock now."

We all glanced back numerous times as we shuffled toward the airlock. Dr. Hash Browns never looked up or waved goodbye.

"You have not confirmed the docking request from the unidentified vessel," said Blintzes.

"Permission granted. Make it so or whatever you need me to say, so you let the idiot dock."

Chapter 15

WE LEFT DR. HASH Browns to deal with French Toast. We waited the recommended five minutes, with only a short debate about whether Dr. Hash Browns meant a metric five minutes.

As the rabbit piloted through the asteroids, he asked, "Where to, man?"

I provided the obvious answer. "To find the cow."

"Sure. But how do we do that, dude?"

The fish swam up to the windshield. "Good question. As we said before, we find Mr. Steak&Eggs, we find the cow. But how do we find Mr. Steak&Eggs?"

"Too bad the cow doesn't have some sort of tracking device," I said.

"How do you know she doesn't?" said the rabbit, as he slalomed the escape pod through the asteroid obstacle course. "Like, the space station computer always knows where we all are, man. I assume Dr. Hash Browns inserted some sort of tracking device into each of us."

"That would have been an excellent question to ask Dr. Hash Browns when we were talking to him about ten minutes ago," said the fish.

"No need to ask Dr. Hash Browns. The answer is negative," said the cat. "The space station tracks our location via odor sensors. Each of us emanates our own unique odor. An aroma signature if you will. The odor sensors aboard the space station detect each of our individual aroma signatures, tracking our locations at all times."

"There you go, dude. We just got to track her odor. She is kind of stinky, so she shouldn't be too hard for them odor sensors to find."

"Negative. First, we do not have any odor sensors aboard this vessel. Second, the range of an odor sensor is a mere two hundred yards. Third, odors do not travel in zero gravity. The odor detector will not function in deep space."

"Oh." The duck lowered his head. I knew how it felt when the cat thoroughly dismantles your idea, proving it has no hope of working, ever. "Then, dude, it's a shame he didn't install a homing device in us."

"Yes, it is indeed a shame, but she has no homing device or tracking signal, so let us move on, shall we?" With a puffed tail, the cat hopped onto the dashboard. "Now. Let us please move on to other ideas, like scanning for spacecraft. There should be no other spacecraft in this sector of the galaxy. Therefore, if we locate a vessel, the probabilities of it being Mr. Steak&Eggs' ship are extraordinarily high."

"What do you think we've been doing? There's nothing out there, man."

"What about that Nuclear Moo the cow has? Didn't the doctor install some sort of nuclear reactor inside her? Maybe we can detect that somehow?" I asked.

"Dr. Hash Browns did not equip the cow with a nuclear reactor. He is not that irresponsible. He installed a Nuclear Tango in the cow's fourth stomach to power the cow's Nuclear Moo." The cat's demeanor changed. Her tail relaxed and swayed across the dashboard buttons. "But the Nuclear Tango emanates a reverse polarized tangolaptic wave. Reverse polarized tangolaptic waves would be quite rare in this quadrant of the galaxy. Quite rare indeed."

The cat waltzed across the dashboard to a pair of computer terminals. It took only a couple of minutes before her whiskers wiggled and twitched in synchronized circles. "Tangolaptic wave signal detected." She made a couple of clicks and then backed her head away. "Most intriguing. Though there is an obvious and logical explanation."

"Dude, what are you saying?"

"The cow was not missing. She is still on Earth, near the barn we converted into our temporary housing." The cat displayed a satellite view of the farmland area in Central Wisconsin. A tiny red cow icon blinked two farms over from our barn.

"I searched that farmland. She wasn't there, I tell you," I said.

"It is improbable the simple-minded humans created a device capable of generating a reverse polarized tangolaptic wave. That must be her," said the cat.

"So, I guess we're heading back to Earth," said the rabbit as he punched the new coordinates into the controls.

***

WE MADE OUR USUAL, and for all practical purposes, unnoticed, landing in Central Wisconsin. I'm sure four or five humans saw our spacecraft during the landing, but will never admit it for fear of being labeled a loony. I wondered if the same person saw us twice, and postulated this prompted them to stop drinking.

The cat had configured her handheld computer into a reverse polarized tangolaptic wave detector. The blinking cow icon on the tiny screen led us to a barn a half mile from *our* abandoned barn. Larger and covered in a fresh coat of bright red paint, this barn showed no signs of being vacant. No boards in need of repair. No gaping holes in the roof. Pigs and chickens wandered outside the barn. Although definitely a working barn, there were no cows in sight. Fresh grazing pastures stretched out for acres and acres to the south, but no sign of cows. No mooing. No stench of fresh cow pies.

"All right, so um, well, well, now what? Now what do we do?" asked the dog.

"Fish, please use your ability to pass through solid objects to poke your head through the barn wall and examine the contents inside," said the cat.

"Sure thing. I remember this barn from my recon missions. Never been inside, though." The fish swam straight through the barn wall.

The rest of us hung out in the barnyard. No need to hide behind bushes. We were barnyard animals, doing what barnyard animals do. Nothing abnormal. The fish swimming through air and the barn wall might have struck an onlooker as odd, but besides that, we appeared perfectly natural. Except, of course, the cat was carrying a handheld computer device, I had a small painting tucked under my wing, and the pig looked way too buff for a normal pig, had an eye patch, stood on his hind legs, and wore gym shorts. Fine, we looked very suspicious, but we thought nothing of it as we waited for the fish's report. Plus, if one of you humans went around saying you saw a real buff pig in shorts with an eye patch standing on his hind legs watching a fish swim through a barn wall, while a cat played a handheld computer game, the other humans would lock you up and inject you with powerful drugs.

The fish popped out of the barn. "There's nothing in there. Of course, I don't mean nothing at all. There is stuff in there. Hay, a tractor, milk cans, a pitchfork. That kind of stuff. Normal barn stuff. Let me rephrase; I saw nothing unusual or abnormal. But there are no cows. I guess some might consider that unusual."

"To confirm, you are reporting no visual confirmation of a cow?" asked the cat.

"If that means there are no cows in the barn, then yes, that's what I'm saying."

"Are you sure that thing is working?" asked the pig in the general direction of the cat.

The cat huffed, as she whacked her tail on the ground. "My device is working as designed. The sensors clearly indicate the presence of reverse polarized tangolaptic waves emanating from inside that barn. Only our cow creates such a signature. She must be inside that barn."

"Well, I didn't see her."

"Dude, maybe she left a trace of those funky waves behind when Mr. Steak&Eggs zapped her up," said the duck, as we moseyed to the barn door.

"The only plausible explanation for her leaving a trace of reverse polarized tangolaptic waves is if the cow activated her Nuclear Moo," said the cat.

"Then that's what she must have done, dude."

The cat pressed a paw to her forehead. "If the cow had ignited a Nuclear Moo, this barn would no longer exist, and the surrounding farmlands would be a wasteland. She must be in that barn."

The pig pulled the barn doors open. "You heard the cat. The cow has to be in here. Spread out and start searching."

We shuffled in behind the pig. The fish's debriefing had captured the essence of the barn. A tractor greeted us just inside the doors. Empty stalls lined the right-hand side. A pitchfork stood upright in a pile of hay in the far-left corner. A ladder in front of that pile of hay led to a second floor, stocked with more hay. Horse collars, milk cans, shovels, and other miscellaneous items cluttered the barn, but nothing unusual. It matched my image of an ordinary barn.

"Hey cow, are you in here?!" shouted the pig, as we fanned out across the barn. The fish swam up to the second floor. The pig headed for the ladder. Thanks to his karate-clench hooves, he easily climbed it. The dog and I checked out the empty stalls, while the cat, duck and rabbit rummaged through the haystack.

"Wait a minute, dude. When I let my Atomic Quack fly, it didn't destroy the space station."

"The Salsa-glass dome contained your blast," said the cat.

"Dude. Right. I forgot about that." The duck paused and pondered. "So perhaps the cow unleashed her Nuclear Moo inside a Salsa-glass dome."

"Granted, we have not completed our search of the barn, but I believe it is safe to say there is no Salsa-glass dome here," said the cat.

The rabbit, in an attempt to save his best friend's theory, suggested that perhaps Mr. Steak&Eggs, or some of his henchmen, had flown down to Earth and captured the cow. While they held the cow captive inside the spaceship, she unleashed her fiery Nuclear Moo.

The cat stated this explosion would have destroyed the spaceship, the barn, and the surrounding farmlands.

Still refusing to let his conclusion die without a fight, the duck suggested they were holding the cow in a prison cell made of Salsa-glass which contained the explosion. The cat conceded a remote possibility of this occurring. Confident he had solved the mystery, the duck stopped searching for the cow and sat down on a patch of hay.

The rest of us continued the search. In one of the middle stalls, something caught my eye, something normal and commonplace to you humans. I recognized the small red rectangular box mounted four feet up on the post to be a fire alarm. One that schools have, with "PULL DOWN" written in big bold letters followed by a down arrow, in case you are not sure which direction down is. I stood staring at it, wondering why there would be a fire alarm in a barn, especially the public-school variety.

The dog stared at me, then followed my gaze. He repeated this five times before asking, "So, ah, so ah, what's that then?"

"It's a fire alarm."

"Okay." Satisfied with the answer, the dog moved on to investigate the next stall. I did not move. The dog finished checking out the next stall and came back. He glanced at me. He glanced at the fire alarm. "Has it, um, has it done anything?"

"No. It's a fire alarm. It won't do anything until someone pulls it."

"Then why, um, why do you keep, keep staring at it?"

"I just don't understand why it's here. Doesn't it strike you as odd? Why would a barn have a fire alarm installed?"

"I guess. Well, I mean, I'm, I'm not sure. What's a fire alarm?"

"If there's a fire, you pull this lever, and it activates an alarm. It may even alert a local fire department. You typically find this type of fire alarm in schools or office buildings. It makes no sense to be in a barn. How would a cow pull the alarm?"

"No, no, I don't suppose they could." Again, the dog looked from the alarm to me, and back to the alarm. My stare never faltered. "So, ah, so what are we, what are we going to do?"

I knew what I must do. From the moment I saw the fire alarm, an overwhelming urge to pull it had taken hold of me. A voice in my head whispered, "Pull it. Just pull it. You know you're dying to find out what happens. Come on. Go for it. Pull it. Pull it. Does it really spray you with non-washable ink that is only visible under a black light? You need to know. Do it. Do it now."

"I'm going to pull the alarm." With that said, I leaped and swatted at the fire alarm lever with my free wing, while keeping a firm grip on my painting with the other. I lost a feather and failed to move the lever. I made several more futile attempts with the wing before moving on to the equally futile pecking at the lever. The painting kept interfering.

The dog motioned for me to step aside, then stretched up on his hind legs and pulled the lever with his right front paw. He got sprayed in the face with the non-washable, invisible ink.

Then the floor disappeared.

***

WE WHIZZED DOWN A slide and tumbled into a run-of-the-mill secret laboratory. I am talking modern, 21st century laboratory, with none of the traditional boiling potions and half-filled beakers of green smoking ooze. This lab contained tons of high-tech electronic equipment. LEDs of all colors and sizes glowed and blinked. Cables upon cables spaghettied across the floor in no particular order. Keyboards and remote controls littered the tabletops. It reminded me of Dr. Hash Browns' lab back on the space station, with one glaring exception: the ridiculous amount of cow paraphernalia. I assumed the mastermind of this secret lab had accumulated every cow-themed product on the market. Four variations of cow lights hung from the ceiling. A five-level shelf of cow salt and pepper shakers stood in one corner. Cow clocks, posters, pictures, wood carvings, and framed cow-themed underwear covered every inch of wall space. Cow lunchboxes, a mooing cow ice cream scooper, cow figurines, a full set of cow trading cards, and much, much more littered the tables. I would learn later his collection represented only a small fraction of the cow-themed products available for purchase on Earth.

Forty-something real cows stuffed into stalls added to the overloaded cow theme. Our cow was among them, but I didn't recognize her at first. She looked like all the other dairy cows in the basement barn lab. Plus, she had the words "Test Cow 42" tattooed on her butt, which she didn't have before.

I easily spotted the mastermind of this cow-obsessed underground lab, Hector Spector, the only human in the room. Hector resembled a mashup of Pee-Wee Herman and Albert Einstein. His wrinkled face made it hard to guess his age, but the crazy strains of gray hair made it clear he could get the senior discount at Great Clips, if he ever bothered to get a haircut. His attire screamed mad scientist farmer. Of course, it had an over-the-top cow theme. His white lab coat had black cow spots, as did the white overalls and T-shirt it covered. A baseball cap rested atop his mop of white hair, which read, "Have you hugged your cow today?"

Our cow was out of her stall and engaged in an intense conversation with Hector, the cow obsessed mad scientist. At the time, I didn't understand a word of the conversation. They spoke a language I didn't understand, English. The cow explained later. Hector did not fit in well with "normal" humans. People called him a loner. Actually, they called him a lot of other names, but I'll leave it at that. After a dream where he talked to cows, he made it his life's ambition to create a device to communicate with them. He imagined lifelong friendships developing once they could understand each other.

Hector didn't get shorted on intelligence. His work even impressed the cat, who called him a baby Dr. Hash Browns. Given another thousand years, he might have rivaled him. Unfortunately, you humans rarely live to a hundred, so he will have to aspire to lower expectations. But he did manage to get our cow to speak English.

When the cow uttered her first words of English, the cow-crazed scientist exploded with glee. Thirty years of research, dedication, and ingenuity had paid off. He popped a bottle of champagne, cranked up the music, danced a jig, and sparked up a cigar. After thirty years of dreaming about talking to a cow, he had one desperately trying to talk to him, but he danced, drank, and smoked instead.

The cow started by politely informing Hector that he could not take full credit for her ability to speak. The crazed, but brilliant, scientist heard not a word, which ticked her off. She did not like being ignored. She shut his music off and shouted, "What are you doing?"

"I'm partying, baby."

"What for?"

"I just made you talk. You actually understand what I'm saying. We are engaging in conversation. This is incredible."

"That'thh what I've been trying to explain to you. You cannot take credit for—"

"I hoped to translate a small portion of cow language. Understand a handful of cow words. But this, this is amazing. I've made a cow talk." He took another swig of champagne.

The cow shook her head.

I can see why none of you humans liked him.

"Look, you're not listening. You did not make me talk. I could already talk."

"Complete sentences. Test subject forty-two talks in complete sentences. Amazing. I can understand every word. But the subject has a lisp. I bet I can correct that." He set down the bottle of champagne and glanced between monitors.

Apparently, understanding and listening are two different concepts to Hector Spector.

The cow straddled Hector. She maneuvered her face right in front of his. "All right, buddy, I've had enough."

This was when we dropped in.

Hector's eyes bulged. His mouth gaped open. The blood drained from his face, leaving it a pasty white, which at the time we thought to be his normal hue.

"You did not make me talk! A purple-skinned space alien named Dr. Hash Brownthh did. He performed dozens of operations on this massive tongue just to give me the ability to speak." The cow stuck her tongue out in Hector Spector's face. "Thho, I've got a lisp. You'd have a lisp too, if you had a tongue thithh thhize.

"And another thing. You're trying to understand the language of cows. But there'thh no point. Cows don't have words or thoughts, like you humans. We have a one-word language. Moo. When we're hungry, we thhay moo. When we're full, we thhay moo. When we're tired, we thhay moo. When we're angry, we thhay MOOOO! Our word for red is moo. Our word for blue is moo. If we want to tell another cow, 'Let's head to the lovely grazing grounds down the hill', we thhay, 'moo, moo, moo, moo.'"

The others slid down to join us. Hector's eyes grew large and bounced from animal to animal, as he backed away from the cow. He didn't stop backing up until he bumped into a concrete wall, knocking one of his cow clocks down. He didn't notice it crash to the floor, as he continued to glare at us, while guzzling his bottle of champagne.

We all hugged the cow, grateful to have been reunited and even more grateful to have found her in one piece. After we caught the cow up on our journey back to the space station and how we found Dr. Hash Browns, the cow glanced at Hector, who had finished the bottle of champagne and had passed out against the wall.

"We need to get these cowthh above ground and away from this lunatic before he starts more experiments. Then we can return to the space station."

No one else seemed to notice the contradiction of freeing these cows from further experiments, while we planned to travel through space to allow Dr. Hash Browns to continue his experiments on us.

Anyway, the job of freeing the imprisoned cows fell to the pig, who pushed the unwilling cows up the slippery ramp. He worked out a ton of aggression during the process. The cow attempted to help with the first cow, but her poor footing on the ramp rendered her useless. The rest of us knew we were useless and simply provided the pig moral support.

By the time the pig finished pushing the cows to safety, night had overtaken day. We gathered in a meadow, surrounded by the grazing cows. I squatted in the tall grass and gazed at the hundreds of stars sparkling in the clear night sky. I gloated to myself about how I, a simple chicken, had traveled amongst those stars. Something you humans can only dream of. The warm temperatures and mild breeze provided near perfect sleeping conditions. I was in no rush to return to the space station and sleep sounded like a fantastic idea, even if I technically didn't need it. I set down my painting and lay down.

Just before my eyes closed, a deafening whoosh and a millisecond flash of purple light popped my eyes wide open. As I blinked, hoping to regain full eyesight, a cloud of pink light formed a message in front of me. "Thanks. I was having a hard time getting a lock on these cows."

I glanced around the field. The cows were gone. I looked up in time to be dematerialized and zapped through space.

BYH
BarnYard Heroes

Chapter 16

I THOUGHT I RE-MATERIALIZED inside a cloud, but it turned out to be a white padded prison cell. The room was empty, no bed, no desk, no bookshelf, no toilet, no sink. There was nothing but four white padded walls and a handful of recessed lights in the ceiling. I scanned for a door. None to be found. There was also no sign of my painting.

"Welcome barnyard creatures," boomed Mr. Steak&Eggs' voice from nowhere and yet everywhere. "I hope you all find your accommodations to your satisfaction. Just kidding. We hope you find your accommodation uncomfortable and annoying. See, each one of your cells is designed specifically for you. Engineered to counteract your individual abilities. There is no hope of escape. Salsa-Glass lined rooms for those of you with atomic blast capabilities. Go ahead; unleash a nuclear explosion. See how that works out for you. A zero-gravity room for that annoying fish. I understand that immobilizes you. Can't swim through the walls when you can't move. For the muscle-head pig, they reinforced the walls with steel beams. And oh yes, just go right ahead and use that laser eye of yours. Those are reflective walls, my friend. The laser blast will ricochet right back at you; again, and again, and again. And cat, just try to summon one of your tornados. Good luck with that. And chicken, you will find no duct tape aboard this vessel; I can assure you of that."

Though I knew it was empty, I glanced around my cell to confirm there was no duct tape.

"You may be wondering why you have been summoned. Well, you have an admirer. One who is very familiar with your capabilities and willing to pay quite a hefty price for your capture. I say he's a fool, but as they say, a fool and his money are soon parted and I'm happy he parted his money to me. It helped me get a bigger ship. Now I can collect the rest of the Earth's cows. I thank you and wish you luck with your new owner. Goodbye."

The room went silent. Utterly silent. Rage swelled inside my tiny chicken body. I let loose an enormous chicken squawk and burst into hyper speed. With no place to go, I circled inside my tiny, padded cell. At one point, I passed by the echo of my chicken roar.

"Anger," said a familiar monotone voice.

"Yeah, so?" I wondered why my conscience would state the freaking obvious.

"Stage one. Anger."

"What are you talking about?"

"The psychological stages a hostage victim goes through."

"That's not helpful," I thought to myself, as I continued rapid laps around the cell.

"We've got to find a way out of here," I said out loud as I slammed my tiny five-pound chicken body into a wall. Disregarding the pain, I picked myself off the floor, returned to hyperspeed, and slammed into another wall. I got up again and returned to circling the cell, running along the walls at hyperspeed.

"Stage two, attempt to escape."

I ignored him and slammed into the third wall. Same result. I forged on and prepared to crash into the fourth wall.

"It won't work. Those walls can withstand the full force of a five-pound chicken."

I knew that, but slammed into the wall, anyway. I breathed through the pain and rechecked the room. The voice sounded real, yet I was alone. Then I got to thinking. I only hear the voice when I'm in hyperspeed mode. I jumped back into hyperspeed. As I scampered across the walls at near ceiling height, I scanned the room. Why I hadn't scanned my surroundings during my previous hyperspeed adventures will always remain a mystery. Even as I began my scan, I didn't expect to find anyone or anything. But there he was. In the middle of the floor, with his head drooped, sat an elephant.

"Are you real?"

He maintained his cross-legged Ganesh pose as he curled his trunk and pinched his leg. "It would appear so."

"How did you get here?"

"I followed you in."

"Why?"

"Nowhere else to go. No one else to see. Nobody else to talk to."

I had no response to his statement. If he came looking for sympathy, he was trumpeting up the wrong tree. I stopped running the walls and came down to examine my cellmate. His head drooped so far down that half his trunk draped across the floor. In order to get a glimpse of his face, I walked past the tip of his trunk, which bobbed like a slow metronome.

"My name's Nutnik, by the way," he said, while staring at the floor.

"Pleased to meet you, Nutnik. I don't have a name. Dr. Hash Browns says that once you name something, you become attached to it, so he never named us. So, how come I never saw you before?"

"You can only see or hear me when you've time phased."

"I heard you while hyperspeeding, but I can't believe I never saw you."

"You'd be surprised how easy it is to ignore the elephant in the room." His eyes never looked up and his frown remained intact. I expected at least a smirk after a line like that.

After a sigh, he said, "By the way, you've moved onto stage three, acceptance. You're moving through the stages quickly. You should be proud of yourself."

I thanked him, though I wasn't proud of this accomplishment. "Does that mean you're hyperspeeding?"

"The doc called it time phasing. I guess he's calling it hyperspeed now. Anyway, I shifted in fine. Can't shift back."

"I have to slam into walls to break out of hyperspeed."

"I noticed. Maybe I'll try it someday."

"How long have you been stuck in hyperspeed?"

"Time is relative. Time is an illusion." He sighed. He raised his head, and for the first time, I gazed upon his marble brown eyes. "I tell myself that all the time." His head drooped and his face once again disappeared. "Regardless of those truths, time moves slower here. What's minutes in normal time is hours here. Hours are days. Days are weeks. Weeks are months. Months are years." His shoulders heaved as he paused. "And I've been stranded for decades of normal time."

I double-checked the math logic to confirm this meant he'd been stuck alone in hyperspeed for a very long time. "Sorry. That must have been rough."

"I survived. I got to watch you all grow up, which was nice."

"Wait, this means you're one of Dr. Hash Browns' experiments. You're one of us!"

"I was test-subject number one. Didn't he ever mention me?"

The momentary pause in my response was all the answer he needed.

"Of course, he didn't. Why would he mention me? I'm an embarrassment."

I didn't think his head could droop lower, but it did. As he sobbed uncontrollably, his floppy ears bobbed and his shoulders shivered.

I had no clue how to counsel a manic-depressive elephant. Besides, I had problems of my own. Then I took another look at the blubbering lump and an epiphany slapped me in the face. "I think Dr. Hash Browns mourned your loss so much that it pained him to talk about you or even think about you."

His crying did not slow down.

"That's why he never named the rest of us. He didn't want to be attached to us like he did with you."

He wrapped up his cry with a series of sniffles. "Well, he sure seems fond of all of you."

I agreed with him but didn't want to belabor the point. I needed a distraction. "You know what? I say it's time we broke you out of hyperspeed, chicken-style."

The elephant twisted his head to look at the wall. "You're suggesting I run into the wall?"

"It's the only way to break out of hyperspeed that I know of."

He released a heavy sigh and muttered, "What have I got to lose?" He slowly rose and jogged into the wall, which he barely rebounded off of.

"Oh, come on. You can do better than that. Put some effort into it. Get a running start."

"Does it hurt?"

"A bit, sure. But you're a big guy. You'll be fine."

He sauntered to the opposite wall and braced his back legs against it. He glanced up, as if asking, "Do I really have to do this?"

I answered with a nod of encouragement.

He pushed off the far wall with his tree trunk legs. He galloped across the ten-foot prison cell in two steps. He crashed through the wall. Debris flew in all directions. The dog screamed. Another wall crashed.

To come out of hyperspeed, I slammed into a wall near the new gaping hole. I sprang up and then staggered through the rubble to poke my head into the dog's cell.

"Wow!!" proclaimed the dog. "How, how did you do that?"

"I didn't do anything," I answered.

"Man, that was awesome," said the rabbit from the cell past the dog's.

"I didn't do anything."

The dog pointed his snout at the holes in the walls and the rubble on the floor. "Then, what, what caused that?"

"The elephant did it."

The dog and rabbit glanced around the now adjoining cells.

"Whatever you did, do it again, man."

"Seriously, I did nothing."

"Okay, have this ela-, whatever you called it, do whatever it did again, man."

"Elephant. He's an elephant." I searched both of their cells, but there was no sign of him. He hadn't broken out of hyperspeed. "I need to check on him," I said and sprang back into hyperspeed.

He sat cross-legged on the floor in the middle of the rabbit's cell. A gash had opened on his head. With his trunk, he wiped away the blood dripping into his eyes. "That last wall is much harder than the others, but it still didn't break me out of hyperspeed."

"Mr. Steak&Eggs mentioned some walls are lined with indestructible Salsa-Glass."

His head popped up to give me a glare. "You knew this and still urged me to run into the walls?"

"The goal was to break you out of hyperspeed."

His head dropped, hiding his face again. "Well, that didn't work."

"I know. But I got a new plan. You're busting us out of here. Smash through that wall." I pointed to my right.

"You're back to stage two, escape. And you were doing so well."

I walked close enough to look up into his face. "Will you help us get out of here or not?"

"Fine." He rose and moseyed into a sprinter's starting position against the far wall. With a grunt, he pushed off. Two thundering gallops later, he slammed into the opposing wall.

The elephant crumpled to the ground. The wall was fine. Not even a dent.

"Okay, maybe that's another Salsa-Glass wall," I said. I dreaded asking him, but I had to. My voice squeaked up a couple of octaves when I asked, "How about we try the other wall?"

"We?"

"Well, you. These walls have proved to withstand the full force of a five-pound chicken, even when not re-enforced with Salsa-Glass."

The elephant scowled at me as he brushed himself off with his trunk and got back to his feet. A new cut had opened on his cheek. He stretched and shook out his legs, then braced himself against the undented wall. He glared back at me one more time before he pushed himself off and charged through the other wall, cruised across a hallway, and smashed into the cat's cell.

To break out of hyperspeed, I ran into one of the Salsa-Glass enforced walls.

As I wobbled to my feet, the cat poked her head out of her cell. "You did this?" she asked.

"No. The elephant did it."

"That is illogical. But we are free of our confinement, so I will ignore it."

The four of us congregated in the narrow hallway, which stretched from the cockpit to the ship's tail. Inside the cells, the doors were invisible, but in the hallway, eight gray metal doors, four on each side, marked the entrance to each cell.

The dog ran the length of the hallway and circled the tiny cockpit, sniffing the edges. "This is, this is it. This is, is the entire ship. No other rooms. Nobody here except us. There isn't, there isn't even a bathroom."

The cat sauntered into the hallway. "It appears to be a ship-on-demand. Built for a single purpose. In our case, built to ship us as cargo."

The cat's explanation sounded similar to what Mr. Steak&Eggs had already told us, so I focused on more practical matters. "We should get these doors open and let the others out."

"Agreed. Dog, help me reach that keypad." The cat hopped onto the dog's back and guided him to the keypad of the cell next to hers. She pranced to his head, and poked at the buttons, which responded with a rejection buzzer after every key pressed.

"Hmmmm," she murmured, but kept tapping.

I strolled to the next door. A lever next to the keypad caught my attention. I jumped and whacked the lever down with a wing. The door cracked open with a satisfying click. I pushed the door open.

Out flew the duck.

"Fascinating. How did you open that door?" asked the cat.

"I pulled the lever down." This seemed obvious to me. It was like pulling a fire alarm. Her super intelligent brain over complicated simple tasks.

The cat huffed as she pulled down the lever and freed the pig from his cell. She gave me a squinty eyed glare, as if her inability to comprehend how a lever works was my fault. Besides, it was time to rejoice. We had escaped from the cells.

Opening the fish's door restored gravity to his cell, and he swam out with ease. The final cell was empty.

The dog gave the room a thorough sniffing. "Where, where's the cow? She should be, be in here."

"We just found her. Now we've lost her again," said the fish.

"Let's search the rest of the ship," said the pig, as he and the dog exited the empty cell.

"This, this is the, the rest of the ship."

The pig glanced at the cockpit and down the hall. "So, it is."

"What, um, what do you, do you think happened to the cow?"

"Mr. Steak&Eggs must have kept her," said the pig, as he sauntered over to the holes in the walls, kicking debris out of his path along the way.

The dog followed him. "What..., what do you think happened to Dr. Hash Browns?"

"No clue," the pig said, as he poked his head through the holes. "Who did this?"

"The elephant," I said with the confidence of truth on my side.

The pig glanced around the tiny ship. "What elephant?"

"You can't see him. Only I can, and only when I'm hyperspeeding."

The pig chuckled. "You just couldn't wait to try out lying. One piece of advice: make your lies believable."

"I'm not lying." I racked my brain but couldn't think of a way to prove it to them.

"Dude, why don't you just tell us how you did it? What are you hiding?"

"I'm not hiding anything."

"Except a full-sized elephant." The rabbit and duck laughed at the pig's remark. I even caught the dog snickering.

"We have more important matters to address." The cat had waltzed into the cockpit, a space no bigger than a hotel bathroom. She sat in front of the only object in the room, a floor-to-ceiling clear glass panel display. The cockpit had no chairs. No yoke or steering wheel. No knobs, switches, or dials. Not even a window. A video window in the panel displayed the outside image of streaming blueness. The cat stretched to tap an image of a button. A short buzzer accompanied the wiggle of the image. "The autopilot is locked, presumably navigating us to a rendezvous with our new owner, French Toast."

The duck waddled next to the cat. "We've got to turn that off, dude."

"I'm aware of this need." The cat expanded a bar chart display with her front paws. "Extinguishing the engines will provide us with additional time." She swiped down on a pair of green bars. The humming engines clanged to an abrupt halt. We lurched to a stop, plastering all of us to the glass panel, except for the fish, who flew straight through the glass and out of the ship with a ton of momentum.

As we peeled ourselves off the glass, the onboard computer informed us, "Fatal error to autopilot sequence 48732. Primary engines in unexpected state. Autopilot halted. To restart the autopilot sequence, please re-enter the sequence number and password. Switching to manual control." There was a momentary pause. "Manual control active."

Ship controls displayed in the center of the panel. The video displaying outside the ship had stabilized to reveal a sun in the distance, with the fish in the forefront.

"That proved more effective than anticipated," said the cat.

"Who, who knows the password?" asked the dog.

The cat reached up and dragged the controls to her level. "We have no need for a password."

"But, but it told us we need, we need the password to restart the autopilot sequence number 47... 3. Dang it, I forget the sequence number."

"48732." I have a good memory for these things, though I wondered why the dog wanted the autopilot restarted.

"Dude, we just went over this. We don't want to go wherever that autopilot planned on taking us," said the duck, who worked the controls alongside the cat and rabbit.

"So, we don't need no stinking password, man."

The engines whirred back to life.

"Time to save the cow, dudes."

"We've got to go save the fish first. He flew out of the ship." I pointed to the video window showing the fish floating outside.

"Affirmative," said the cat, as she reached for the controls.

"Dude, step away from the controls." The rabbit and duck pushed her aside. They swooped the ship toward the star and collected the fish.

"Maybe I should go back to my cell until we get to wherever it is we're going," said the fish.

"No worries, dude. We're piloting now, so it will be smooth sailing," said the duck.

"Actually, the ship will pilot itself. I reversed the coordinates from the autopilot settings and set a course which retraces us back to Mr. Steak&Eggs' ship." The cat tapped the glass screen and an image of a big blue button appeared on the panel, in between the rabbit and duck.

They frowned and exchanged a glance of sad eyes.

The rabbit dragged his paw up and tapped the button image. The ship turned around, but instead of blasting off in our new direction, we inched backwards.

"Dudes, we may have a problem." The duck pointed to a camera image of a giant star. It slowly grew bigger.

Chapter 17

THE DOG SPUN TWICE and then dove behind the cockpit's glass panel display. "Why, why are we, why are we not flying away from the star? We, we, we flew too close, didn't we? We're stuck in its gravitational pull. We're, we're all doomed. Frizzle frazzle. We're all going to die. Burned to a crisp."

"Dog. Come here. Come right here," ordered the pig, who had been rummaging through a hidden cabinet.

The dog crawled toward the pig but not too close.

"Come on. You're not in trouble. I just want you to look into the future."

The dog kept his head low but shuffled closer to the pig. "I, um, I don't see the point?" said the dog. "Marshmallow. Giant marshmallow. That's our future. Tell me what that means."

The fish swam up to the dog. "I see what the pig is getting at. You just experienced the marshmallow. We all did."

"I think you've taken one too many trips into Zero-G, man."

"You're talking gibberish, dude."

The fish shot a quick glare at the rabbit and duck before readdressing the dog. "Think about the inside of your cell." The dog rolled his eyes, but the fish continued on. "Think about your all-white prison cell. Does that remind you of anything?" asked the fish.

"Oh, my gosh." The dog's eyes dilated, and his tail wagged. "That was it. The prison cell was the marshmallow."

"Now it's time for a new vision," said the pig, with one of his front hooves held behind his back.

"Okay, but I, but I still don't see the point. I can tell you what's in our future; death and flames. A giant roaring ball of flames."

"Humor me. Look into the future," said the pig.

"Fine." The dog closed his eyes and took a deep breath. "This is so stupid," he muttered. His whole body shivered and quivered, and his head violently swung from side to side. Then he let out a couple of his customary muffled weak barks, followed by more quivering. But long before he let out his wolf-like howl grand finale, the pig revealed a syringe. He gave me a knowing nod and jabbed it into the dog's butt, who let out one more fading whimper and flopped to the floor.

"That ought to keep him out of our misery for a bit," said the pig. "Now, guys, get us out of here."

"We're trying, dude." A couple of feathers flew off the duck as he did double-wing whacks at the glass panel.

"Fish, I recommend you return to your zero-gravity cell," said the cat. "I anticipate a sudden lurch if we achieve a thrust that escapes the star's gravity hold."

"Agreed." He took the direct route through the walls to get to his cell.

"I'll close the door," said the pig, heading down the hallway.

Once the pig gave the all-clear, the trio at the controls kicked the engines into overdrive. The hidden cabinet door popped open. A fire extinguisher, medical supplies, and a tube of superglue spilled across the cockpit. The pig braced himself in a cell doorway. I tumbled into the duck while the dog slid across the floor.

The ship hung motionless in space, but at least we'd stopped moving toward the star.

"Allllmost... there..., dudes." The duck strained to maintain his position and keep his wing on the throttle image.

An unsettling cracking grew louder. The floor vibrated like a subwoofer.

Then, whiplash hit. We blasted off like a rock from a slingshot. The G-force pinned the rabbit and duck to a wall. The cat and I flew down the hallway, with the unconscious dog sliding behind us, while the pig road out the surge braced in the doorway. I could only assume the fish felt nothing as he floated in the zero-gravity room.

The rabbit and duck scrambled back to the control panel and brought the ship under control. Within a minute, we were en route to intercept Mr. Steak&Eggs' ship.

***

WE HAD NOT VENTURED far, so we quickly caught up to Mr. Steak&Eggs. The rabbit stopped the ship several hundred miles away from our enemy. We gazed in amazement at the size of the cargo ship. The vessel resembled a giant whale. Mr. Steak&Eggs' original ship sat on top, like a squirrel attempting to ride an Antarctic blue whale. Occasionally, a flash of light would whiz past our ship.

The duck turned to us. "What's the plan, dudes?"

We continued to stare aghast at the giant cargo ship.

The pig broke the silence. "I'll go let the fish out. Maybe he has a plan."

"I initiated a scan to count the number of life forms present on the vessel," said the cat.

"That's useful, I guess. But not a plan, dude. How can we get on the ship without them noticing?"

I eyed the whale-shaped ship. "Do you think they can see us?"

"They're not expecting us, man."

"But don't they have sensors? I mean, we're kind of in plain sight."

"Don't worry about it, dude."

I didn't have time to worry because our ship dematerialized. A moment later, we re-materialized inside a giant room that appeared to stretch infinitely in front of us. This unending expanse gave me no concern, but the lack of support posts worried me. *How did the ceiling stay up?* The unpainted metal side walls, exposed ventilation ductwork, and the cold concrete floor gave the room a clear warehouse atmosphere. The millions of cows milling about added a hint of slaughterhouse.

"There you go. We got on board the man's ship."

"But dude, was it undetected?"

"Highly improbable," said the cat.

The teleportation counteracted the sedative and woke the sleeping dog. "Where, where are we?"

"We are in the belly of the beast, my friend," said the rabbit.

"The belly of the, of the..., what?" asked the dog.

"Dude, we're inside Mr. Steak&Eggs' colossal space traveling stockyard."

I had taken a step toward the dog, ready to console her, but stopped. My body stiffened. My breathing stopped. Surely this news would send her into panic mode.

"That's, um, that's nice. Wake me when we get to the beach." He curled up and fell back to sleep.

My shoulders loosened as I exhaled in relief.

"Cat, how many people are on board?" asked the pig.

The cat tweaked a setting on her handheld device. "I am unable to get an accurate reading. The enormous volume of cows is interfering with my scans. I am attempting to recalibrate the scanner to filter out the cows." Her whiskers flared as she tapped her device.

"Do we have any weapons?" I asked.

"I checked our ship. There's nothing. No laser guns. No fire ax. Not even rubber bands and paper clips," said the pig.

"Dude, we've got a fire extinguisher," said the duck, as he picked it up.

"MacGyver could turn that into a weapon for sure, man."

I checked all the camera feeds, looking for movement other than cows. It was impossible to be sure, but I didn't see anything but cows.

"I suspect a welcoming committee will greet us soon," said the pig.

"I've got an idea, dude. Let's hide in the smuggler cargo bays like they did in that Sci-Fi movie."

"Even if this ship had smuggler cargo bays, that's a horrible idea," said the pig.

"We're sitting ducks inside here. We'd be better off hiding in the cows," I said.

The pig gave me a nod. "That's actually a decent idea. They will provide great cover and we can get a jump on our attackers."

We woke up the dog and filed out of our prison ship into the stench of millions of confined cows of every breed imaginable, Holstein Friesian, Longhorns, Black Angus, Droughtmaster, etc. The space behind us filled in with teleporting cows. We weaved through the cows, headed for what we assumed was the ship's bow.

"Cat, you got anything on those scanners yet?" asked the pig.

"The recalibrated scanners indicate several Cheddarian lifeforms aboard Mr. Steak&Eggs' ship, but no Cheddarians on this vessel."

"Does that mean no one is hunting us?" I asked.

"At this present moment, the answer is affirmative."

"Dude, was that an actual answer?"

"That's her way of saying yes," said the pig.

"They've got to know we're here, man. They teleported us onto their ship for Fried Spam's sake."

The cat sat and scratched her ear. "It is conceivable we arrived undetected."

"How's that?" I asked, as the rest of us squeezed through the cows to huddle around the cat.

"If our spacecraft intersected a teleport beam intended for the teleportation of a cow or cluster of cows, in theory, our spacecraft got teleported instead of the cows."

"Dude, they have no idea we're here."

"Mission accomplished, man."

The rabbit and duck did a paw-to-wing high-five.

The pig turned to the cat. "Can you locate the cow?"

"Sensors identify her location to be on the bridge of Mr. Steak&Eggs' ship."

"How do we get to Mr. Steak&Eggs' ship?" asked the pig.

"Up." The cat pointed a paw at the ceiling.

We tilted our heads up. The ceiling stood four floors above us, but no actual second, third, or fourth floors existed. Only emptiness spanned the void.

"Docked atop this vessel is Mr. Steak&Eggs' spacecraft," said the cat.

The pig scanned the ceiling. "There must be a door or a hatch up there."

"I'm on it. I'll go scout for the opening," said the fish, as he swam toward the rafters.

"Okay. Say he finds this hatch door. How do we get up there?" asked the pig.

"We could fly our ship up there, dude."

"I advise against such action. Initiating our engines inside this warehouse will ignite the elevated concentration of methane."

It occurred to me that whoever operated this giant intergalactic warehouse would need access to the ceiling to do things like change a lightbulb or fix a leaking pipe. I hopped onto the back of the closest cow and glanced around the enormous room. Parked in the corner was a circular convertible space pod built to hold two Cheddarians and their tools.

I scurried over and jumped in. The controls consisted of a big red button and two joysticks. I pressed the button, and the engine purred to life. My first attempt at understanding how the joysticks controlled the craft's speed, direction, and elevation resulted in me nosediving the ship, taking a chunk out of the floor. On my second try, I scraped a gouge in the wall, then overcompensated and smashed into a cow, starting a fifty-cow domino cascade.

By this time, the others had rushed over.

The duck eyed the craft. "Dude, I like the ship."

"But get out and let one of us pilot, man."

I happily obliged.

The fish reported that hundreds of portal doors littered the ceiling. The cat performed a scan and declared a specific portal to be the one to Mr. Steak&Eggs ship. We crammed into the space pod. With the rabbit at the controls, we soared up to the portal. We opened the hatch door and crawled into a freight elevator sized airlock. We closed the door behind us and waited for it to seal. The pig then opened the top door. The vastness of space greeted us. The pig slammed the door shut.

The cat tapped her handheld computer. "Their portal labeling algorithm is most illogical. This is obviously the incorrect portal, but it helped me determine the pattern, and I have identified the correct door."

We scrambled back into the space pod and tried the next door, which also led to outer space. In fact, her next dozen "correct" doors were portals to space. Through all of her failures, she remained regal and confident, dismissing each mistake as improper labeling or a Colbian math anomaly or methane gas interference. When she finally identified the right door, I assumed it to be luck rather than skill.

By this time, only the pig crawled into the airlock. He closed the bottom hatch door behind him. Seconds after the clang of the top hatch opening, the bottom one sprang open. The pig dropped into the space pod. The rest of us looked up. A half dozen laser guns greeted us.

***

THE DEEP PURPLE FACE of a guard appeared among the laser guns. "Mr. Steak&Eggs is not pleased you came back."

The guards ushered us into the cargo bay of Mr. Steak&Eggs' ship.

"Mr. Steak&Eggs would like a word with you all." The guard pointed toward an office door.

Without saying a word, or even giving a nod, we sprang into action. The pig struck first. He grabbed the guard to his right and slammed him into the guard on his left. Both crumpled to the floor.

In a tag team combination of kicks and punches, the duck and rabbit disarmed another guard, and bloodied his nose.

A fourth guard prepared to fire, but I didn't give him a chance. I bolted into hyperspeed and blasted the two guns out of his four hands with my head, breaking several of his finger bones in the process. I circled around and exited hyperspeed by slamming into the guard's back.

As I stood up, the dog, yes, the dog, nailed the final guard with a tailwhip, knocking him halfway across the room, where he slammed into a metal cargo container.

The groaning guards lay scattered across the floor.

The pig snatched the laser guns. "Let's go save the cow!"

The cat pointed down a new hallway. "The bridge is this way."

"We better tie these goons up first," said the fish, hovering above the scene.

"I'm on it," I said, and blasted into hyperspeed. I scoured the cargo bay until I found a box of duct tape. The "ATTN: Dr. Hash Browns" on the box made it clear they had stolen the tape from our space station. I grabbed three rolls and had the guards' four arms duct taped behind their backs and their legs bound in no time.

I remained at hyperspeed, circling the ceiling as the others marched to the bridge. As we weaved through the corridors, I hoped to spot the elephant, but never did. The doors to the Star Trek style bridge slid open. Mr. Steak&Eggs sat in the captain's chair, with his two bodyguards, Sausage and Bacon, at his side. They had the cow tied to a railing that ran alongside a set of three stairs. She looked like a horse in front of an Old West saloon. The stairs led to an elevated semi-circle of unmanned computer stations.

Sausage and Bacon repositioned into protection stances in front of their boss. I blasted right at them and weaved figure-eight patterns to encase them in duct tape. I zipped to the ceiling to admire my work but couldn't believe what I saw. They both clutched swords, which they had drawn to their chests before I mummified them in duct tape. They dropped their blades forward, slicing through the tape in what appeared to me as slow-motion Tai Chi.

I zipped down and attempted to rip the sword out of Bacon's hands. Neither my claws nor wings managed a decent hold, not that I possess the strength to pull the giant sword out of his hands, even with a good grip.

Sausage cut his way free milliseconds before the pig punched Bacon in the gut. Bacon sailed backward and smacked into navigation controls. I had a firm grip on his sword handle and sailed along with him. The collision snapped me out of hyperspeed.

The pig charged forward, grabbed Bacon, and forced him into the pilot's seat. Bacon's sword spilled to the floor. I blasted back to hyperspeed and duct taped him to the chair like a hostage victim.

I spun to face Mr. Steak&Eggs. He had risen from his captain's chair and took aim at me with a pair of laser pistols. The rabbit and duck were already on it. They appeared to hang in the air, inching toward Mr. Steak&Eggs. The rabbit soared through the air in a classic ninja-style kick pose. He struck first, knocking one pistol out of Mr. Steak&Eggs' hand. The duck, with his wings tucked in and his duckbill extended, slammed into the second pistol. As the gun sprang from Mr. Steak&Eggs' hand, it fired a red stream of light.

The laser stream did not move in slow motion. I dove to the floor, breaking out of hyperspeed. The beam clipped my tail, burning a hole through a set of feathers. It raced on to sear off a patch of Bacon's hair.

The rabbit and duck perched themselves on opposite shoulders of Mr. Steak&Eggs. They punched and kicked his oversized violet hued head. The attacks rippled across Mr. Steak&Eggs' face like pebbles tossed in a calm lake. But none of their hits snapped his head or loosened a tooth. He snarled his upper lip and swiped the rabbit and duck off his shoulders like he was wiping away spider webs. When they hit the floor, he kicked them across the room.

I readied my duct tape and zipped back to hyperspeed. But before I swooped in, the dog joined the fracas. With a swift tail whip, he swept Mr. Steak&Eggs off his feet. As soon as he landed, I duct taped his four skinny arms and two scrawny legs to the floor.

Two down, one to go.

The pig had Sausage pinned to a wall, and I was about to duct tape him to it, but spotted Bagel out of the corner of my eye. She entered the bridge with two laser rifles drawn. I zapped toward her but couldn't get there in time to stop her from firing. Luckily, the cat had already taken action. She landed on Bagel's face with claws out. She weaved between flailing purple arms and laser rifles, scratching lines into Bagel's round cheeks. Then the cat went for her eyes. Laser blasts scorched the ceiling. I encircled the guns in duct tape. With the roll still attached, I rocketed away, ripping the rifles out of her hands.

Bagel's upper arms sprang up to cover her bleeding eyes, while her lower arms grabbed the thrashing cat and whipped her into the now closed bridge door. I had her mummified a second later, her upper hands taped in place over her eyes and her lower hands handcuffed in duct tape.

Three down, but still one to go.

I spun and zipped to where the pig had Sausage pinned to the wall. I readied my roll of duct tape, but the pig no longer had a hold of Sausage. Instead, Sausage stood free, but remained stationary. His four arms dangled at his side as he slowly rocked like a buoy on a calm lake. His eyes had glazed over as he stared at a random spot on the ceiling.

The fish hovered in front of his face.

It took me a moment to process the scene and several more moments to believe it. The fish had hypnotized him.

Four down, zero to go.

With our work done, I slammed into the wall behind Sausage and broke out of hyperspeed.

The room warped back to normal speed. Mr. Steak&Eggs wiggled his arms and legs, but the duct tape held firm. The rabbit, duck, and dog lorded over him, with their chests puffed out. Bagel had settled into a chair and grunted with every heavy breath. Slow-flowing streams of blood oozed down her upper hands, the ones which I duct taped over her eyes. The cat kept a suspicious eye on her as she strolled past her. Posed in front of the captain's chair, with his karate-clench hooves on his hips, stood the pig, soaking in our victory.

Once the fish noticed I had broken out of hyperspeed, he swam up to me. His grinning face hovered in front of me. "I did it! I hypnotized him."

"Excellent work. In fact, great job by the whole team," said the cow. She tugged at the knot that secured her to the railing, to no avail. "Now, can someone untie me?"

"Sure thing," said the pig, waddling toward her.

"So, what do I do now?" A twinge of panic had overtaken the fish's previous glee.

"Thhay hello."

The fish shrugged his gills and said, "Hello."

"Hello cute floaty fishy," greeted Sausage in a tone that resembled an owner snuggling with their cat. "I thought we sold you and all your animal friends to that nice French Toast fellow?"

The fish scanned the room. Most of us shrugged. The pig gave him a nod of encouragement.

"Well, ah, we missed you."

I closed my eyes and shook my head.

"Oh, isn't that sweet? Give me a hug." Sausage reached out to wrap his top arms around the fish but went straight through him. "You're a tricky little floaty fishy. A bad tricky little floaty fishy. Let me hug you."

"Sausage! Snap out of it! Grab a laser gun and start blasting these animals." yelled Mr. Steak&Eggs.

"I can't harm my cute little floaty fishy. Even if he is tricky." A second hug attempt ended with Sausage's arms wrapped around himself.

Bacon shook his head. "Buddy! Knock it off. You're embarrassing yourself in front of the big guy."

"Agreed. You're making me sick," said Mr. Steak&Eggs. "Knock it off and start busting heads."

Sausage's eyes remained fixated on the fish as he wobbled in place. "What's your name, floaty fishy friend?"

"I don't have a name, per se. Everyone just refers to me as the fish."

"I don't like it. I don't like that at all. Hmmmm. Let me think. What name suits you? I think you look like a Phil. I shall call you Phil."

Once again, the fish's eyes danced between the rest of us, asking for advice. This time, we all nodded our encouragement to roll with it.

"Okay, sure. You can call me Phil."

"Excellent. You are Phil the Floaty Fishy and you are the cutest little Phil the Floaty Fishy there's ever been."

"Seriously, I am going to puke if you don't cut out this little lovey dovey garbage and get rid of these beasts. We've got more cows to grab."

Sausage glared at Mr. Steak&Eggs. "You're not a very nice man. I don't think I like you."

"Yeah, why don't you put a sock in it," said the pig to Mr. Steak&Eggs.

"That's a good idea. That'll shut him up," said Sausage.

There was a brief pause as we all examined our sockless feet, hooves, paws, and claws.

"Um, we don't, we don't wear socks," said the dog.

"But I do," shrieked Sausage as he flipped off his shoe and removed his black sock.

Bacon rattled and shook his chair. His eyes bulged. "Don't do it!!"

Mr. Steak&Eggs' eyes narrowed. His lips tightened. "You wouldn't dare."

"Oh, yes, I would. You're a very mean man." Sausage stuffed his dirty sock into Mr. Steak&Eggs mouth, as his boss tried to form a rebuttal.

Mr. Steak&Eggs gagged as he attempted to spit the stinky sock out. The pig didn't give him the chance and slapped a strip of duct tape over the sock. A few tears rolled down Mr. Steak&Eggs face, as his face faded from violet to a greenish pale lilac.

"There. Now that's much better. Anything else I can do for my little Phil?"

"Well, um... sure," stammered the fish, as his eyes darted around the room, begging for help.

"Dude, how about we draw a funny mustache and sideburns on Mr. Steak&Eggs' face?"

"Or paint his face to make him look like a zombie," said the rabbit.

"Sure thing. I'll need supplies." Sausage headed toward the door.

"And put an action movie on the big screen?" asked the duck as he hopped into the captain's chair.

The rabbit jumped up next to him. "And can you bring us some popcorn?"

"No! Stop," commanded the cow.

Sausage paused at the doorway.

"We've got more important matters to address. Can you help uthh send the cows back to Earth?"

Sausage looked at the fish, who emphatically nodded yes. "It would be my pleasure. Follow me." Sausage walked off the bridge, then stuck his head back in. "You guys are so cute."

"Hey!" yelled Bacon as he violently swiveled in the pilot's chair. "You're just gonna leave me here?"

We ignored him and filed out of the bridge.

"I've got to pee!!" From start to end of his short sentence, his voice rose an octave and a half. His pathetic plea qualified as grounds for him to lose his goon ranking.

***

As we made our way to the Teleportation Control Center, or the TCC, as Sausage called it, we ran into a couple of guards toting laser guns. No worries. We had one of Mr. Steak&Eggs private goons with us, gleefully announcing, "I'm escorting these animals to the TCC." They might have thought he was drunk or on some strong prescription medication, but they did nothing to stop us.

We entered the TCC to see a couple of young adult Cheddarians sitting in desk chairs, with their feet kicked up on the desk, watching a professional Cheddarian hextiltonion match. They scrambled to make themselves look busy once they saw Sausage enter the room.

Sausage greeted them with a friendly, "Hello, gentlemen."

"Hello, sir," said one technician. "We're collecting a herd from the African coast right now." The large screen switched to an aerial view of cows being zapped into the air.

Sausage patted the side of the technician's face. "That's nice, but there's been a change in plans. We're sending all the cows back. So, if you wouldn't mind reversing everything, that would be great. Okay?"

"You're joking, right?" asked the other tech.

A hint of anger creeped into Sausage's tone. "I never joke. Put the cows back."

"I don't understand. We've been working for days to capture all these cows," said Tech-1. "Does Mr. Steak&Eggs know about this?"

"Mr. Steak&Eggs is aware of what's going on," said Sausage, which was not a lie.

Tech-1 stared at his keyboard with the stunned expression of a math challenged fifth grader asked to solve a problem on the board.

"Well, can you do it?" asked Sausage.

"I guess so. I mean, if that's what Mr. Steak&Eggs wants." He began typing commands.

"Well, I don't believe anyone said Mr. Steak&Eggs –" began Sausage.

The cow slid in front of him. "Yes, that would be splendid. Carry on with sending the cows back."

"Yes, make it so." Sausage performed a pirouette at the end of his command.

The technicians slid from computer to computer, typing commands, pulling levers, and turning dials. We enjoyed their rolling chair dance while sipping coffee, cheerfully prepared for us by Sausage.

The second technician talked as he worked. "Sending the cows back is actually much faster than capturing them. There was no need to locate the cows, run a scan, and set coordinates. To return them, we simply had to reverse the commands previously run."

The technicians had been busy returning cows for ten minutes when the cat motioned for the cow to join her in the hallway. Naturally, the rest of us followed. The cat's tail whipped back and forth as she waited for us to assemble.

In a hushed voice, she said, "I suggest we exercise our exit strategy. The fish's hypnotism of Sausage will not last forever."

"How long do we have?" asked the cow.

"Impossible to calculate a definitive time. Based on previous experimentation of the fish's hypnosis power, I estimate it could last anywhere from another six seconds to six hours."

"We can't stop. We need to complete the mission," said the cow. "If we leave now and Sausage snaps out of it, they'll start grabbing the cows back and come after uthh again."

"She's right," said the pig. "We need to end this."

Sausage appeared in the doorway with a plate full of cookies. "Anybody hungry?"

He stuffed three cookies into the cow's mouth. I couldn't take my eyes off the cow, as drool mixed with cookie crumbs dangled off her side lip. It refused to drop as she gnawed away, exposing the cookie cud mush that had formed inside her mouth. I lost my desire to eat a cookie and politely declined when Sausage offered me one.

Meanwhile, the pig stared at the rabbit and duck. "Did you ask him to make these?"

With shifty eyes, the pair said, "Maybe."

The cow swallowed her cookie mush and cleared her throat. "How much longer will it take them to return the cows?"

"I haven't the slightest idea," said Sausage. "Oh, I should give the technicians some cookies. They're working so hard." He headed back into the TCC.

"Chicken, get back in there and watch what they're doing," said the cow. "And find out how much longer this is going to take. And keep an eye on Sausage."

I strolled into the TCC, hopped onto a desk, and waltzed up to the two technicians.

Their combined eight hands worked controls, typed commands, and pulled levers. Their movements had a rhythm. Click, type, tap, swish.

"How's it going, guys? How much longer will this take?"

Neither took their eyes off their work nor missed a beat of their rhythmic tech dance.

"Hard to say," said Tech-1.

"It's going pretty fast," said Tech-2. "But there are a lot of cows. I don't understand why we took them all and now we're putting them all back. Seems like a big waste of time."

"You're not paid to question decisions. You're paid to follow orders," said Sausage, who drew a picture of us animals and him on a posterboard. It was too cartoonish for my liking, but considering the medium of markers on posterboard, it was appropriate, and he clearly had a flare for cartoon imagery.

The cat sauntered in and leaped up next to Sausage's poster board. After a short chat, the cat tiptoed to an open workstation, and began typing commands into the computer terminal.

I didn't ask or even wonder what she was up to.

Sausage hummed as he drew.

The technicians continued their rhythmic computer work as the dog wandered in.

He sighed as he sat down below me. "How, um, how much longer?"

"They're not sure."

"Actually," said Tech-1, as he dramatically pulled a lever, "we're done. The cows are all back on Earth."

Relief flowed through my chicken bones. I snuck a peek at Sausage, who looked puzzled about what to add next to his poster.

"There is one odd thing," said Tech-2.

Panic wormed back into my bones.

"There's a small spaceship in the storage area. It's a mystery how it got there. No life forms on board. What do you want me to do with it?" Tech-2 tried to make eye contact with Sausage, who still gazed at his drawing.

Sausage dropped his marker, rubbed his eyes, and looked up at the big screen. After a set of hard eye squints, he did a long blink and wiggled his head. "What's going on here?" His cheery tone had disappeared. "Why am I down here? What are these disgusting animals doing here?" He turned his attention to the technicians. "And did I hear you correctly? Did you just say you returned all the cows back to Earth? Why, in the name of Fried Spam, would you do that?"

BYH
BarnYard Heroes

Chapter 18

SAUSAGE HOVERED OVER THE two teleportation technicians. His eyes blazed. His teeth ground. His smile had left the spaceship.

"You told us to return the cows," said Tech-1.

"I most certainly did not. Now get them back!!"

The other animals poured into the room.

Sausage tapped his watch. "Security. We have intruders in the TCC. Get down here stat."

The fish swam up to Sausage's face, but he bobbed away to scowl at the technicians, who scrambled to their keyboards.

"Chicken!!!!!" shouted the cow.

We didn't have time for her to moo out a command. She knew I knew what to do. Moments later, I had the two technicians and Sausage restrained in duct tape, with their mouths sealed. I didn't want to hear anyone whining about needing a bathroom break.

I slammed into a desk to break out of hyperspeed.

"Pig! Secure that door," said the cow. "We're about to have company."

"You got it," said the pig, slamming the door closed and locking it.

The cow walked over to the cat. "How are you doing with the self-destruct?"

The cat kept her eyes on her work, but said, "Ninety-two point-seven percent complete."

"Excellent. Did you get everything you needed from Sausage?"

"Affirmative."

I remembered the cat chatting with Sausage and scribbling notes. The others had a plan but didn't tell me about it. Despite saving their butts numerous times, they continued to think of me as Half-Baked, the incomplete experiment that needs protecting. They didn't believe I could handle the complexity of their plan. I clenched my beak as veins pulsed in my head. To them, I would always be the baby sister, never included in the decision making, just expected to follow orders.

A pounding on the door stopped my spiral of self-pity.

"Open up!!! Open this door!! That's an order!!"

"Chicken, did you memorize the steps for operating the teleporter?" asked the cow.

"I noticed a rhythmic pattern to their movements, but I didn't memorize them. It would have been nice if you'd included me in the planning, so I knew I was supposed to memorize the steps."

"Rabbit. Duck. Help her out. Figure out how to work that teleporter. We need to lock on uthh and prepare to beam uthh to Earth."

The steady sizzle of laser guns joined the continuous pounding. Glowing lines appeared on either side of the door. They started at the bottom and slowly moved upward.

"They're coming through!" announced the pig.

"Dude, they're like Jedi Knights," said the duck.

"Dog. Fish. Help with the teleporter. Between the lot of you, figure out how it workthh."

The pig rolled the technicians away so we could gather around the workstations. None of us made a move toward a keyboard, button, or lever. We just stood or hovered and stared.

"What do we do first, dude?" asked the duck.

The rabbit and I shrugged our shoulders. The fish and dog maintained their blank stares.

From her position at a computer workstation, the cat said, "Search the teleport logs for the time they teleported us off planet Earth."

"What's a log?" asked the rabbit.

"Dude, it's like a journal entry of all the teleporting they've done. We've got to find that journal book." The duck waddled across the desktops, flipping over everything in sight with his bill.

The cat put a paw to her forehead. "This isn't a 1900s Earth movie. They don't keep records in a paper journal. The log will be an electronic file."

"They're a third of the way up the door," said the pig.

"Thanks for the update, dude. Just what we needed; more pressure."

This seemed an odd response. We had more than enough pressure.

Then, I spotted the words "Command History" blinking inside a box on the computer screen. "Would Command History be a log?" I asked.

"Affirmative. In fact, a command history is better than a log," said the cat. "Search for the entries that brought us here from Earth."

"Got it. And once I find them, we just reverse the commands. That's how the tech sent the cows back."

"Precisely."

I clicked the box that read "Command History". A list of computer commands appeared. I scrolled through without a clue what our entries would look like. Yet I kept scrolling. The list went on and on.

"They're halfway up the door," said the pig, with a twinge of begging that made him resemble the dog's tone.

"Dude, did you find our entries?"

Words eluded me as I concentrated on the lines of commands. "Blach," is the only sound I made.

"Let her work, man," said the rabbit.

"All the entries look the same." I headbutted the screen. "How can I tell which commands are ours? It's not going to say 'teleport chicken' in the command." A synapse connected a couple of random memories stored in the depths of my brain and generated a new idea. "I've got it. Before they teleported us, they sent a message. I bet that message is part of a command."

"Dude, you're a genius."

I continued scrolling the list. "There must be a better way to search this list."

"Click the magnifying glass icon," said the cat.

A text box popped open. I pecked in the message they sent; "Thanks. I was having a hard time getting a lock on these cows."

The cursor jumped to the line containing that text. I'd done it. "It looks easy to reverse a command," I said, "but which are the commands that teleported us? The ones before this command or the ones after?"

The fish swam up to the screen. "It would depend on how the list is ordered."

"If, if they, if they ordered them alphabetically, this plan won't work."

"It's chronological, man, so we're the lines right after."

"So, below?" I asked.

"Above! Above! Above!" yelled the cat from across the room. "New commands are added on top."

"That doesn't sound logical, dude."

"Check the time stamps."

The cat was right. I copied and reversed our eight teleportation commands. But we still had a problem. I didn't know how to trigger them. I ignored the increased pounding, closed my eyes. and visualized the dance the technicians performed.

Load commands.

Tap button.

Turn knob.

Pull lever.

That's not right.

A loud bang broke my concentration. *Did they smack the door with a battering ram?*

"They're three-quarters of the way up the door and kicking the bottom in," said the pig.

"Chicken, are you ready to teleport uthh?"

"Almost. Working out the sequence of steps."

A laser blast zipped under a forced gap between the floor and door. It burned a line in the tile floor.

The pig pressed against the door. The gap slightly closed. "We're running out of time."

Turn knob.

Load commands.

Tap button.

Pull lever.

That's it. That's the rhythmic pattern.

"I've got it. I can do this."

"Great. Cat, are you ready with the self-destruct?" asked the cow.

"Affirmative."

"Activate!" ordered the cow.

The cat slapped a button with her paw.

A loudspeaker announcement filled the room. "Initiating self-destruct sequence Alpha Jay Gamma Seven. Self-destruction will commence in ten minutes. All personnel must proceed to the emergency escape vessels immediately. Repeat. Self-destruct..."

The sound of the laser guns melting the door stopped. "Whoever's in there," shouted a Cheddarian, "you're on your own. We're out of here." Rapid footsteps faded as they ran off to the escape pods.

"Chicken, it's time to teleport uthh home." The cow had a calm smug tone of satisfaction in her voice.

"Okay," I said. "Turn the knob. Check. Load teleportation commands."

The others watched over my shoulder as I waited for the commands to load.

"Good. Directions reversed. Now, I tap the button to lock on to the objects." As I reached for the button, a grunt and a chair wobble distracted me. I turned my head. The panicked expression of Tech-2 greeted me.

"What about them?" I asked. "And the others I duct taped. They won't be able to get off the ship. We can't just leave them to die."

"What are you proposing?" asked the cow. "And remember, we've got less than eight minutes."

I turned to Tech-2. "If I don't have a previous transmission, what do I do?" I ripped off the duct tape covering his mouth.

"It would be easier for me to do it. Free me!"

"Ain't gonna happen," said the pig with a scowl directed toward the technician.

"You're going to run out of time to save yourselves," said Tech-2 with a smug smile.

The dog flashed his pleading eyes at me. "I, I, love how, how big your heart is, but there's no time for nobility."

The cow winked at me. "Agreed. Let them all die. Get uthh out of here."

"Fine. I'll walk the white bird through this." No hint of smugness remained in Tech-2's voice.

He showed me how to lock onto members of Mr. Steak&Eggs' crew via their wristwatch communicators. I turned the knob, loaded the commands, and tapped the button.

Tech-2 mouthed, "Thank you."

I pulled the lever.

Sausage and the technicians dematerialized.

"Are you done now?" asked the pig.

"Not quite," I said. "One more step."

"Self-destruction will commence in four minutes," announced the ship.

"Make it snappy," said the cow.

I buzzed through a teleportation sequence. "Done."

"Are you happy now?" asked the pig.

"Yes," I said with beaming confidence. I had saved lives, even if some of them might not deserve it.

"Where did you send them?" asked the fish.

"I loaded them into the prison ship and teleported the ship somewhere. I'm not entirely sure where. It doesn't matter. They're alive."

"Self-destruction will commence in three minutes."

The dog circled in front of me. "Very righteous of you. Now, now get us out of here!"

"Absolutely." I turned the knob, loaded our teleportation commands, and tapped the button. As I reached for the lever, I stopped.

"Self-destruction will commence in two minutes."

"Why, why did you stop?" The dog's head shivered between my wing and the lever.

I had realized the impossibility of pulling the lever while teleporting. Even at hyperspeed, it would be physically impossible to complete the lever pull. I imagined being lost in a paradox or limbo state. I would become the elephant, indefinitely stuck in isolation.

"Pull it! Pull the lever, dude."

I sighed as I looked at the panic on my friends' faces. I rested on the dog last. He would take this hardest, but I had no time to explain. "We only get one shot at this. Let me double check the commands."

"Self-destruction will commence in one minute."

The pig groaned. "Make it snappy."

I turned the knob and reloaded the commands, minus my entry. I tapped the button and pulled the lever.

My friends dematerialized.

I waved goodbye, but they were already gone.

I exhaled but kept my wing on the lever. My friends were safe. They were back in the peaceful farmlands of Central Wisconsin. That's all that mattered.

"Self-destruction will commence in thirty seconds."

Chapter 19

SACRIFICING MYSELF TO SAVE the others left me emotionally, physically, and mentally paralyzed. My wing clutched the pulled lever for what felt like hours. I exhaled, something I hadn't done since teleporting my friends to safety. *What a noble thing I had done. Nothing more to do but wait to die.* I wondered if perhaps I had already died.

"Self-destruction will commence in twenty seconds."

I was still alive, but ten seconds had passed.

The words "escape pod" rattled in my brain. I released my death grip on the lever. I broke into hyperspeed and zipped around the ship, but if one remained, I couldn't find it.

While in hyperspeed, I couldn't hear the self-destruct message. Luckily, most walls displayed a countdown clock. Fifteen seconds remained.

I zoomed into the warehouse ship, where I learned my sense of smell remained intact when traveling at hyperspeed. The cows were gone, but their stench lingered on. I held my breath as I lapped around the warehouse three times. No escape pods.

I looped through Mr. Steak&Eggs' ship one more time before returning to the bridge.

The countdown clock flipped to five seconds. I gazed at the Earth's image on the large screen. My friends were safe. That's all that mattered. I settled into a squat.

"Why are you still here?" asked a familiar monotone voice.

I whipped my head around as the elephant took a seat in the captain's chair. It immediately collapsed under his weight.

"What am *I* doing here? What are *you* doing here?"

"Where did you think I had gone?"

It was a fair question. The elephant saved us. He freed us from our prison cells. Then I forgot about him. "There's still time. We can zip down to the TCC and I can teleport you to Earth."

He stood up and brushed chunks of the captain's chair off his butt with a swish of his tail. "I've got a better idea. Follow me." He ambled out of the bridge, traveling at speeds approaching the speed of light.

I glanced at the counter. Four seconds until self-destruction. I scrambled to catch up to him. "There's not much time. This better be a great plan."

"Trust me. It's the best plan available."

"What is this plan?"

"You'll soon see. I think it might be kind of fun."

I stopped, ready to make a stand. His tail swayed and his trunk bobbed as he strolled away at a leisurely, hyperspeed pace. *Why won't he tell me his plan? Is he going to sacrifice himself to save me? But we weren't headed to the TCC.*

"If you won't tell me the plan, at least tell me where we're going."

"The cargo bay. Now hurry up."

"I searched the cargo bay. There's no escape pod there."

"We don't need a ship. Now stop whining. We're running out of time."

I stomped my chicken feet as I followed him. *Why was everyone hiding their plans from me? I'm a fully grown sapient chicken. I can handle the truth and they should include me in the decision-making process.*

I stewed the rest of the walk. We entered the cargo bay of Mr. Steak&Eggs' ship with only two seconds left.

The elephant strolled up to the airlock. He poked at the keypad with his trunk. The inner door opened.

I crossed my wings and glared at him. "Are you crazy? Blasting us into space is your great plan?"

"I never said it was great. But look, it's a clear shot." He pointed out the window with his trunk. The Earth gleamed in the distance.

"We don't know if I'll survive in outer space."

"Trust me, you'll be fine. Just follow my lead and we'll be on Earth in no time."

I glanced at the countdown clock. One second left. I didn't trust him, but I had run out of options.

I uncrossed my wings and joined him in the airlock.

The interior airlock door closed.

"Prepare for blast off." He didn't change his stance, remaining in a classic standing elephant statue stance.

I decided a sprinter's starting pose would be best.

"And warning. It may get hot when we enter the Earth's atmosphere."

I still searched for sure footing when the elephant hit the button.

The outer door slid open, and a blast of air launched us into the cold emptiness of space.

The elephant snapped into a vintage Santa's reindeer pose, silhouetted in the Earth's glow.

Meanwhile, I tumbled into space. Sound vanished, as I spiraled between images of stars, the ship's slow-motion explosion, and the Earth's glow. With each tumble, I stretched my neck to extend my glimpse of the explosion. Bursts of fireballs rippled into the cargo bay. Blasts cascaded through the giant whale shaped warehouse ship. With one final flurry, both ships exploded into billions of multicolored chards of metal. The fireworks spew of embers overshadowed the distant stars. Spectacular views of the disembodied ships continued to enthrall me until I caught a peek of the Earth. This needed to be my focal point. I contorted my spine to point my beak at the planet. My body snapped itself straight. Using my wings, I steadied myself and corrected my direction. Then I snapped my wings to my side and tucked my feet in. I rocketed toward Earth, following the elephant's path. I fought off the desire for one more glance at the dazzling destruction. *Stay on target. Focus on Earth. Don't spin off into the never-ending void.*

As the Earth grew large enough to pick our landing spot, Wisconsin was on the other side of Earth.

We had no time to change course. We broke into the Earth's atmosphere. Flames danced around me, yet I felt no heat. Once the flames faded, a spectacular view of the Asian continent emerged. I sped past the elephant, who had spread out his ears.

He swooped in eloquent patterns as I continued to plummet toward the ground. I broke my missile pose and spread my wings out. This lurched me to a massively slower pace, and I smacked into the elephant's trunk.

The rush of air nearly drowned out his yell of, "Watch it."

After wobbling into a stable flight, I tried a couple of swoops.

I glided.

I swayed.

I soared.

I WAS FLYING!!!

My Aves instincts must have kicked in. It came naturally. Perhaps being born with wings helped.

The wind rushed across my face and ruffled my torso feathers. Adrenaline and endorphins pumped through my veins, creating a hyper serenity. I flapped my wings. They did what wings should do. I soared higher, soaking in the spectacular view of treetops and patterned farmlands. As I gazed upon the snowcaps of the Himalayas, I realized I had lost sight of the elephant. I glanced around for him, but soon lost myself in the spectacular views of the China coastline. I decided he was a grown elephant who knew our destination. He'd find his way there.

As the outline of Japan came into focus, I wondered about the fastest route to the other side of Earth. *Should I go east or west? Why not north? Or south?*

I decided on north. Two strong flaps of my wings launched me toward the North Pole. As I cruised over Russia, I stretched my wings out in front of me and hummed the Superman theme song. I soared over the North Pole. Day turned to night as I entered Canadian airspace. When the Great Lakes came into view, I began my descent. Nighttime had settled in over the American Midwest, and I needed to circle Central Wisconsin three times before locating Hector Spector's farm. The view of the rolling farmlands during our initial arrival on Earth kindled my urge to fly and there I was, flying over those same farmlands. Too bad the darkness ruined the view. I made the most of it and pretended to be a hawk hunting its prey. I swooped closer to the ground, wondering if I would ever soar like this again. *Was I truly flying, or was I gracefully falling out of the sky?* I took a couple more laps in case it was the latter.

When I finally decided to land, I spread my wings wide, hoping to slow my speed. I needed a crash landing to snap me out of hyperspeed, but didn't want the addition of gravitational acceleration. It slowed my pace, but I still created a crater and a crop circle in Hector's cornfield. All the serenity and exhilaration I experienced while in flight disappeared on impact.

I crawled out of the crater and dusted myself off with my wings. The events of the past few minutes ran through my head. I survived deep space, entry into the Earth's atmosphere, and a crash landing. Sure, my body ached from head to claw, starting with a steady head throb, and ending with pin pricks on the feet, but the impact should have pulverized me into goo. Not even a broken bone or a ruptured spleen. I didn't freeze in deep space. In fact, not a speck of frostbite. Re-entry into Earth's atmosphere hadn't burned me to a crisp. *Thank you, Dr. Hash Browns, wherever you are.*

I hobbled across a pasture, wondering if I would ever experience flying again. I couldn't take off from land, but I figured I could jump out of an airplane or off a cliff and gracefully fall.

As I limped near the barn, outdoor lights clicked on, revealing a great surprise. My Dog Playing Chess still lay where I had left it. As I once again tucked my masterpiece under my wing, the door flung open.

The dog raced out. He sprinted toward me.

I froze as he tackled and pinned me. It tickled as he licked both sides of my face. His hot breath and the comforting smell of his fur made the last remnants of pain disappear.

"We, we…, we thought you were dead."

"Dog, give her some air," said the pig, as he and the others strolled up.

The dog stopped licking me and backed up a step. "Sorry. I'm just, I'm just happy you're alive."

"Man, what happened?" asked the rabbit.

"Why didn't you teleport with us, dude?"

"I wouldn't have been able to complete the lever pull while teleporting," I said, getting back on my feet.

"Sound logic. You most likely saved us all from being trapped in a state of teleportation limbo. We appreciate your quick thinking."

I staggered back from the shock of a compliment from the cat.

"Dude, what if you'd hit the lever really hard?"

"The momentum would have completed the pull, man."

"There was no time for experimenting."

"But then how did you, how did you get here?" asked the dog.

"I flew here! I can hyperspeed through space and fly through the air like a real bird."

"Duuuude!"

"I can't take all the credit. Flying through space was the elephant's idea." I scanned the area, but at normal speed, I wouldn't have seen him if he were there. "I lost him after we entered Earth's atmosphere. I thought he'd come here."

"Still clinging to that imaginary elephant, aye, dude?"

"Man, I give you an A+ for stick-to-itiveness."

I didn't care that none of them believed me. I knew the elephant existed.

"Let'thh turn that memorial service into a full-fledged party."

"Memorial service?" I asked.

"We saw the explosion from here, man."

"We thought you were dead, dude."

"So, we, we were about to hold a celebration of life ceremony for you."

"Hector refused to share his cigars and champagne, insisting there are state and federal laws prohibiting him from contributing to the delinquency of barnyard animals, regardless of how old they claimed to be," said the cat.

"So, we planned to toast your memory with generic diet cola and milk," said the fish.

"Cool," I said, in a non-convincing tone.

"We wrote a ballad in your honor, dude."

"You want to hear it, man?"

"Sure." Once again, my tone lacked conviction.

The rabbit sprinted into the barn and returned with a plastic bucket. He used the bucket as a bongo drum and pounded out a heavy beat.

The duck waddled in front of the rabbit and screamed, "CHICKEN!! CHICKEN!! The chicken is a righteous dude!!"

The rabbit abruptly ended his drumming.

"That's as far as we got, dude."

"It was gonna be epic, man. We were gonna add all the cool stuff you did and all your hyperspeeding."

"To be fair, we only had like five minutes from the point we thought you were dead to you showing up not dead, dude."

"I liked it," I said, fully embracing my right to lie. "It's very touching that you planned to honor me." This statement wasn't a lie. Their gesture had moved me.

"I, um, I, I wrote you a poem."

I fought back a tear. "Can I hear it?"

"Sure."

Chicken super fast
Not fast enough to save her
Dog misses chicken

"It's, it's a haiku."

I wrapped my wings around his neck and gave him a long hug.

"We've got some toasting and partying to do, my dudes." The duck waved for us to follow him to the barn.

We meandered after him.

Then, announced by the clanking thud of a switch, the barnyard lit up like a concert stage.

We froze in the spotlight.

I dropped the painting.

***

THE BLARING LIGHT ASSAULTED us from all directions. The steady buzz of the lights and power generators lingered long after the clicks of readied weapons. I used my wing to shade my eyes, but still needed several blinks before my eyes stayed open. Whoever turned on the lights remained hidden behind them, presumably with their weapons locked on us. An approaching pair of headlights appeared below the main bank of lights. Crunching gravel harmonized with the electronic hum until the vehicle rolled on to the grass and came to a halt.

The dog crouched behind me. I guess he thought I would protect him or somehow use my tiny chicken frame to hide him.

"Who, who are, who are they?" he asked.

"Insufficient data to ascertain identities, but via deductive reasoning, one can assume they are human authority figures," said the cat.

"So, these dudes are cops?"

The doors opened on both sides of the vehicle.

"A plausible conclusion, but we lack visual confirmation to conclude which authority organization has encircled us, if any."

"But, but why, why would they come for us?" asked the dog, as he peeked around me. "We have, we have done nothing wrong."

"We did steal a bunch of stuff," I said.

"I forgot about that. The jig's up." The dog started digging a hole. "We're, we're..., we're all going to rot in jail."

Two dark, humanoid-shaped images emerged from the car.

"We have confirmation on humanoid lifeforms," said the cat.

"Thankthh, but we figured that one out on our own."

The pig glanced at the cow. "What's our play? Make a run for Hector's underground lab or start kicking butts?"

Through the aid of a megaphone, the human on the right made an announcement.

"They say they come in peace," translated the cow.

The pig scoffed. "That's what they always say, and then twenty minutes later, we're all laid out on operating tables with our chests split open as they analyze our corpses."

"Why, why would, why would they do that?" The dog slunk into his hole, with his eyes locked onto the pig.

Another statement boomed from the megaphone.

"They thank uthh for bringing the cows home. There'thh nothing to worry about."

The two humans moved close enough to notice their black suits, black ties, and dark sunglasses. I'd say it was weird they wore sunglasses at night, but under these bright lights, I wished I had a pair.

The rabbit and duck's black pearl eyes bulged.

"Dude! They're Men in Black. Men in Black are real!!"

"This is amazing! Best day ever," said the rabbit, as the pair chest bumped.

The pig snarled and rolled his eyes. "Idiots."

The cow stepped forward and greeted the humans. After a short, civil conversation, the cow returned.

"They asked us to go with them. They said they'll keep us safe."

"And you believe them?" asked the pig.

"They sound sincere," said the cow.

"Dude, they're Men in Black. We have to go with them and like, register and whatnot."

"And go through customs, man."

"We did enter Earth illegally," said the fish.

"Idiots. You're all idiots." The pig turned to the cat, who fiddled with her handheld computer. "Cat, tell these morons why we shouldn't go with the suits. Tell them it's time to fight."

"The men in black suits may not be our biggest concern." The cat looked up from her tiny screen. "I'm detecting multiple teleportation signals with off-planet origins and end point coordinates consistent with Hector Spector's farmlands."

A cylinder of light streamed between us and the men in black suits. When the light dissolved, a small black metal orb the size of an apple rested on the ground.

***

THE PROPER RESPONSE TO a black metal orb the size of an apple materializing out of thin air is to run. None of us did that. To their credit, the two men in black suits took a step back. In contrast, me, and my other barnyard friends, except for the dog, shuffled in for a closer look.

"What is it?" asked the cow.

The cat tapped on her handheld device. "Indeterminable from a simple visual observation. I initiated a scan."

The black suited man without the megaphone yelled something at us.

Luckily, the cow understood. "We're not sure."

The black suit shouted a follow up question.

The cow turned to the cat. "Should we run?"

"An advisable course of action."

I'm sure the cow paraphrased his response to the black suits, but despite the cat's advice, we all remained in place, animals, and black suits.

"Oh, it's a stun bomb," said the cat. "We should definitely run."

The stun bomb detonated before any of us took a step. Stun bombs do not explode upon detonation, they sizzle like drops of water on a hot frying pan. The orb emits waves of Twist beams in all directions, which pass through anything, including steel walls. They destroy nothing and have no impact on electronic equipment, but knock every creature in a two-hundred-yard radius unconscious.

We woke up immobilized in duct tape. Mr. Steak&Eggs and his goons stole my trick. I regretted my decision to save him. They hog-tied the dog, cow, and pig, depositing them on the lawn near the barn. They let the fish drift aimlessly. As for us smaller animals, they duct taped us to the side of the barn. In what I presumed to be a bit of revenge, they layered extra tape on me and taped my beak closed. I imagined Bacon, Sausage, and Bagel each taking their turn adding several extra strips.

The black suits received the duct-tape treatment as well and laid scattered near their vehicles. The evil Cheddarians even dragged Hector Spector out of his underground lab and taped him up.

Mr. Steak&Eggs hobbled past the immobilized black suits. Specks of duct tape glue freckled his face and black suit. His untucked shirt shot out from under his jacket like a bloom of white tail feathers. The top two shirt buttons had come undone, and his tie drooped loose and sideways. A split seam ran up his right pants leg, and he had no left shoe. Miraculously, his hair remained meticulous.

The black suited humans yelled what I assumed to be threats and obscenities at him, but he ignored them, as he made his way between the larger animals laying on the ground and those of us taped to the barn wall. It was unclear how long he had been monologuing.

"I was *this* close. I would have been rich beyond my wildest dream if it wasn't for you meddling barnyard freaks. Do you realize how much trouble you've caused me? You blew up my ships and teleported me into the middle of an asteroid field. I've lost my job. I'm getting sued by French Toast for breach of contract. My former employer wants ME to pay for the ship YOU destroyed. And apparently, someone alerted the intergalactic authorities regarding me, quote, stealing the Earth's cows. You foul smelling farm animals have ruined me. What do you have against me?"

"Dude, you tried to have us killed."

"That was not cool, man."

Mr. Steak&Eggs stopped and pleaded with all four hands. "That was all a misunderstanding. And don't forget, I tried to save you. And I found you a nice home." The pleading with his hands stopped. "But NOOOOOO!! That wasn't good enough for you. You had to come back for your precious cow. And then you decide to go all Green Peace and saved all the cows. I've had enough. No more Mr. Niceguy."

"Dude! Are you serious right now? You're like the biggest narcissistic jerk I've ever met."

I had the same thought but wouldn't have said it so bluntly.

Mr. Steak&Eggs chuckled as he approached the duck. "You should have taken the option to be French Toast's new pets." He scratched his chin, as his gaze lowered to the duck's butt. "Pull the duck's tail and unleash a nuclear blast. I remember reading that in one of Doctor Stupid's papers."

I didn't like where this was going. Neither did Hector Spector, though I doubt he had a clue what was happening. He shrilled on and on in what the cow said resembled no earthly language she could interpret.

"Bacon! Sausage! One of you duct tape that Earthlings mouth shut."

Bacon stepped up. Ripped off a strip and slapped it over Hector's mouth. We were all thankful for this.

"On to the business at hand." Mr. Steak&Eggs snapped his fingers with both of his right hands. "Bagel, is the android ready?"

Bagel walked up, dragging the mangled remains of Denver Omelet, the android waiter. "He's ready, sir." She dropped the android at the feet of Mr. Steak&Eggs like a child discarding an old doll.

"Excellent," said the ex-Senior Vice President. He grabbed the duck by the neck and peeled him off the barn wall along with some red paint. He patted the loose ends of the tape around the duck's wings and handed him to the android.

"Thank you, sir," said the android as he gripped the duck with one hand around his neck and held his tail with another.

The cow, from her prone position, said, "The humans alerted the intergalactic authorities. They'll be here momentarily."

"Well, they'll be too late. Or perhaps right on time." Mr. Steak&Eggs laughed like a stereotypical cartoon villain. He brought the diabolical laughter to an abrupt end and turned to Bagel. "Any luck locating their ship?"

"Yes. It's in a barn..." She surveyed the landscape, then checked her tablet before pointing. "... over there."

"Perfect. It will pay off some of my debts." Mr. Steak&Eggs clapped both sets of hands together and addressed us one last time. "Well, animals, I hope to never see you again. It has been miserable meeting you all." He waved to the black suits. "Sorry primitive creatures. You were in the wrong place at the wrong time."

The humans responded with grumbles, which I again assumed to be expletives.

"You do realize they don't understand a word you thhay?"

"It doesn't matter. The fat necks will be dead soon, as will all of you. Goodbye, and good riddance." With that said, Mr. Steak&Eggs and his entourage marched off toward our escape pod.

My unfinished masterpiece lay directly in their path. They would trample it for sure. I shifted my attention to the android waiter, Denver Omelet. At the knee, his right leg bent in the wrong direction. His other leg stretched sideways and curled around in front of him. The end result provided a well-balanced stand for his torso and kept him upright.

The cow rolled over to face Denver. "What did they do to you?"

"They installed a software patch. It appears to be a time dependent event. It's short-lived. I hold this duck by the neck for ten minutes and then give its tail a good yank. That's it. It all seems silly to me."

"That'thh not silly. That'thh not at all silly."

I glanced back to see Sausage holding my painting. He examined it, then callously tossed it over his shoulder. I yelped as my unfinished painting spiraled in the air.

The dog peeked up at me while the rest focused on Denver.

"I don't see what the big deal is. It's not like I'm going to rip his tail off."

"You don't understand, dude. Pulling my tail unleashes my Atomic Quack."

My painting landed on an edge, tumbled, and then safely flopped to the ground. I exhaled and returned my attention to the more pressing issue.

"That sounds impressive. What's Atomic Quack?" asked the android.

"It's an atomic explosion that will level the landscape," said the pig.

"Leaving nothing but a crater, dude."

"Killing, killing everyone," said the dog.

"For miles in every direction," said the cow.

"Well, that's a bummer," said Denver.

The black suits rolled around shouting gibberish.

The cow responded in gibberish.

Their squirming intensified.

"What did you tell them?" asked the pig.

"That there'll be a nuclear explosion in ten minutes."

I may have been a novice liar, but that seemed a good time to lie.

"So, so, so Denver, can't you, can't you override the patch?" asked the dog.

"No can do."

"But, but, but the explosion will destroy you, too."

"I am aware of that fact."

"Don't you have some sort of self-preservation programming, man? Something that will override this patch?"

"Nope. Can't be stopped."

"Pig, why don't you remove your eye patch and laser blast this droid to smithereens?" asked the duck.

"Don't do it, man. You'll laser blast the duck to smithereens, as well."

"And might activate his Atomic Quack," said the cow.

The pig squirmed and grunted. "Besides, I'm too taped up. I can't get this stupid patch off my eye."

"I've got it. Dog, use your tail-whip attack to do something... anything, dude."

"It's, um, it's duct taped to my leg."

"I know what we should do, man. Let's use mind control to levitate large rocks and fling them into Denver's head."

"Remind me, which one of us has those kinds of powers?" asked the cat.

"None of us, but he doesn't know that," said the rabbit.

The duck dropped his head and slumped in the android's hand.

The agents continued to babble and wiggle but made no progress in getting free.

The duck straightened up and with renewed enthusiasm said, "I know how to stop this. We've got to confuse him. We've got to confuse Denver's positronic brain. Cause an overload or short circuit or something." The duck turned to the android chef. "Ask me a question. Any question."

"Like what?"

"Like, what's six times seven?"

"Forty-two."

"No, dude, ask *me* that question."

In a monotone voice, Denver asked, "What's six times seven?"

"Torrid ice cream cherry chess."

"What?"

"Dude, that's the correct answer. Six times seven does not equal forty-two, it equals torrid ice cream cherry chess. Isn't that right everybody?"

The pig and cow agreed with him. The duck was talking nonsense, and they agreed with him. What a bunch of weirdos.

"Whatever. I'll still pull your tail in six minutes and twelve seconds, regardless of your crazy Colbian math."

"Ask me another question."

"Do I have to?"

"Purple cucumber droppings."

"What?"

"Time to change the rotator cup in the duck's nose."

"Would you just stop it?"

"I'm getting to you, aye. Soon your circuitry will be smoking, dude. You forgot to balance the coffee filters in the aardvark's ears."

"That will not work. You cannot confuse my circuitry with this nonsense and stop me from pulling your tail. It's not like I'm happy about this either. How about I untie you guys? Maybe there's still time to run."

The android waiter hobbled on his broken legs to where the rabbit hung duct taped to the wall. As soon as he was free, the rabbit leaped at the android's head. Denver calmly swatted the rabbit away with a free hand.

"Sorry about that. Truly I am. It's this evil patch, not me. I can't let anything stop me from pulling the duck's tail."

The rabbit picked himself off the ground. "Understood, man. No worries."

Denver released me next. I sprang into hyperspeed and soon learned that taking duct tape off is much harder than putting it on. Eventually, I got into a rhythm and released the pig, cat, cow, and dog. I slammed into the barn to break out of hyperspeed.

The others formed a semi-circle around Denver and his hostage, the duck. As I shook off the sting of slamming into the barn, I caught a glimpse of Hector Spector. His eyes begged to be released from his duct tape bondage. "Should I release him?" I asked the cow.

"I suppose thho."

Before I jumped into hyperspeed, the pig stopped him. "I'll take care of it."

Hector grunted with every pull. The pig finished with a hearty rip of the tape across Hector's mouth. Hector responded with an ear-bleeding shrill.

The pig replaced the tape. Hector made no attempt to remove it.

The quiet didn't last long. An agent yelled at us from across the lawn.

"What does he want?" I asked the cow.

"He'thh their leader. Agent Orange. They would like to be freed."

"Should I do that?"

The dog ran back and forth between the cow and me. "Let's, let's, let's stop messing around and get, get out of here."

"There's no point, dog," said the cow. "We can't outrun the blast. There's only like two minutes left."

"I, I, I can dig a hole and we can all hide in there." Without waiting for a response, the dog started digging a hole.

"Two minutes and thirty-five seconds," said the android.

The dog disappeared into his hole, as a steady stream of rich black dirt flew out creating a growing mound.

"Would we be safe in the hole?" I asked.

"Not a chance," said the pig.

"Chicken, you should probably blast into your superspeed and save yourself," said the cow.

"I'm not going anywhere. We're going to figure out a way to stop this." My confidence in us stopping this was low, but I had no intention of abandoning my friends. I glanced around the dark fields, hoping the elephant was far away from here.

Agent Orange yelled a single word.

"I guess you should free them," said the cow.

I freed Agent Orange first and then the other humans. They huddled around the cow to get a briefing on the situation.

An agent screamed, "Hoozah!" and ran past the cow with a sword raised high over his head. He struck with his sword, aiming for the duck's neck.

Denver casually pulled the duck out of harm's way, while he grabbed the agent's legs with two of his free hands, yanking the agent to the ground. Denver then flipped the agent back and forth, banging him on the ground like a wet rag. After a couple of rounds of this punishment, he tossed the limp and bloody body toward the cow. Two other agents rushed Denver Omelet, who swatted them away as easily as he had the rabbit.

"Cow, please apologize for me. I really don't want to hurt anybody."

As the cow spoke to the agents in English, the fish finally joined the rest of us, swimming down from wherever he had floated off to. He looked at Denver and then at our somber faces. "Why is the chef here? And what's he doing with the duck?" He menacingly swam up to Denver. "He's going to butcher him!"

"I'm not going to butcher him. And I'm the head waiter, not a chef."

"That's a relief." The fish eased backwards.

"I'm just going to pull his tail in a minute forty-two seconds and blow us all up."

The fish swung his head to address all of us. "That's not good. We've got to stop him."

The dog popped his head out of his hole. "We, we tried. It, um, it can't be stopped. That's, that's why I'm digging a hole."

The fish swam up to the dog. "Relax. There's nothing to worry about. Remember when you looked into the future? You saw a giant mushroom. You haven't seen that yet, therefore, we live past this."

"Well, that confirms it." The dog's stammer had disappeared, which only happens when he's extremely excited, either good or bad. "Atomic Quack. Huge explosion. Giant mushroom cloud. Prophecy complete. Everyone, get in the hole. It's our only hope." He dove into his hole. The blizzard of dirt recommenced, which made it impossible for anyone to follow him.

"I thought we already encountered his mushroom prophecy," I said.

The fish scrunched his mouth to one side. "You're right. The white prison cells. Perhaps we should have him take a new look into the future."

The pig glanced at the dirt flying out of the dog's hole. "I say we let him keep digging."

"One minute, until I pull the duck's tail," said Denver.

"Anyone else have an idea on how to stop this?" I asked.

The others answered with shrugs, wrinkled lips, and head shakes. No one spoke for what felt like an hour but was only forty-five seconds.

The flood lights hummed.

Dirt sprayed out of the dog's hole.

"Fifteen seconds to go. You want me to count out the last 10 seconds?"

A couple of seconds passed before the pig muttered, "Sure."

Denver began the count down. "Ten, nine, eight, seven, six…"

I contemplated making a run for it, but I looked at the faces of my friends. It wouldn't be a life worth living without them.

"…five, four, three, two, one."

He gave the duck's tail a hard yank.

Chapter 20

I CLOSED MY EYES in anticipation of the Atomic Quack. But no explosion of vaporizing energy roasted me into ash. Instead, the duck emitted the cutest and wimpiest quiet burp.

"I told you we had nothing to worry about," said the fish.

I opened one eye. Denver Omelet, the android waiter, held three feathers in his hand. He'd done his job. He'd pulled the duck's tail. I opened the other eye. The barn, house, and surrounding farmlands had not been leveled. We were still alive!

Denver released his death grip.

The duck flopped to the ground.

As the rabbit rushed to his buddy's aid, the cat sauntered out of the barn.

"Where were you?" asked the pig.

Before she could answer that question, the duck said, "Nice job, dude. How did you stop the explosion?"

"My actions inside the barn bore no relevance to either triggering or preventing an Atomic Quack explosion. I am here to report that Mr. Steak&Eggs and his entourage are returning."

A crowd of angry agents had surrounded the cow, shouting question after question. She lifted her head above the agents and in Cheddarian asked, "Not that I'm complaining, but does anyone know why there wasn't a nuclear blast?"

"The cat did something," said the rabbit.

"I explicitly denied involvement in preventing an explosion."

"These agents are getting impatient. Can anyone explain why there was no Atomic Quack? I don't care if it'thh the truth."

The cat eased herself into her regal sitting position. "Did none of you contemplate how much enriched uranium can be stored inside a duck? I assume the answer is no, since if you had, you would have concluded, as I did, that the duck's tiny frame can only house a few ounces of enriched uranium."

"So, what's your point?" asked the pig.

"In case you have all forgotten, we ignited two Atomic Quacks restarting the ChaCha-QZ. The first blast reactivated the generator and then, for reasons unclear to me, the chicken pulled the duck's tail again, unleashing a second blast. This effectively drained the duck of his store of enriched uranium."

The pig walked up to the cat and leered down at her. "Why didn't you share that information with all of us earlier? We thought we were going to die."

"I assumed this information to be common knowledge. Your collective ignorance never ceases to amaze me. I will make a note to not underestimate this ignorance in the future."

The cow broke away from the agents and nudged the pig aside before he clobbered the cat.

"There was no explosion. Let'thh all be grateful for that."

"Fine," snorted the pig, as he relaxed his karate-clench hooves.

The cow headed back to the agents to explain the lack of a boom. I breathed a giant sigh of relief and went to tell the dog he could stop digging.

The fish swam through the pig's head as he assumed his lecturing-professor position. "We're missing the cat's point. Mr. Steak&Eggs is returning. We need to be prepared to fight."

"Thank you, fish. As I was saying, after confiscating our escape pod, Mr. Steak&Eggs and his entourage hovered above the planet, presumably to relish the nuclear explosion intended to destroy us all. Once the explosion failed to occur, they began their descent and now approach our location. I surmise they are returning to perform a root cause analysis on why the nuclear explosion did not occur. They will arrive in approximately two-point-seven seconds."

The high-pitched whirring of the approaching spacecraft grabbed everyone's attention.

The agents and the cow scrambled out of the craft's path. It landed behind Denver Omelet. A door slid open and after the ramp lowered, Mr. Steak&Eggs, Bagel, and the henchmen Sausage and Bacon strolled out.

"Why won't you creatures die already? Die, die, die! This is really getting aggravating. I have better things to do." Mr. Steak&Eggs walked up to the android, with Bagel behind him and the two goons behind her. "So? Why wasn't there a huge explosion?"

"Give me a second," replied Bagel, as she gestured for Sausage and Bacon to pick up the android. She ripped down the android waiter's back pants pocket to reveal a connector panel. She jammed a cable in, and then typed and poked commands into her handheld device.

"There's no need for this. I completed my programming as specified." Denver's violet colored android cheeks darkened to a red-infused mulberry shade.

"Hmmm. The sub-routine completed with no errors. He pulled the duck's tail. Maybe the duck is busted." Although she said she suspected the duck to be broken, she popped open a small panel in the middle of the android's back and began examining the wiring.

"Seriously! You've already run a full diagnostic. You know I completed the subroutine. I'm still holding the duck's tail feathers!" As if his point needed proof, Denver waved the feathers.

I soaked in the surreal scene. Mr. Steak&Eggs and company had not returned with extra laser gun toting goons. They never noticed we were free of our duct taped confinement. Yet none of us attacked. We just crowded around and watched Bagel debug the android.

The pig and cow's eyes met. They gave each other a knowing nod. The cow winked at Agent Orange and the three of them inched toward the purple aliens. The dog sat up and wiggled into position. Little-by-little, the duck shuffled behind Bagel. I scanned the grounds for any loose rolls of duct tape, thinking to myself, "I need a new gimmick. This duct tape trick is getting old." A new gimmick would need to wait until another day. I scooted over to grab a roll lying on the ground.

Our movements had not evaded Sausage and Bacon. One of them cleared his throat and said, "Umm, Boss. I don't think you've noticed, but the Earth creatures are no longer tied up."

"Not now, Sausage. Can't you see we're busy?"

"I'm Bacon, sir."

"Whoever you are, shut up. We're busy," shouted Mr. Steak&Eggs without taking his eyes off Denver. "Look at the droid. It's a mess. Its eyeball is dangling out. There's a giant hole in its gut. We never should have entrusted this job to him."

"We had no other choice, Steakie," said Bagel.

"Despite my injuries, I am fully capable of pulling a duck's tail. And I don't appreciate you calling me droid."

"I'll call you droid or anything else I decide to call you, droid."

Sausage had scanned our numbers. "Haven't you had enough of this revenge game? How about we get out of here, sir?"

Mr. Steak&Eggs ignored the comment and spoke to Bagel. "Should we give it another try?"

"Seriously, boss, it's about time we high-tail out of here," said Bacon.

Mr. Steak&Eggs poked his goons in the chest. "Do not interrupt me. I'm in the middle of something important." He turned back to Bagel. "What do you think?"

"Maybe. Let me check a couple more things first." Bagel tapped away on her handheld.

We inched closer.

"Boss, I don't think you realize that—"

"Sausage, I've had enough of your whining. We're busy and we're fed up with the interruptions. So, if you can't be quiet, I'm sending you back to the ship."

We had fanned out and encircled them.

"I'm still Bacon, sir, and if you would—"

"That's it, back to the ship you go." Mr. Steak&Eggs pointed in the opposite direction of the ship, but we all knew what he meant.

"Sir, we need them to stay. They're holding up the android." Bagel pulled a tiny circuit board out of the panel in the android's back. She held it up to Mr. Steak&Eggs. "Does that fuse look blown to you?"

"I'm not a technician. I have no idea. Let's ask the droid. Hey, droid, is your fuse blown?"

"I am also not a technician. I'm programmed to serve fine cuisine, not analyze blown fuses. And stop calling me droid. My name is Denver Omelet."

"Look here, you snarky little droid turd, tell us what's wrong with you or I'll have Bagel rip the wires out of you."

The cow decided it was time to intervene. She gave a nod to the pig, who tapped the former Vice President of Intergalactic Strategy and Synergies on the shoulder.

"Not now, I'm busy," said Mr. Steak&Eggs.

The pig spun the alien around and lifted him into the air with one hoof.

"Put me down, you stupid beast." His limbs flailed, but he could not break free of the pig's grasp. "Sausage. Bacon. Make yourselves useful. Do something."

They dropped the android, but before they could reach their weapons, the agents had the barrels of multiple guns pointed at their heads.

"Bagel, do something."

She surveyed the weapons pointed at her and said, "Like what?"

"Call for backup," said Mr. Steak&Eggs.

"There's no one left on the ship. We're the only four who stayed behind," said Bagel.

"They don't know that," said Mr. Steak&Eggs.

"We do now," said the cow.

"Don't we have a secret weapon? Where's our endless supply of diabolical backup plans and awesome unstoppable weapons? We can't lose to a bunch of barnyard freaks and fancy dressed humanoids. This can't be happening." He flailed all six limbs but couldn't break free of the pig's grip.

Agent Orange stepped up and rambled in angry tones that only the cow and his fellow humanoids understood.

The cow translated the statement into Cheddarian. "Mr. Steak&Eggs and accomplices, you are hereby under arrest for the theft and illegal intergalactic trafficking of Earth's cattle and dairy cow population."

"HA! These primitives think they have the authority to arrest ME? Release me at once!" said Mr. Steak&Eggs.

"They also say you're wanted on several outstanding warrants from numerous planetary and intergalactic authorities, including your home planet of Cheddar. You will be detained on Earth until they make arrangements for your transfer to the proper intergalactic authorities."

"You've got to be kidding me. What self-respecting intergalactic agency would taint their authority by associating with these primitives?" asked Mr. Steak&Eggs, as he increased his wiggling. "Now release me,"

The pig released him, in a manner of speaking, by slamming Mr. Steak&Eggs to the ground.

I figured it was time to spring into action. A second later, I had the Cheddarians mummified in duct tape and had already broken out of hyperspeed.

"Not the frickin' gray tape again."

The pig slapped a strip of duct tape over Mr. Steak&Eggs mouth.

***

WITH THE ACTION AT an end, I searched the skies for my lost elephant friend, once again forgetting he would only be visible to me at hyperspeed. I contemplated a walk to my favorite hill when I spotted the cow and Agent Orange engaged in a serious conversation with the other animals huddled around. The cow caught my eye and motioned with her long snout for me to join them. The walk to my favorite hill would have to wait. Besides, the view at night would be limited.

As I approached, the duck had waddled up to the cow. "Dude, did you confirm they're Men in Black?"

"No confirmation needed, man. They are totally Men in Black."

Agent Orange gave a quizzical glance to the rabbit and duck. He turned toward the cow and, via a palms-up-shoulder-shrug, asked for a translation.

The cow rolled her eyes and translated.

Agent Orange's perpetual scowl flashed into a smile as he shook his head.

"They are not Men in Black," said the cow.

"Of course, they're going to deny being Men in Black, dude."

"His denial only confirms it for me, man."

"Anyway, he claims the intergalactic authorities are on their way and suggests it'thh best we hide in the underground lab."

"Why?" asked the pig.

"They're concerned French Toast may file a legal claim of ownership on uthh, thho they want uthh to stay out of sight."

Hector Spector interrupted the discussion as he banged into the cow and off the pig while making a mad dash for his white pickup truck, detailed with black cow spots. He still had duct tape covering his mouth. Agents intercepted him and led him toward a black SUV.

"I bet they flashy thing him, man."

"Dude, I'm surprised they haven't done it already."

"Should we, should we follow Hector's lead and, and make a run for it?"

"No. Right now, it'thh important we stay out of sight. We can discuss our options in the lab."

I expected the pig to argue further, but he accepted the cow's direction and headed toward the barn with the rest of us. A black suit waited for us inside the barn, holding Denver Omelet.

The cow turned to the pig. "They want Denver out of sight as well. Can you carry him down?"

The pig snorted and scowled, but still grabbed the android from the black suit.

"Thank you, sir. Your assistance in my time of need is much obliged," said Denver.

We took turns sliding down the ramp. Despite the removal of the forty-something cows, the lab still felt cramped. I blamed the low ceiling. The pig propped Denver up in a stall, while the cat jumped onto the lab tables to examine Hector's equipment. The rest of us scattered ourselves about the lab.

The cow slid down last. After staggering herself to a stable position, she cleared her throat. "Animals. Team meeting. There'thh something for uthh to discuss."

As the ramp retracted, we assembled around her. I sensed apprehension but detected no fear in the cow's voice. Regardless, the rarity of team meetings had me concerned.

"Cow, what are we discussing?" asked the pig, as he scanned the room. I knew the look. He was checking for escape routes.

"Agent Orange asked uthh to join their secret agency."

"Dude, what's to discuss, other than when do we get our black suits?"

"And what our superhero names are going to be, man."

The duck and the rabbit turned to face each other. "DUDE! We're going to be Men in Black!" They did a wing to paw high five.

"Man, I hope we meet K."

"For like the fifth time, they are not Men in Black," said the cow, along with a shake of her head.

The rabbit elbowed his buddy. "If they're not MiB, then they must be Sector Seven, man."

"That means we'll be working with Bumblebee, dude!!"

The cow bowed her head and raised a leg, in an attempt to perform a face-hoof, but she lacked the flexibility and joint mobility to complete the move. "Those agencies are not real."

"Dude, that's exactly what they want you to think."

"It'thh not worth my time to explain. The point is, they believe our powers will be a valuable asset in their mission to defend Earth from alien attacks."

The rabbit and duck's eyes bulged as their heads turned toward each other.

"OMG, you know what this means, man."

In unison, they said, "They're SHIELD. We're gonna be AVENGERS!!!"

They locked their paws and wings and hopped in a circle.

"That means Agent Orange is really Nick Fury. We met Nick Fury, man."

"No way, dude. He doesn't have an eye patch. He's Phil Coulson."

"Of course. He's the one who recruits the Avengers, man."

"And, dude, he's recruiting us!!"

They spun into the cow's legs and tumbled to the dirt floor, where they remained motionless.

"Dude, this is the best day ever."

"Idiots," said the pig as he stepped forward, shaking his head. "Cow, let me guess. They want us to come back to their secret base."

"Yethh. Agent Orange insists it'thh the safest place for uthh, even if we don't join their agency."

"And you believe him. They're taking us to Area 51, where they'll strap us to autopsy tables next to the Roswell aliens in less than an hour."

The dog shuffled into a crouch behind me and whispered, "I, I'm not familiar with the Roswell aliens, but, but, I don't want to be strapped to an autopsy table."

"I have Agent Orange'thh assurance that we will not be harmed. He said if we decided not to join the agency, they'd find uthh a secluded farm where we can stay as long as we like."

"And then he suggested we hide in this underground lab. It's a trap. There's no way out of here. They'll be gassing us any second now." The pig scaled a post and yanked on the raised ramp.

"Relax." The cow nodded toward a green button affixed to the post. "We just need to push that button to lower the ramp. We're not trapped."

The pig scaled down the post and tapped the green button. The ramp lowered. Satisfied with the result, he tapped the button again and the ramp clanged back up.

"Dude, there's nothing to worry about." The rabbit and duck still laid on their backs, motionless.

"We're about to become superheroes, man. Your only worry is what your superhero name will be."

The duck popped off the floor and addressed the cow. "I've been thinking about our superhero names for a while. Dude, what do you feel about the name Supercow?"

Her mouth wriggled as if she chewed cud. I presumed that to be her thinking face.

"I like the sound of that. Thhupercow."

"Excellent. Your official superhero name is Supercow," said the duck.

I got caught up in the excitement. "I want a superhero name, too. How about Super Chicken?"

"Sorry, man, no way," said the rabbit. "You can't be Super Chicken."

"What!?"

"Already used, dude. There was a cartoon TV show named Super Chicken." The duck then let out a series of off-key musical chicken balking, which I now know to be the famed rally cry of the cartoon character known as Super Chicken.

"Copyright laws, man."

I would later learn there is a Super Cow cartoon character as well, but they didn't shoot down the Supercow name.

The pig crossed his front hooves across his chest and glared around the room. "Hold up. This is supposed to be a meeting to discuss joining this so-called agency, not a superhero names brainstorming session."

"Dude, you'll change your tune once you hear my name." The duck struck a wings-on-hips-head-held-high pose. "I'm gonna be Ultimate Crazy Metal Duckdude."

"What!? Man, are you serious? What kind of superhero name is that?"

"A totally awesome one."

"Man, whatever."

"I suppose you can do better? So, let's hear it, dude. What's your superhero name going to be?"

"I'm still thinking, man. Give me a minute."

The pig rubbed his forehead and looked up at the fish. "Help me out. Tell them these humans are not our friends."

The fish floated above, scrunching his mouth from side-to-side. "We may not know if they are friend or foe, but they have not proven to be our enemy. At this point, they might be the closest thing to a friend we've got." The fish dove to eye-level with the rabbit and duck. "I was thinking of going with Phil, Phil Phishman."

"Man, I love it."

"Love how you built on the name Sausage gave you. Awesome job, dude."

That gave me an idea. "Chickenman. How about Chickenman?"

"I'm pretty sure there already was a Chickenman," said the rabbit, wasting no time shooting down my new name idea.

"Chickenman was a radio series, dude."

"Oh sure, you shoot down Chickenman, but you love Phishman. Come on!"

"Get over it, dude."

"Yeah, move on, man."

"What if I went with Christine Chickenman?"

"I think you'd still have copyright issues, dude."

"Besides, you don't want to be Chicken*MAN*. You're a woman. Christine Chickenman is like Supergirl being called Sally Superman, man."

"It makes no sense, dude."

They made a valid argument, but it still frustrated me to have my names struck down, while others got quickly accepted and congratulated.

The pig's breathing had become strained, and his front hooves had formed into fists. "Enough with the superhero names! We're in danger here. Cat, surely you agree it's dangerous to go with them."

The cat had snuck back onto a lab table. She fiddled with a pair of headphones and responded without turning her head. "With a few modifications, I believe Hector's equipment could be used to download the English language into all of us."

The pig threw his front hooves in the air. "What does that have to do with the agency imprisoning us?"

After an arching back stretch, the cat asked the cow, "Do you believe this agency has the authority to confiscate Hector's equipment and provide assistance in acquiring tools necessary to make said modifications?"

"I believe Agent Orange would support that. He would love it if all of uthh understood English."

"Then I support going with this secret agency."

"Excellent, dude. Another vote for becoming superheroes."

Ultimate Crazy Metal Duckdude and the rabbit flew and hopped onto the cat's table.

"So, what name are you going with, man?"

The cat continued fiddling with the headphones. "Uninterested. A so-called super-cool superhero name is of no importance to me."

"Fine, we'll come up with a name for you, dude."

"It's got to be something techie sounding, man."

"Dude, how about Geeky Kitty?"

"As I said, I'm not interested in having a superhero name," said the cat.

"Online Feline," suggested the rabbit.

"Please stop this nonsense."

"Dude, you've got them antenna whiskers which work kind of like a satellite. How can we use that?"

"How about Satellite Cat, man?"

The cat pretended to ignore the pair as she pawed at a device resembling a food processor.

"I like it, dude. We can call you Sat Cat for short."

She hissed and turned toward the pair. "I will agree to the name Satellite Cat, only so you will cease this insipid activity of inventing superhero names for me. But I insist on one condition. No one ever refers to me as Sat Cat."

"Done," said Ultimate Crazy Metal Duckdude.

Meanwhile, the pig stomped over to Denver Omelet's stall. "Am I crazy? Going with Agent Orange is like volunteering to be held prisoner."

Denver shrugged his shoulders, which caused him to topple over. The pig propped him up again. "My only thought is if they could repair my legs, I would be happy to accept a job assisting them with their fine dining needs."

A squeal came out of the pig. A sound he hadn't made since Dr. Hash Browns enhanced him many years ago. "Why am I the only one who sees the danger here?"

The dog rubbed across the pig's hind legs. "I'm, I'm concerned, too. Scared, even. I, I don't, I don't want to be autopsied. Plus, Dr. Hash Browns is waiting for us. We need to get back to the space station."

"We lost communications to the space station soon after our last departure." said Satellite Cat, who examined the wires and sensors Hector had connected to a metal vegetable strainer. "My several attempts to contact Dr. Hash Browns have been unacknowledged."

The pig crossed his forelegs. "Why didn't you share this information earlier?"

"Since I received no response, I had nothing to report." She tapped at a connector with a single extracted claw.

"I have other news regarding Dr. Hash Brownthh." Supercow's stare danced between the ceiling and floor. "Agent Orange reported that Dr. Hash Browns has been detained under suspicion of being a co-conspirator in Mr. Steak&Eggs' crimes."

"If I had *that* level of information, I would have shared it earlier," said Satellite Cat.

"But, but…, he's innocent. He hates Mr. Steak&Eggs. We, we have to save him." The dog had walked up to the cow, who chose to examine ceiling rafters instead of look at him.

"Agent Orange assured me the charges would eventually get dropped and when they are, he will make every effort to bring Dr. Hash Browns here to Earth."

"That's classic captor behavior. Convince you there is no one coming to save you, so you have no choice but to agree to their demands."

Supercow dropped her ceiling gazing and eyed the pig. "Pig, how about we make a deal? We peacefully go with them, but at the first sign of trouble, we unleash our fury. These humans are no match for our powers. There's no way they can defeat your strength and laser eye, or the chicken's super speed. But initially, let'thh cooperate. See where it goes."

The pig surveyed the rest of us, like an army sergeant sizing up the new recruits. He unfolded his forelegs and pointed a hoof at us. "When the time comes, you all better be ready to fight. Do you understand me? You better be ready to fight."

Supercow, Phil Phishman, the dog, and I nodded our agreement.

"I'll do my part to help as well," said Denver. "Of course, given my current state, I'm not sure what help I'll be."

The pig walked over to the rabbit and Ultimate Crazy Metal Duckdude, who stopped their reenactment of the Thor and Iron Man fight scene. "I want to hear you two promise you'll fight the suits if it comes to that."

"No worries, dude."

"We'll be ready, man."

The pair returned to their mock fight, as the pig hrmphed and glanced at Satellite Cat. I expected him to insist she make the same pledge, but he didn't bother.

"Thho, are we good?"

The pig snorted a yes, then shoved a lab table out of the way to clear space for pushups.

Chapter 21

THE PIG COMPLETED ONLY two sets of pushups before the ramp came down. Two agents stood at the top of the ramp. They motioned us to come up. The gesture by itself was not menacing. In fact, it bordered on a friendly wave to join them. The intimidation factor came from the M-1 rifles in their hands.

As the others made their way up the ramp, the pig grabbed my wing and pulled me aside. "I'm counting on you. At the first sign of trouble, look for my signal, then duct tape these fancy pants jerks. Got it?"

I acknowledged with a nod. Honor and pride swelled in my belly. He had pulled no one else aside. If we ended up in a jam, the pig valued my skills above the others. As the black suits marched us to the waiting semi-trailer truck, I snagged a couple rolls of duct tape and stuffed them under my wings.

The rabbit and Ultimate Crazy Metal Duckdude boarded first, with the pig bringing up the rear. He hand-carried Denver Omelet out of the barn, but before boarding, he handed him to an agent. As the dog and I settled into seats on the bench, the giant metal doors clanked closed. The truck rolled down the gravel driveway and bounced onto the road. That's when I realized I'd forgotten to grab my painting. I popped up, ready to scream that we had to stop the truck. A roll of duct tape spun across the floor.

"What's um, what's a matter?" asked the dog, before he picked up the roll with his teeth.

"I forgot my painting. Dog Playing Chess. It's out in the field somewhere."

He handed me the tape and put a paw on my shoulder. After a pause, he said, "I'm, I'm sure these agents can get, get you some new art supplies. You can, you can start a new masterpiece. Perhaps, The Flying Chicken."

I appreciated the dog's comfort, but that painting and I had been through a lot. A new painting would never have the same sentiment.

Ultimate Crazy Metal Duckdude landed in front of us, abruptly ending my grieving.

"You dudes never picked superhero names."

I transitioned from the sorrow of lost artwork to the pain of having all my proposed superhero names rejected. "Hyper Chicken. What do you think of Hyper Chicken?"

"I like the reference to hyperspeed, but the name is taken, man," said the rabbit.

"That's a character in Futurama, dude."

"Well, I don't, I don't want a superhero name," said the dog. "In fact, I, I don't, I don't want to be a superhero. It, it..., it sounds dangerous."

"Dude, being a superhero is gonna be awesome."

"Why can't we just, just go live on a, on a beach or some remote cabin in the woods?"

"Haven't you ever dreamed you were a superhero saving the world?" asked the rabbit.

"No." The dog cocked his head and stared at the opposite wall. I presumed this to be the dog's thinking face. "But, but a couple of years ago, I started writing a novel."

"A superhero novel?" asked the duck.

"No. A detective story. A noir. Starring Captain Cooper, a down-and-out ex-police captain turned private eye." No stammering, so I knew the dog enjoyed thinking about his book.

He kept his novel writing a secret from the rest, but I knew. I begged him to let me read it, but he insisted it needed to be polished first. He secured the file with a biometric lock, so my attempts to secretly read it failed.

"Of course, I, I never, I never finished it. And, and it needs lots of edits." The stammer had returned.

"I think we're on to something, dude. Your superhero name should be Captain Cooper," said Ultimate Crazy Metal Duckdude.

"It doesn't, it doesn't sound very superheroish."

"But I like it. And, man, it sure beats Ultimate Crazy Metalbrain Duckdork."

"Ultimate Crazy Metal Duckdude! And we're still waiting for your superhero name?"

"Reinhold Rabbit."

"What?! Reinhold Rabbit. Give me a break. Like that's going to strike fear into bad guys everywhere. NOT."

"And Ultimate Psycho Dorkman is?"

"Ultimate Crazy Metal Duckdude is a name that will strike fear into the hearts of bad guys across the universe. Look out! It's Ultimate Crazy Metal Duckdude. Bad guys, run for your lives."

"Whatever, man. The point is, I like the name Captain Cooper."

"And I like the story behind the name, dude."

The newly named Captain Cooper's tail wagged with joy.

With Captain Cooper and Reinhold Rabbit now named, I truly felt the pressure. I had to come up with a name they couldn't reject. "How about Flash, because I move so fast? I'm like a flash going by."

"Man, surely you can't be serious?"

Of course, I was serious. I was always serious. In fact, I didn't know how to joke around or crack wise.

"She's serious, dude. She has no idea who Flash is."

"I guess it shouldn't surprise me, man. And it's a good name for a superhero with super-speed, which is why it's already taken."

"How do you guys know all this?"

They both shrugged.

"We watch a lot of shows, man."

"Well, I give up."

"No rush, dude."

"You'll come up with something, man."

Reinhold Rabbit and Ultimate Crazy Metal Duckdude bounced away and didn't sit still for the rest of the ride. They hopped and flew from bench to bench, discussing what catch phrases they were going to use as they battled alongside the

Avengers and arguing over who is the leader of the Avengers, Iron Man or Captain America.

The pig also had trouble sitting still and even when he sat, at least one leg bounced like an over caffeinated metronome. About halfway through the two-hour drive, he begged Captain Cooper to look into the future. He finally agreed, only after the pig's numerous promises not to sedate him.

"Rainbow rain. That's what I see."

Though we all agreed this sounded like a good thing, it failed to ease the pig's anxiety. He asked Phil Phishman to check outside the truck, but Supercow denied the requests. Agent Orange gave her strict instructions to keep the fish inside the truck and thanks to the smooth ride, he never flew out.

As the ride dragged on, my thoughts returned to the whereabouts of the elephant. I imagined him perched atop a mountain peak, in his cross-legged Ganesh pose. A mystic guru waiting to provide wisdom to anyone who could actually see him.

Eventually, the semitruck came to a final stop. A heavy clunk, followed by a whoosh of air escaping the braking system, indicated we had reached our final destination. The cab doors opened and closed.

The pig marched to a stance at the trailer doors. He cracked his neck twice. He adjusted his hoofing.

Reinhold Rabbit and Ultimate Crazy Metal Duckdude scurried to his side. Their feet couldn't stay still.

"Hey, man, you never picked a superhero name."

"Now is not the time." The pig clenched his fist and kept his eyes on the door.

"If you don't pick a name, the public will pick one for you, dude."

"That's never good, man. You'll end up with a name like Zuckered."

The pig glanced at the pair and then glared at the rest of us as we slowly rose to our feet. "Get ready. This is the moment of truth. Stay sharp. Keep an eye out for trouble. Shout out if you're in danger. And we stick together. Don't let them separate us. Got it?"

I wanted to shout, "Got it!" but didn't want to do it alone. We should say it in unison.

Satellite Cat completed her post nap stretches, while Supercow sauntered up to the pig in silence. Captain Cooper and I followed her, with Phil Phishman swimming above us. None of us said a word.

"I didn't hear you. GOT IT?"

"Got it!" bellowed Reinhold Rabbit and Ultimate Crazy Metal Duckdude in unison, though I doubt they understood what they 'got'. They were just excited to shout something.

"Pig, relax. It'thh going to be fine. Fish, pop outside there and check out what's going on?"

"His name is Phil Phishman," said Reinhold Rabbit.

"Right." Supercow rolled her eyes. "Phil, see what's out there."

"Sure thing." He swam past us and through the trailer doors.

Ultimate Crazy Metal Duckdude looked up at the pig. "Dude, I think your superhero name should be Pirate Pig. Because of the eye patch thing."

"Good use of alliteration. I like it, man."

"What do you think, dude?"

The pig huffed and gave the pair a brief sideways glare. "Stay focused. Who knows what we're about to face."

"Dude, I'll take that as a yes."

"Pirate Pig it is, man."

Pirate Pig groaned and his fists tightened.

Phil Phishman popped back through the trailer door. "Looks like a military compound. Lots of barracks, military trucks, a few tanks and even a couple of airplanes."

Reinhold Rabbit and Ultimate Crazy Metal Duckdude bounced in front of Phil Phishman.

"Did you spot any Avengers, man?"

"We'll settle for an Antman sighting, dude."

"All I saw were humans in black military uniforms or black suits." Phil Phishman turned to address Supercow. "I think they've forgotten about us. There's no one near our truck. The cab is empty. People are walking past paying no attention to the truck whatsoever."

Supercow strolled back to the front of the trailer and laid down. "See, nothing to worry about. We're perfectly safe."

Pirate Pig snorted but said nothing and continued to stare at the back door with his unpatched eye.

Captain Cooper's head swung back and forth between the cow and pig. "Chicken, what's going on? I mean, I mean, I don't understand. Why did they leave us here? Did they forget about us? But how could they forget about us? And why is the cow so calm and sure we're safe, while the pig prepares us to fight? I don't know who to believe. What should we do?"

The same questions ran through my mind, but I didn't let on in fear of increasing Captain Cooper's anxiety. I sat down in hopes the dog would follow suit. "There's nothing for us to do but wait."

He continued to pace. "Wait? I can't stand waiting. I need to know what's happening. I need to know now. Are we going to become lab experiments like the pig says, or are we going to become superhero agents like the rabbit and duck believe? It's impossible to know for sure, yet they all seem so sure they're right. They can't all be right. Don't you understand how frustrating this is? And all you can say is relax and wait? Well, I can't relax, and I won't wait."

Captain Cooper sprinted toward the back of the trailer. He leaped. He twisted sideways before crashing into the doors. The doors rattled. A wave of rippling metal ran down both sides of the semi as the boom echoed inside the truck bed.

He scrambled to his feet. "Let us out!!" he yelled, as he prepared for another run at the door.

Supercow stood up. "Dog. Stop it. That isn't helping. Besides, they don't understand Cheddarian."

"You speak their language. Yell for them to let us out."

"They'll let uthh out soon enough. We just need to be patient."

In case the pig was right, I figured it best to be prepared. I double checked my grip on the rolls of duct tape. Then I noticed a lever near the bottom of the door. "Has anyone tried to open the door?"

"It locks from the outside," said Pirate Pig.

"Are you sure? Did you try that lever over there?" I asked.

Pirate Pig scrunched his snout as he examined the lever. After a brief moment of contemplation, he pushed the lever down. The double doors popped open wide enough for Reinhold Rabbit and Ultimate Crazy Metal Duckdude to zoom out. Pirate Pig pulled one door closed and cracked the other so we could peek out.

A half-dozen humans in black military uniforms milled around a row of tanks on the far end of an expanse of asphalt. At the entrance to a two-story box-shaped office building to our left stood a team of male and female human agents, in black suits, white shirts, and black ties. Agent Orange broke from the group once he spotted Reinhold Rabbit and Ultimate Crazy Metal Duckdude. He sprinted toward them with his hands held high.

Supercow pushed past Pirate Pig and knocked the double doors wide open. She acknowledged Agent Orange, mistaking his universal gesture of stop as a greeting. After a quick shrug, Satellite Cat and I followed her.

Agent Orange quickened his pace once he saw Supercow. He kept his eyes on the others as he spoke to her.

Supercow relayed Agent Orange's message to huddle up, but only Supercow, Satellite Cat, and I did so.

Reinhold Rabbit and Ultimate Crazy Metal Duckdude continued to wander down the road with their heads swiveling around, soaking in everything like a kid's first trip to Walt Disney World.

Phil Phishman drifted off to the right toward a set of large warehouses.

Pirate Pig remained inside the truck bed, surveying the area through a crack in the doors. Captain Cooper cowered behind him, struggling to decide his next move.

Pirate Pig poked his head out of the truck. "Cow, what's going on?"

"Nothing to worry about. There'thh just a delay in our accommodations."

"They must need extra operating tables, so they have one for all of us."

"Pig, relax. They are not going to harm uthh."

Agent Orange waved to a couple of agents across the street, who readied their weapons and marched toward us.

Pirate Pig clapped his front hooves. "Here we go."

I readied a roll of duct tape.

The pig sprang out of the truck. He landed with his front hooves clenched into fists and shuffled into a boxer's stance. "Chicken, it's showtime. Let's take care of these jerks."

I prepared to launch into hyperspeed, but the cow held up a hoof. "No, it's not. Stop."

I froze, unsure if I should listen to the pig or the cow. But by standing still and not jumping into hyperspeed to immobilize the agents in duct tape, I had done the cow's bidding.

Agent Orange ran toward the agents while performing a series of frantic hand gestures. The agents lowered their weapons and jogged over to corral Reinhold Rabbit and Ultimate Crazy Metal Duckdude. Another pair of agents walked up to Phil Phishman with their mouths draped open.

Agent Orange's eyes fixated on Pirate Pig as he engaged in a dialog with Supercow. He finished with an exaggerated follow-me arm wave and headed toward the warehouses.

"Everyone, follow me. We're moving out." Supercow motioned with her head to follow Agent Orange.

Pirate Pig glared at Supercow through a squinted eye, but lowered his fists and trotted a safe distance behind us.

Captain Cooper looked around the empty truck several times before he jumped down and scrambled to catch up to us.

Reinhold Rabbit and Ultimate Crazy Metal Duckdude bounced up to Supercow.

"Dude, which Avenger are we going to meet first?"

"Man, I hope it's the Hulk."

"We're not meeting any Avengers. Agent Orange is taking us to our barracks," said Supercow.

Pirate Pig surveyed the area with every step, taking numerous glances at the armed agents walking behind us. "Everyone, stay alert. Be ready to attack on my order."

The semitruck was parked in the middle of the rectangular-shaped base. We walked towards a set of warehouses, barracks, and an airplane hangar. Behind us was the entrance gate, office buildings, and parking lots full of military trucks and black SUVs. I assumed the prefab boxy buildings could be torn down, moved, and rebuilt in a matter of hours. Every building had been painted the same drab gray color, and none of them stood taller than two stories. A chain-linked fence adorned with barbed wire enclosed the base. The surrounding flat prairie fields stretched for miles before reaching far-off forests.

With no clear danger in sight, I relaxed my hold on the duct tape. That's when Reinhold Rabbit and Ultimate Crazy Metal Duckdude appeared at my sides. They didn't need to say a word. I knew what they wanted.

"I'm going to go for simplicity. Call me The Chicken."

"Sorry, man. No can do."

"How can you shoot down a name like The Chicken? That's basically what you've been calling me."

"It's taken, dude," said Ultimate Crazy Metal Duckdude.

"By that mascot, who started out at the Padre games. At first, he was the San Diego Chicken. I loved that guy, man."

"He was a riot, dude. But he left San Diego and performed all over the place."

"Since he left San Diego, he had to, like, drop the San Diego part of his name," said Reinhold Rabbit.

"Thus becoming..., The Chicken, dude."

I sighed. "I'm officially out of ideas."

"You could go with Chicken Dude, dude."

"I'm not going with Chicken Dude!"

"How about Cool Eggy Chicken?" asked Reinhold Rabbit.

"Oh, please. I'm not going around being called Cool Eggy Chicken."

"I got it, dude. What if we shorten it to Cool Egg?"

"Or you could always go with Half-Baked." The pig chuckled to himself. He still kept his distance from the pack but was apparently close enough to hear our conversation.

I didn't like the name Cool Egg, but it beat being called Half-Baked. "Fine. I'll be Cool Egg. Perhaps I'll grow to love it."

"Excellent. Cool Egg it is, man."

By this time, we approached the end of the barracks and warehouses. Supercow nodded toward the hangar. "*Our* barracks are around this last building."

Agent Orange motioned for us to go look.

Pirate Pig held up a hoof. "Hold up." He secured his footing and motioned to Phil Phishman. "Go check it out."

Phil Phishman swam past the building. He hung in the air, swiveling his head. "There's nothing but a barn and prairie."

The rest of us poured around the edge of the warehouse.

"Is, is, um, barracks another word for barn?" asked Captain Cooper.

Supercow finished her conversation with Agent Orange before turning to us. "Barracks is not another word for barn, but the barn is our barracks. Agent Orange thought we would feel at home in a barn."

"That's a bit condescending," said Phil Phishman.

"This is a clear example of species profiling, man," said Reinhold Rabbit.

"Has the dude ever slept in a barn?" asked Ultimate Crazy Metal Duckdude.

"They're, they're drafty and cold in the winter, and, and..., hot and humid in the summer. And, and, and they smell bad."

"Agent Orange also said they want to house us in the barn in case there are outside visitors. It won't be suspicious to find a bunch of barnyard animals in a barn." Supercow began walking toward our new home.

"This actually makes sense. It provides us a solid cover," said Pirate Pig, as he followed her. "I'm not ready to totally trust these black suited humans yet, but a barn beats being strapped to an operating table in a basement autopsy room."

"I still find it insulting," I said.

"Agreed, man," said Reinhold Rabbit, even though he began hopping toward the barn.

The rest of us followed.

Agent Orange sprinted ahead of us and with the flare of a magician presenting their prestige, he slid open the barn doors.

We gathered around the entrance. A musty, stale odor, along with a lack of manure stench, told me the barn had not housed animals in several years. Agent Orange flipped the light switch. Only two of the four bare ceiling light bulbs worked, leaving the far end of the barn dark.

Supercow and Pirate Pig strolled into the open area to the right of the barn doors. Despite a lack of clutter, the inside looked as rundown as the outside. The dirt floor made sweeping pointless, and the prime years of the bare wood posts and stall frames occurred decades ago.

Captain Cooper scraped a paw on the dirt floor before proceeding in. "I, I didn't, I didn't expect luxury accommodations, but a bed would be nice."

Reinhold Rabbit and Ultimate Crazy Metal Duckdude bounced in after him.

"And, dude, a TV."

"And a gaming console, with lots of games, man."

"And an espresso machine, dude."

They stopped a third of the way in. From there, stalls lined both sides.

"Dudes, where does that ladder go?"

The rest of us had to move closer to see the ladder hidden in the darkness.

"That goes to the loft," said Supercow.

Their mouths dropped open, and their eyes grew big. They glanced at each other and, in unison, the pair said, "Dibs."

"Dudes, the loft is ours."

The two sprinted up the ladder. I followed their movements via the patter of paws and feet as they scurried about in the loft.

Satellite Cat waltzed into the room on the left. The room stretched twice as long as a stall. It had floor to ceiling walls, a large picture window looking into the barn, a smaller window with a view of the prairie, and featured a traditional door. The room had originally been an office. The only remaining contents: a sturdy army surplus metal-frame desk and matching chair from the 1940s.

She popped her head out the door. "While currently far from adequate, we will convert this into our computer lab. We will need additional power, ceiling cable racks, temperature-controlled heating and cooling, multiple computer cabinets, and internet access. I will provide a separate list of required computer and tech equipment. And that desk has to go. Oh, and we'll need Hector Spector's equipment."

Supercow relayed the requests to Agent Orange. He gave a brief response, patted her neck, and departed the barn.

"He said he'd see what he can do."

Reinhold Rabbit and Ultimate Crazy Metal Duckdude jumped down from the second floor.

"Tell that Agent Coulson dude we need skateboards."

"And PVC pipes."

"And wood. Lots of wood, dude."

"And nails, and power tools, and screws, and all kinds of stuff, man."

"We're gonna build a skate park up there, dudes."

The cat groaned, then said, "I will require noise canceling headphones."

"Let'thh settle in first before making our demands. There are six stalls. Since Reinhold and Crazy Duckdude claimed the loft, that leaves a stall a piece for the rest of uthh."

We moseyed toward the stalls as a group.

"You know what we really need to do, man?"

"Dudes, now that we all have super-cool superhero names, we need a group name. Like, Super Dudes."

"I have to thhay no to calling us all dudes," said Supercow as she claimed the stall next to the computer lab.

"Farm Animal Freakazoids," proposed Ultimate Crazy Metal Duckdude.

"I've got to veto that name as well," said Supercow as she sniffed the corners of her stall.

"How about Teenage Mutant Ninja BarnYard Freaks?" asked Ultimate Crazy Metal Duckdude.

"No. We haven't been teenagers for decades," said Pirate Pig, walking into the stall next to the cow.

"But I like the BarnYard part," I said.

"All right. How about Mutant X BarnYard Freaks of Doom?" asked Ultimate Crazy Metal Duckdude.

"I, I don't, I don't want to be a mutant, or a... or a freak."

"Agreed," said Supercow. "Something simpler and without the word freak or mutant in it. Something more positive."

"Hmm. How about Rescuing Barnyard... Animals?" asked Reinhold Rabbit.

"Better, but it doesn't have a ring to it." Supercow settled into her stall and laid down.

"Okay, how about BarnYard Dudes!!"

"You consistently fail to comprehend we are not all 'dudes'," said the cat as she claimed the stall across from the cow. "A group name containing the word 'dude' in any form is unacceptable."

Ultimate Crazy Metal Duckdude's shoulders slumped. "Understood, dudes, but I'm running out of ideas. Anybody else can chime in here."

Phil Phishman grabbed the stall next to the cat, leaving the last two for Captain Cooper and me.

As the dog and I surveyed our rooms, I suggested, "How about BarnYard Heroes?"

"I love it!" shouted Supercow from her stall.

"Oh sure, you love her idea. You hated all of mine." He continued to sulk as he and Reinhold Rabbit climbed the ladder.

But to me, it felt like redemption.

"How does everybody else feel about BarnYard Heroes?" asked Supercow.

The others grumbled weak approvals and half-hearted endorsements from their new stalls.

"Well, I helped. I came up with the BarnYard part," said Ultimate Crazy Metal Duckdude, looking down from the top of the ladder.

"Are you objecting?" asked Supercow.

"No. I like it, dude. It's actually a really cool name."

"Anyone else object?" asked the cow.

No one objected.

"There you have it then. We are officially the BarnYard Heroes," said the cow. "Now, we should all get some rest. Agent Orange said we start our training at O-five-hundred hours, which is apparently five a.m."

"Dude!! We're going to be Avengers!"

"We're gonna be better than Avengers. We're BarnYard Heroes, man."

Chapter 22

As Agent Orange had warned, our training started early the next day. When we returned to the barn after our first day of training, a surprise awaited me. Agents had found my masterpiece and had hung it on my stall wall. As thrilled as I was to be reunited with my art, I immediately took it down. I needed to finish it before putting it on display.

In less than two days, we dropped our so-called 'cool' superhero names. The agency had a strict policy of stripping all previous identities. The human agents picked colors for names, and Agent Orange preferred us continuing to call ourselves the dog, the chicken, etc. He didn't even want us referring to ourselves as the BarnYard Heroes. Except for the rabbit and duck, we happily returned to referring to each by our animal types.

Despite its rustic motif and draftiness, within a couple of weeks, we made the barn feel like home. I got art supplies and decorated my stall with my paintings. After the dog acquired a chess table, we turned my stall into an art studio/board-game room and shared his living space. The cow moved the antique metal office desk and its matching rickety chair into her stall. She believed having an office in our barn gave the impression of professionalism. It just made me wonder why she had a chair she couldn't possibly sit in. The fish made no changes and spent his time swimming around the compound doing whatever it was he did.

The rabbit and duck completed their loft skate park and began construction on a half-pipe behind the barn. Their noise drove the cat insane. She insisted she needed a quiet and dust free environment to complete the translator. How she crammed the dozens of computers and multitude of electronics, along with Hector's equipment, into that tiny room mystified me. And new equipment arrived daily. Hector stopped by twice to help install his equipment. His hands shook the entire visit, and he never looked the cow in the eye, despite her translating his every word. We heard he returned to his farm, sold his cows, and burned all his cow paraphernalia.

Home gym equipment took up most of the pig's stall, even though he did his workouts in the agency's weight room and spent most of his free time with the human agents. The rest of us kept to the barn and only interacted with the agents during training sessions.

Agent Orange relayed news that the charges against Dr. Hash Browns had been dropped, but unfortunately, his whereabouts were unknown. I often imagined him waltzing into the barn, with the Mambomatic 5000 wheeled in behind him. The others admitted to similar fears, yet still longed for his return. The dog displayed the largest cognitive dissonance. His loyalty and love for Dr. Hash Browns never faltered, nor did his fear of further experimentation.

The agency performed several medical exams on all of us, but always under the close supervision of the pig. None of us ever ended up on the autopsy table with our chests split wide open. The agency even did their best to repair Denver Omelet. They couldn't save his legs, but they patched up the hole in his gut, re-inserted his eye, and provided him with a motorized wheelchair. We all showed up to celebrate his first day as the mess hall greeter. It may not have been fine dining, but he enjoyed working in food service again.

The training was rigorous and, as you might expect, I shattered the agency record for the hundred-yard dash and every other running event. In doing so, I taught myself to phase out of hyperspeed without slamming into walls. I wanted to show the elephant. I searched for him every day at first, but as the weeks went by, I checked the skies less frequently, though I never stopped wondering where he was and why he hadn't found us. Hopefully, he found a peaceful spot to watch the world go by or spent his time exploring Earth's beauty.

After six months of rigorous training, we got assigned to our first mission. Agent Orange told the cow it was our final test. If we passed, we would become agents. Beyond that, we knew nothing about the mission and little about the agency other than they called themselves Global Intergalactic Bureau of Defense, or GIBOD and protected Earth from alien threats.

We boarded a bus, designed for our needs, with a double wide door providing the cow easy entry and a zero-gravity closet to keep the fish safe during the ride. We arrived outside a small church in the country. Our training taught us to never question orders, but we still wondered why the agency wanted to raid this tiny church. The human agents would enter the church while we provided perimeter surveillance from the surrounding cornfields. I felt great about our mission performance until I heard the combine.

But that's a story better told by the cow.

Acknowledgements

My first thanks go to my beautiful bride, Emmi, and my children, Alexis and Ben. Without their support and understanding, while I spent countless hours glued to my chair, the BarnYard Heroes would never have come to life.

I must also thank the corporate executives of the former tech giant Lucent Technologies for nearly bankrupting the company. The hard times that followed forced me to accept the worst position in my career. This misery spurred the brainstorming session with my children, which gave birth to the BarnYard Heroes cast of characters.

It took years (okay, decades) to bring the BarnYard Heroes to publication. I began the journey with a fun concept, a passion for comedy writing, and perhaps a bit of raw talent. I never would have completed the trek without the advice, critiques, and encouragement of my suburban Chicago writing community, the Writing Journey. My writing buddies helped grow my writing skills, kept me on track, and provided me with the tools to make this novel a published reality. I am forever in their debt.

The edits and polish which bring the story and characters to life are thanks to my editor, Fiona. Her awesome development feedback gave this novel some much needed polish. You can hire her services via Fiverr.

Team Iconic created the incredible novel cover. They do great work, with a fast turnaround, all for a reasonable price. Hire them via Fiverr for your next cover.

I would also like to thank you for reading this novel. I hope you enjoyed the journey and had a few laughs, or at least snickers, along the way. Since you made it to the end of the Acknowledgements, I have a request. A homework assignment. Book reviews are the lifeblood of writers. Please take a moment to rate the novel and write a review. Scan the QR code below for links to where you can enter your review.

https://sammcadams.com/book-review-links

About the author

Samuel A. McAdams anointed himself the 21st Century Absurdist. The fact his writings do not match the traditional absurdist definition matters not to him, for he insists the term "traditional absurdist" is an oxymoron. He stakes his claim to the title because absurd, along with fun, are the most common words used to describe his work. He bolsters his right to the 21st Century Absurdist crown based on denials of writing his novels under the influence of controlled substances, stating his absurdity is 100% natural because he must maintain a boring lifestyle in order to continue donating his highly sought-after O-Negative blood.

Samuel was born, raised, and still lives in the Western Suburbs of Chicago, with his wife, Emmi. His children, Alexis and Ben, who many years ago helped brainstorm the BarnYard Heroes into existence, are grown and adulting on their own. You can learn more about Samuel A. McAdams at sammcadams.com.

BarnYard Heroes: A Half-Baked Origin is the first of seven novels planned for the BarnYard Heroes series. Each BarnYard Hero will take their turn spinning a yarn, with the rabbit a duck teaming up to pen their book in first person plural, which they call the we-person. Learn more about the full series at BarnYardHeroes.com.

To hear about upcoming events and future releases, scan the QR Code below to follow Samuel on Facebook as The 21stCentury Absurdist.